Edward W. Randell, Sr.
His Flight Thru Life

Marjorie Irish Randell

Order this book online at www.trafford.com
or email orders@trafford.com

Most Trafford titles are also available at major online book retailers.

Print information available on the last page.

ISBN: 978-1-4907-7830-3 (sc)
ISBN: 978-1-4907-7829-7 (e)

Trafford rev. 11/10/2017

www.trafford.com

North America & international
toll-free: 1 888 232 4444 (USA & Canada)
fax: 812 355 4082

This is Edward's story,
the story of his
'flight' through life, if you will.
It is Edward's story as told through
letters, memories and pictures.
Told with love in my heart
for the man of my life.

~ Marjorie Irish Randell

Chapter One

There is an enlarged, framed black and white photo leaning against the wall on top of tall bookshelves in our living room. It shows five children sitting on the steps of what is presumably their home. One of the larger boys is holding a toy airplane as he absentmindedly twirls the propeller. All of the children in the picture seem happy except one; one who peers out from behind his two older brothers. He looks either unhappy or distressed.

"Is that you behind Jim and Bud?" I ask.

He nods.

"Why are you looking so anxious or unhappy?"

"That airplane should have been mine," he replies, wearing the same anxious scowling look on his adult face.

"My dad should have given that to me!"

This scowling little boy was already set in his mind to take to the skies. The love of airplanes became his life.

See the photograh on page 2.

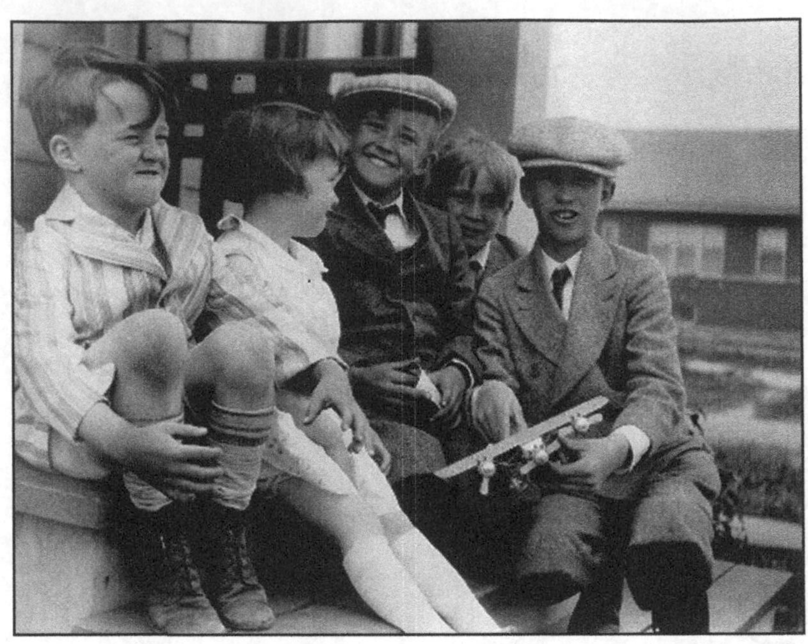

Randell kids on the porch

The scowling little boy was Edward William Randell, born on the 28th of April, a Wednesday in 1920. He was the third son for James and Dorothy Randell. His parents lived in Chicago but Edward was born in a hospital in Evanston, Illinois, just north of Chicago itself.

The Randell family lived on Lunt Avenue in Rogers Park on the north side of Chicago. There was a fourth boy and a little girl born after Edward making him definitely the "middle child."

Life was good in the area of Rogers Park in those days and there were many vacant properties and a lot of wide, open spaces for the four young boys to roam and play their childhood games. Their mother, however, was constantly reminding them, "Look out for your sister.Be careful of your little sister."The boys preferred to leave "little sister" at home with her mother and they soon named her "Sister."

The boys, Jimmy (James Pratt Randell), Bud (George Milton Randell) and Eddie (Edward William Randell) played endlessly in those wide open spaces and the gravel pit nearby and were soon joined by Jack (John Rogers Randell), born in 1922. There were Indian dress ups, explorers, treasure hunting, tag and much digging in the sandy soil.

In a computer search I found the following information about the American Indians in the Chicago area at that time…

> *The Rogers Park area was developed on what once was the convergence of two Native American trails, now known as Rogers Avenue and Ridge Boulevard, predating modern metropolitan Chicago. The Pottawatomi and various other regional tribes often settled in Rogers Park from season to season. The name of Indian Boundary Park west of Rogers Park reflects this history, as does Pottawatomie Park near Clark Street and Rogers Avenue.*

I'm sure this had a great influence on the boys' games of playing Indians. There had also been Indians in the Seattle area where their mother (Dorothy Pratt Randell) grew up. She had baskets and several mementoes from them that she kept carefully through the years.

Why oh why did we chase all of those Indian people out of their homes? What in the world gave the English the right to do that? Cruel. This country was ***their Native Land****…and we took it all away from them! I feel shame and heartache for them today after all of these years.* ***It was cruel and unfair.***

Sorry. I digress.

I've just found a letter to "Eddie" from his Grandfather Pratt, who was his mother's father. I'll copy it here. The envelope is postmarked 1931 making Edward eleven years old on the birthday his grandpa is writing about.

> *Eddie boy,*
>
> *I believe now you are remembering to do what the teacher asks you to do. Think of it real hard as she asks you to do some extra schoolwork and if it is homework please do not put it off 'til some other time. Think what is necessary*

to do to have a neat paper. Of course you can do your work as neatly as Jimmie or George by trying, and their orderly habits will be of use to you all your life.

Grandma and I are sending a little present for your birthday next week and hope you will have a pleasant one.

For several days I have been quite sick with a cold, which I suppose can be called influenza, and am still too weak and ill to work in the garden. It began ten days ago. We had planned to be with the Nelsons for the opening of the fishing season on the 15th. While we were eating an early breakfast Mr. Dines, another fishing fanatic, joined us. Wasted the best part of the morning on the nearby river, water too high. Then "three men in a boat" on Lake Sammamish—after an hour or more I got a strike. Wham! The tip of my rod went two feet under water in the wink of an eye. Getting squared around to "fight the fish" he soon broke water some 40 ft. away and after a few minutes of reeling in the line and giving out more—finally worked him within reach of the landing net, 13 1/2 inch cutthroat trout—soon after—a crash on the water beside the boat—then another on the opposite side, and I got a good look at a monster trout. It was Nelson's fish and for a while he had all he could handle—diving, leaping streak of green & silver—I had the net and at what I thought was a favorable time I raised him out of the water. With the running waves of a breezy day and a fighting fish it wasn't easy to get him head first into the net, so he lay across the frame. But I swung it over the boat and a three pound 20 1/2 inch trout was ours! That was all we got.

The day didn't improve my cold and I haven't been able to do anything since—.

April 23, 1931

G. H. Pratt
Our love—
Grandpa–
Kirkland, Wash.

Edward in front of the Randell home on Lunt Ave

ALWAYS CARRY THIS OPERATOR'S LICENSE WHEN DRIVING

1\. NAME Edward W. Randell.

2\. STREET AND NO. R. #1

3\. CITY OR POST OFFICE Coopersville, Mich.

4\. Signature of Licensee Edward W. Randell

SEP 29 1941 B 281867

Expires License No.

	AGE	COLOR OF EYES	COLOR	WEIGHT
5.	18	grey	white	150 LBS.
	SEX	COLOR OF HAIR	HEIGHT	PREVIOUS LICENSE NO.
6.	M	brown	5 FT. 10½ IN.	A801737

V H P

Is hereby licensed to operate a motor vehicle in accordance with the provisions of Act No. 91 of 1931, as amended

STATE OF MICHIGAN

Leon Case
SECRETARY OF STATE

Ed's drivers license

The four Randell boys grew and played together and went to the Eugene Field Elementary School until beginning their High School years. Then it was Lane Technical High School, which was a distance from their home on Lunt Ave. They used the public transportation of a streetcar to get there.

These school years of the late twenties and early thirties were during a national depression in the United States..

It was during the Depression Years Edward's parents lost their home in Chicago. What were they to do? Where in the world could they go?

As the result of Edward's father's real estate business he owned a small forty-acre farm in Michigan, which proved to

All five Randell children grown up

be one answer for their dilemma of what to do and where to go. James Randell had someone living there caring for the place before but now they were asked to leave and the small farm became the Randell family home.

The children felt definitely displaced. At least the boys did. Because Jimmy was a bit older, he had a good job and was contemplating marriage. He stayed in Chicago living with Aunt Isabelle, his father's sister. George was particularly upset he might have to finish his senior year at the small town high school in Coopersville, Michigan. He went back to Chicago. Edward wasn't as upset, although he would have preferred to stay in Chicago. He adjusted to the change, made friends, found a girl friend named Faye and attended Coopersville High School for his freshman year. Both Edward and George stayed on the farm in the summers and worked hard for their father, milking cows and working the land. John and Edward were both under twenty-one, so young when their parents made the move they *had* to stay with them while George could stay in Chicago.

Following is a letter written by Dorothy Pratt Randell to two of her children who had been sent to Chicago to stay after a *fire completely burned down their farm home* the week before Christmas in 1934.

Dear Sister and Jack:

Your pretty card came this morning. We are at Mr. Durphy's now just north of Rachael's house. The mail is left at the Post Office for us. We drove to Mr. Brown's the lumberman yesterday afternoon. It was awfully cold and snow over the roads. He let us have lumber if we would give a mortgage so your father and Mr. Durphy drove to Grand Haven and the court house to record it. We are at the farm now and a load of lumber has just come. Mr. Veeneman is going to saw it in the barn and a lot of men are coming from the church to help.

Friday

The church ladies are planning to give a dinner for the men the day we sheath up the house. It is to be at the min-

ister's home. Mrs. Strong invited us for dinner and supper yesterday. She gave me pieces for quilt blocks she thought I could sew while the house was being built. The cloth for pajamas was saved from my room so I wanted to make them right away. As soon as we get some money will send you some clothes.

We got Isabelle's & Gabie's letters today and are glad to know you are getting along all right. The second load of lumber has arrived and the boys are clearing the rubbish away to lay the floor tomorrow. We are building 2 rooms + bath in this first section. Haven't decided all interior details yet. (She drew a little sketch of two tandem rooms with bath between.)

We went over to Westrates about 11:30 and she had a big ironing so I ironed while she got dinner for us. Mr. Westrate was driving to Grand Rapids this morning and the rain froze on his windshield so he could hardly see. He was almost to Marne when he saw a man waving his arms in from of him and he jammed on the brakes and skidded into a telegraph pole crushing fender, bending axle and bending frame so the door won't close.

Marie wanted to write you a letter and Ted sent one to Jack. Scotty (the dog) was so glad to see us when we reached the farm today. He sat on the car step and laid his head on my lap and cried. Bud and Mr. Veeneman have sawed 2x4s for studding. We found the parts of the sewing machine in the wreckage. The tub melted and the sink was folded up. The chimney blew down Tuesday night in a gale. Had a regular blizzard in the night. Wed. was -6 degrees.

We sang "Happy Birthday to you" at breakfast for your father. I told Mrs. Durphy it was his birthday. She had a little candle at each place for Christmas dinner and a pond with cotton sprinkled with snow. She had a couple of Santa Clauses going down a chimney and poinsettias around the candlesticks. The Westrate boys loaned Bud a suit and shoes to wear and Ed a pair of pants, to come to Christmas din-

ner with the Durphy's. The Walcotts and Miss Gray came in the evening and we made ice cream using snow to freeze it. Miss Gray gave us a five-pound box of candy and a— (Can't decipher the words on a fold of the paper!)

Must get this in mail. The hankies are so cute. I never saw any just like them and I know the collar will be too beautiful to wear. Jim started wearing his socks right away. The boys are delighted with their mufflers. Where is the egg case? Can't write a decent letter my mind is too much like hash yet. We are sleeping a little better. Going out to dinner tonight. With love, Dot

Indeed her mind must have been hash. She signed a letter to her children with her first name instead of signing Mom or Mother. She did well to write at all.

Later, while Edward was on the farm working, twice a day an airliner flew over going from Grand Rapids to Muskegon. He always stopped to watch it dreaming of flying some day himself. He kept going to the Muskegon airport to watch the planes coming in and taking off.

He worked hard, saving every penny he could and finally earned enough to begin taking flying lessons from Sinnie Sinclair at the Muskegon Airport. He was thrilled with *at last* being in the air! He used to tell the story of his taking lessons and how one day when they went out to the plane for a lesson Sinnie said, "I think you're ready to take her up on your own today."

For just a moment Edward panicked, then began to practice what he had been taught.

He soloed that day, receiving a diploma from Mr. Sinclair. Edward kept that tiny diploma. He saved it for writing his autobiography.

Directly across the road from the Randells on the farm were neighbors by the name of Busman. Tony was the same age as Edward and the two became good friends. They hatched up a number of great ideas, one of which was to establish a roller-skating rink. They investigated thoroughly, found a vacant building just west of the farm in a valley and rented it. A special skating floor was installed, skates were purchased, advertising was written and published, signs made up. *They were in business!*

Following is a write up from Coopersville, Michigan's weekly newspaper, the

> ***Coopersville Observer***
> *"Coopersville Men To Start Skating Rink"*
>
> *"Two of our Coopersville young men, Tunis Busman and Edward Randell have started on a new business venture. They have remodeled the building west of Coopersville known as Wa-Be-Kark and have installed a skating floor. John Randell will manage the lunch counter and will serve light lunches and soft drinks. This will be a good place for the young people to spend a pleasant evening at slight expense. Positively no liquor is allowed. An A.M.L. machine will provide music for the skaters.*
>
> *"The opening of Sleepless Hollow roller skating rink Saturday, March 9th, was a grand success. Every skate was sold by 8:30. A nice orderly crowd of young people from the surrounding country attended and everyone voted it to be a fine place to spend an evening. A public address system furnished music for the skaters. We wish the boys good luck in their new venture. The rink will be open on Wednesday and Saturday nights."*

I contacted Tony and asked for his input on this Roller Rink story. The following paragraphs are written after I received his letter.

The Randell's small farm in Coopersville was at the southwest corner of 88th Ave. and Arthur St. At one time Edward and Tony got enough of some wire to stretch across the road and establish their own phone line. There was no ringer and no way to contact each other; they just grabbed their phone and hollered, hoping the other one would hear the call. In 1936 Tony and his family moved into the village of Coopersville and the two boys saw each other only occasionally. Around 1939 they somehow got together and decided to open a roller rink. They rented the old "Wha-Be-Kark" Road House, which was located on the north side of the old U.S. 16 (now Cleveland Road) just east of 88th Ave. They raised some money and went to Chicago and bought 30 pairs of new skates directly from the Chicago Roller Skate Factory. When opening night came the power had not been connected and a small generator was borrowed from the Ottawa Center Chapel. This was used for two weeks until the power company finally got them hooked up. They had a Juke Box with skating music and Edward's brother John sold candy and popcorn.

Everyone seemed to have a good time with no problems of any kind. Things were going well until the building was sold from under them. The people who bought it thought they could just take over the business but the fellows thought differently, closed it all up and left. The used skates were sold, all the bills paid and that was the end of the venture. The people who had purchased the building went broke and the place was abandoned. It sat there for several years until someone bought it during WWII, tore it down and used the lumber to build their house.

I've scanned a copy, on the next page, of one of the small flyers the fellows had printed and reduced the size. The originals were 6x8 inches.

The years sped on with roller skating, flying lessons and working on the farm, but on April 28, 1941, the very day of his twenty-first birthday, without a word to his father who had insisted he *had* to stay on the farm and work there, Edward walked out the door. He headed for Chicago, not really thinking of what it would mean to his younger brother. It left John with all the work on the farm, the milking of cows, cooling the milk, bottling it and then delivering it on a milk route developed in the village of Coopersville. In the many years since it happened Edward has voiced his regrets again and again for having done such a thing to his brother. John was under heavy pressure from his father to ***"get the work done."***

GRAND OPENING MARCH 9, 1940!

ROLLER SKATE

AT

SLEEPLESS HOLLOW

Wednesday and Saturday Nites

4 MILES WEST OF COOPERSVILLE OR
½ MILE WEST OF DENNISON ON US-16

ADMISSION TO RINK . . 25c

Good Food -- Music

Sleepless Hollow flyer

James Paul Randell was a strange man. He thought he couldn't do physical work himself, so he ordered the boys to… "***Do it! Do it! Do it!***" There was no letup and no way for John to get away from it.

He snapped.

One day John bought a gun somehow. I have never learned exactly what happened that dreadful day, but it ended up with his sister Dorothy going into Coopersville for help. Police were involved and John was sent to Kalamazoo, Michigan to an institution established for treating mentally disturbed and violent people. He spent the next twenty years there.

John's life was taken away from him. Sad. He was never the same again, even after many years later when he was released. Edward still felt strong regrets all the rest of his life for this having happened. He felt he had let his brother down by walking out the door and not looking back.

Chapter Two

When Edward reached Chicago he lived, as did brother George, with their Aunt Isabelle in her apartment on Richmond Ave., on the north side of Chicago. They both went to Lane Tech and Edward graduated from there in 1938. After graduation Edward and George were both back on the farm.

George and my brother Jack (Howard Irish, Jr.) became good friends. Edward was often with his brother George when he came to our home to see my brother. I paid no attention to them. They were just friends of my brother. In later years, Edward came alone sometimes, visiting with my folks. I would wash my hair, study, and even once I fell asleep on the end of the couch while he was there.

Oh my goodness! I did that?

In 1941 Edward was in Chicago staying with his Aunt Isabelle, known to the family as Radda. She acquired that name when Edward's brother Jimmy was little. Isabelle's parents and aunt called her "Bunny" just out of fondness for her. Young Jimmy wondered about that and asked what a "bunny" was. They explained to him about bunny rabbits. In his efforts to say rabbit it came out as "Radda." The name stuck.

Edward wrote letters back to Michigan to his brother John (Jack).

Fri. 13 June '41.

Dear brother John,

Well, I don't know just what to write but if you all pass your letters around you get the general news.

Sunday afternoon Radda, Jim & Mary Lee, a friend of hers and I went for a ride to Fort Sheridan. I wanted to see Howard Irish. We didn't call up beforehand and so he wasn't there. They told me he was somewhere in Chicago. Bud didn't go as he had to practice his scales for Monday. The teacher got tough with him because he didn't do so well on them. He told me he hadn't practiced them once since he started taking piano.

On the ride Mary Lee kept hinting about how she would like to drive but Radda and I didn't catch on. We rode in front, Radda drove up and I drove back. We saw a nasty accident, three women, they were all cut and bruised except the little girl and she was getting a big kick out of it. She climbed all over her mother who was sitting on the ground with a cut knee and was holding her back. Poor lady.

On the way to Chicago I drove from South Haven to Gary. The Ford is a nice car but is awful light. I kept running off the road on the curves.

Sitting next to me is Bud's boat with two engines in it. One is no good. The things develop 13,000 R .P .M. and shake the screws out of the board they tried to anchor it with. So they are waiting to get a piece of aluminum to mount it on. Bud says they will have to steal the aluminum as it is so scarce and so far I guess they can't find any to steal. Also next to me sits Bud's Derby. He looks like a G-Man he thinks, but together we look more like Laurel and Hardy.

Well, according to the Doctor I may as well give up any dreams I ever had about flying with the Air Corps as he doubts very much if they would take me.

Am sending you some pictures a friend of Bud's took. There is a very interesting story behind each one.

We had rain here the last two days and it's nice today, except in this apt. and boy it sure does not cool off much in here even at night.

Bud just called from Crowes. (Crowe Name Plate where he worked.) Says to be ready for tonight we are going to N. U. (Northwestern University) to hear the band at the Commencement exercises.

Am sending you a design of your airplane. Remember the one in which you ran down the field to take off? Some fun.

Bud has won a Scholarship Keychain and knife and also an Honorary Key for playing in the band, 1st Trombone '41. B- average.

Went to N. U. and they do not have an Aviation Engineering course so guess I will have to save my pennies and go to Massachusetts Institute of Technology. The tuition is only $600. a year.

Happy Landings,
Your dear brother Ed Wings Randy

July 29, 1941, 9 PM
Monday

Dear Comrade,

How are you old Bully Boy? That's fine. Yes I have that chemical calculator you speak about. So you would like it, huh? And I also have my Chemistry handbook. You better take it easy on the explosives, or they may blow you to Kingdom come.

What seems to be the trouble with you, Old Salt? You are bilious as hell? I thought I told you never to touch that stuff. Not to smoke too many ears of corn. Do you know what a buccaneer is? Well, it is a heck of a high price to pay for an ear of corn. Corny joke, aye what, old top? I also have that Trigonometry graph. What on earth do you want with that?

So you have the darkroom all set up. Swell. The fixer

is all made up. It is the Hypo. Use it straight. As for the time to make a print you have to experiment a little. I don't remember offhand, but think you hold the white light on 4 seconds, maybe more. As for finishing them, all you have to do is wash the plate in warm water and then cold, dry it and it's ready for use. It does not have to be waxed. Just get off the dirt, lint, etc. Yes, one of those power packs work but it has no condenser in it. It gives off about 400 volts the way it is. Raw voltage. It is not steady. It is pure pause current I believe.

You bet, brother. I'll design anything for you, bridges, dams, cars, or what have you. Now a word for the wise and you'll never go wrong. Always keep the height of the section modulus greater along the vertical axis than along the horizontal. "Formula for Structural Design for the Rectangular Moments of Inertia, Section Modulation." I'll explain it to you some day. The Buick Company down here is to have their plant finished by the first of September and then a lot of the fellows are going to try to get jobs there as engineers.

Hold off on the dimensional statistics a while as I have only gotten as far as Non-concurrent coplanar force systems.

Yes, sir, you just lie back in your little old bed and take it easy like that nice doctor said. Thanks for your Philosophy. How soon do you think you need that calculator? Right away. O.K.

As for entrance into college, look in my bulletin for Mass. Inst. Tech. and you will find that only two semesters are required. (Two units or1 year)

Am sending the title to the Ford for whomever it belongs to.

We are melting away, the temperature here in the flat is 90 F. outside is 99 degrees and 115 in the sun. Well, we had Physics test again today. I got 80 on my last one.

They are starting the boys off down here at 75 cents an hour. That is forty dollars a week. The government defense work is, however, 58 hours with time and a half over forty hours, with double on Sundays. Bud says his boss told him today that he could begin working 78 hours a week whenever he wanted to. Boy that is rolling in the dough... in loaves!

Well I haven't much to write. Say hello to everyone for me. Am also sending a letter to Dot. Say hello to the Bartholomew's for me.

Happy Landings
Your loving brother comrade
"Wings"

Labors 2nd day (1941)

Dear Old Top, Runt, Rock, Carrot, Jack and Stuff,

How are things by you? Swell. That's fine. How are the photos coming? I see where I'll have to come up and print a few for myself, so as to finish my album.

Next Sunday Cousin Foster has invited us three to dine at the Sovereign, and they are making a special cake for Radda's birthday, which she doesn't know about yet. And don't you tell her. It is to be a surprise.

I have done nothing better than sleep over the weekend... catching up on sleep I lost going to school.

It was hard work, but it was fun. But I guess I'll have to forget about school now for a few years.

My dear fellow, do you have any late history books, American History you could loan me, as one of the Air Corps tests is on American History and I need to review it.

Buick has hired me as a floor sweeper, or to work in the assembly line but have not told me when to come to work. They have no need for designers at all, so I was thinking I would pull up my stakes and head west either to Santa Monica, California or Seattle and get in the aircraft industry until the Army calls me.

I know how I can get out there free of charge, but I have a couple hundred dollars debt here to pay off first.

Remember George McDonald? Well, I found where he lives in Park Ridge, and went to see him. Johnny is a sophomore at N. U. studying Chemical Engineering. Richard is working, and George and another fellow own a woodworking shop. Now here is the sad part. George had an awful case of Scarlet Fever four years ago and is all but blind. He said he has been to New York twice but the doctors don't seem to help him and every year his sight is getting less. While I was there his draft card came. He is classified 4F never to be called, physically unfit. I was talking to his mother and she was saying any fellow ought to be willing to serve his country if he was able, for one or two years, than to go the rest of his life blind or otherwise handicapped. Boy I tell you that sure is food for thought and I said to myself then and there I would never complain again and thank God I can still see and enjoy the things of nature. Well, brother, keep looking up, the Lord is coming, and when he does we must all be ready. Don't work too hard. I don't feel so well mentally today, so can't think what to write.

I will drop in to see you before I leave for the Coast.

Say Hi to all the animals and cats and dogs, etc.

I am going to Stewart Warner tomorrow to see about work. We thought maybe we would be up last Sat. but aunty got home first. Will be seeing you in the funny paper.

As always, Happy Landings, Ed.

Maybe I'll come up for a few weeks and we can design a dam. This course I took taught me a few things, and the greatest thing is that I'm not so smart and don't know a thing and am no mechanical designer. The teachers pounded that into us so we wouldn't get the big head.

Your Loving Bro,
Ed.

Monday Noon
Oct. 20, 1941

Dear loving Family,

Well! How are all my happy ones? Enclosed please find a $20. Money Order. My boss has decided to let me work 8 hours a day starting the first so I won't have to quit work *and then I'll have four hours in which to study for my future position.*

I went to see Dr. Penberthy last Mon. and have six cavities. So will be set back another $25.00.

Stewart Warner has written out a deferment blank for me, and I am to take it to my draft board today.

Faye says they are going to have a Halloween party Sat. Nov. 1st and I am invited.

I was out to Buick Mon. last week, and they say they don't know when I'll be called. I have heard some talk that they are going to call in men for work starting Nov. 1st.

How is the silo filling? I imagine it is a problem.

Radda went to Springfield last weekend and Glen Ellyn yesterday. And as per usual, went to see Bud and Violet. Yesterday Bud went to dinner with his old music teacher and Mr. Johnson and Lawrence Salarno, all of WGN. Excuse the misspelled names. He is thinking of getting into radio work. Well, I have to see my Doc and the draft board so will write again.

Let's hear from you all.

Your loving son,
Ed   Happy Landings

Enclosed clipping is from Radda.

In the summer of 1941 my parents and I took my brother, Howard (Jack to close family members) to San Francisco to sail for the Philippine Islands where he was to serve as a Reserve Officer in the 91st Coast Artillery.

Edward had plans for military service about that time also, but for flying, especially flying in the Army Air Corps. He questioned them, tried to enlist and was turned down. He had no idea why. He was required to register with his local draft board, but he had no intention of being drafted.

Form 340 Rev. 8-1-39
PASSENGER CARRYING PROHIBITED

UNITED STATES OF AMERICA
CIVIL AERONAUTICS AUTHORITY
WASHINGTON, D. C.

THIS CERTIFICATE MUST BE CARRIED AT ALL TIMES WHILE PILOTING AIRCRAFT

This certifies that STUDENT PILOT CERTIFICATE NO. S 41422

Edward William Randell
(First Name) (Middle) (Surname)
is properly qualified and is physically able to perform the duties of a Student Pilot.

Address 6509 NorthRichmond St.
Chicago, Illinois

WEIGHT	HEIGHT	DATE OF BIRTH	HAIR	EYES
152½	70	4/28/20	Lt.Br.	Blue

DURATION

This certificate is of 60 days' duration and, unless the holder hereof is otherwise notified by the Authority within such period, shall continue in effect indefinitely thereafter, unless suspended or revoked by the Authority, except that it shall immediately expire (1) at the end of each 12 months period after the date of issuance hereof if the holder of this certificate fails to secure an endorsement by an authorized Medical Examiner or Inspector of the Authority within the last 45 days of each such period, or (2) at any time an authorized Inspector or Medical Examiner of the Authority shall refuse to endorse this certificate after inspection or examination.
The holder hereof is now physically qualified for no higher grade of pilot certificate than that of COMMERCIAL

Date of Issuance 18 July 1940
By direction of the Authority:

Medical Examiner of the Authority

CERTIFICATE ENDORSEMENTS OR REFUSALS TO ENDORSE

MEDICAL EXAMINER'S OR INSPECTOR'S SIGNATURE	Physically Qualified	DATE

LIMITATIONS

Edward William Randell
Signature of Student Pilot

Any alteration of this certificate is punishable by a fine of not exceeding $1,000 or imprisonment not exceeding three years, or both. (over)

Student pilot certificate

Local Board No. 77 61
Chicago City 731
NOV 25 1941 077
2356 West Touhy Avenue
Chicago, Illinois
(STAMP OF LOCAL BOARD)

NOTICE TO REGISTRANT TO APPEAR FOR PHYSICAL EXAMINATION

Nov. 25, 1941
(Date)

You are hereby directed to report to Local Board Headquarters
(Name of examining physician)
at 2356 W. Touhy Ave. for physical examination at 9:30 a.m.,
(Address)
on Thursday, November 27, 1941 Failure to do so is an act punishable by imprisonment and fine, and may also result in your losing valuable rights and in your immediate induction into military service.

W J Fike
Member of Local Board.

D. S. S. Form No. 201 16—17105

Notice to appear for physical

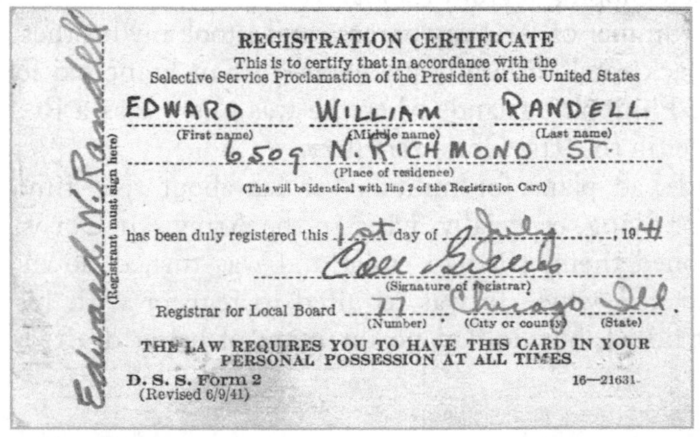

REGISTRATION CERTIFICATE

This is to certify that in accordance with the Selective Service Proclamation of the President of the United States

EDWARD WILLIAM RANDELL
(First name) (Middle name) (Last name)

6509 N. RICHMOND ST.
(Place of residence)
(This will be identical with line 2 of the Registration Card)

has been duly registered this 1st day of July, 1941

Coll Gillis
(Signature of registrar)

Registrar for Local Board 77 Chicago Ill.
(Number) (City or county) (State)

THE LAW REQUIRES YOU TO HAVE THIS CARD IN YOUR PERSONAL POSSESSION AT ALL TIMES

D. S. S. Form 2
(Revised 6/9/41) 16—21631

Edward W. Randell
(Registrant must sign here)

Registration certificate

When war broke out on December 7th Edward was more than ever determined to join the Army Air Corps. This time in January of 1942, the Army Air corps accepted him as a cadet in training.

His real career as a pilot began.

He wrote faithfully to his mother from Texas, always answering her many questions telling of his training experience.

His first penny post card was postmarked 'Waxahache, Texas but his notation was:

> *Muskogee, Okla. Jan. 30, Dear Folks, The trip has been swell. Don't see why I haven't been in the Army before. I get a dollar a day ration money and .03 cents a mile for driving. This is the life only it isn't quite like home. Am trying to make San Antonio tonight.*
>
> *Happy Landing, Ed.*

> *2/11/42*
>
> *Dear Radda,*
>
> *Well, it rained again last night so we sat indoors again. The "doc" here has all the boys gargling and snuffing salt and soda water. Would it be possible for you to send me some oil, don't make a special trip as I still have a little.*
>
> *The days that it doesn't rain it is hot and the ground dries in a hurry and then it's dusty. It irritates my nose and throat on the dry days, and on the rainy days we all get colds, but besides that everything is fine.*
>
> *2/13/42*
>
> *Last night we were given a talk by our Lieutenant on cadet honor plus on the honesty of perspective officers. It was because someone stole $55.and a $35 watch yesterday afternoon after gym class. Most of our privileges are now taken away. We are hardly allowed to turn around.*
>
> *Yesterday we got our footlockers. It is a small-scale trunk. We are already given the opportunity to lead and command our own flight.*

They can really dish out the discipline. Yesterday I had to run around the parade ground because I executed a command wrong. If you get caught talking in mess you have to wash all the barrack porches or the Lieutenant's office floors. Today we go to have an x-ray taken. Mon. I will have another physical. The Army works slow and no one knows what we do next, not even the Lt., but as soon as an order comes thru they say "Okay, men, on the double."

Yesterday while playing volleyball we saw three 4-motor bombers go over on the way to Kelly Field. Boy, they were the most mammoth airplanes I ever saw. They seemed to me to be flying slow, slow, slow. They were so large they made a big target. Some workmen are blasting out some stumps across the road. The blast shakes the barracks. They have public address systems in the barracks hooked up to the front office. They even have an air raid system alarm. The officers at Kelly field have real nice homes. We are not allowed to go to Kelly Field any more. Someone said we are having a movie here tonight. The Lieutenant is coming in for inspection so I'll sign off.

Happy Landings,
Ed.

Ed in cadet uniform with saber

Edward never told the Army Air Corps that he had taken flying lessons and had soloed in a small aircraft.

His first letter home on the following page:

Feb. 19, 1942.
Thurs. Cold.

Dear Folks,

Thanks for your letters. I appreciate them. We all have more work every day and it's getting hard to find time to write. Our only free time is 11:30 to 12:50 (noon) and 17:30 to 22:00. Our time is also most confusing as we are on a 24-hour clock, which is called airtime. It is black as pitch when we march to morning mess.

We had our physical this week and I passed okay. We were x-rayed for tuberculosis and tested for syphilis besides the regular physical exam.

Saturday I have to take a psychology exam. Sat. noon until Sun. at 5:30 we have our first leave.

We are allowed a 200-mile radius from the camp. The Reception Pool is S.W. of San Antonio. Fort Sam is west of San Antonio. We are quite a few miles from each other. The Army and the Air Corps Cadets don't get leave for town at the same time because the enlisted men are jealous of the Cadets and are always trying to start fights.

Today the upper class men were training again with their gas masks on the parade ground. They had the whole field covered with smoke. Boy, you couldn't see a thing. The smoke came up from somewhere in the ground, and the wind blew it over the field. We watch from our parade ground. We were standing retreat at the time.

Where we are is only a reception pool for the Central Part of the country. After 8 to 10 weeks of Officer training and Math we are sent to Primary Flying schools in the Gulf Coast Area, which includes Arizona on the west, Louisiana on the east and Illinois on the north. Some fellows have been sent to East St. Louis, Ill. to Parks Air College. The upperclassmen leave Feb. 25 and then we will be assigned to Squadrons. Then after 5 weeks or more we will be sent somewhere for Primary Training. Then to Basic Flying school. And then to Kelly which is the advanced school. In our barracks we have 55 men. Where I am on the first floor are 23 Misters. The fellow next to me reminds of John. He is always up a half hour after the rest of us have gone to bed just walking around. He is a very nice fellow though. We went to Kelly Field to a show, which was out of bounds. Then he went to Kelly with me to the P. X. I had permission, but he didn't. The poor fellow was caught and has to work 2 hours a day for10 days scrubbing the Lieutenants' offices.

I feel bad about it. They also won't give him the day off with the rest of us. I can't do anything off the straight and narrow path because he says I set an example for him, which he wants to follow. He says he can't figure out why I'm not like the others…playing dice and using strong language at times. I told him I was raised differently. We were just informed (9:00 P.M.) that the upperclassmen are on their way over here to haze us as this is one of their last nights here. Some fun, if you get in the spirit of the thing and don't get angry.

My car is in a parking lot here at the pool. Quite a few Cadets have cars. I think I will get a canvas to cover mine, as there are no garages here. It has been raining lately. The other morning when we woke up it was 35 degrees. Yesterday we got out of calisthenics, as it was too cold and windy. Today we didn't have gym, same reason. (The upperclassmen are upstairs now. They are making the fellows sing the Air Corps song.) However, we do drill as we have heavy mackinaw coats and our uniforms are all wool. The winter issue is olive drab. The summer issue is khaki. The fellows all thank you for your best regards.

We are about 9 miles from town. There are all new barracks. I can use my car on days off and when I get permission. I just got paid $39.77 for travel from Chicago. After I pay Radda back I will be just a few dollars ahead for my day off. I don't have to worry about my car, if I can't sell it, which I don't want to do, I give it to my wife.

We have had grapefruit only once since we've been here.

We have oranges, bananas and apples at breakfast. Yes, we have finally gotten a few papers from home. Chicago. Sunday we got the San Antonio Press. I wear my sweater under my shirt. Yes we have Chapel every Sunday. The Chaplain is a 1st Lieutenant. 9 a.m. is the Protestant service and 10 a.m. the Catholic.

The shows are 20 cents. Good luck with the fresh cows. Faye wrote and told me about her ankle. Some kid. We think the new time is silly, too. It doesn't save a thing. I got my cap insignia and underwear today and my shirt and pants pressed so I'm all set. Please write soon.

Happy Landing…

Ed-Wings-Randy.

P.S. I got Dot's Valentine and letters from Mrs. Irish and Rev. Moffatt.

Cadet Edward William Randell –1942

Mrs. Irish (my mother) was his Sunday school teacher in Michigan, Rev. Moffatt the minister from Rogers Park Baptist Church in Chicago.

March 1, 1942
Sunday, 1400 o'clock
Sunshine.

My Dear Mom,

Thanks for all the letters. I have finally been assigned to a squadron. No. 3 and Flight C. Flight C. is a model or show barracks of the Reception Center. The floor downstairs has linoleum on it, with a two foot insignia of the Air Corps set in it.

The beds are double-deckers. I did have an upper, but I now have a lower because some upperclassmen left for Primary School today. So, I moved my "home." I am in class 42-I. About 1000 men graduated last week and left for Primary. In the morning we drill, have calisthenics, followed by noon mess. Classes are in the afternoon. Our first class is Military Science and Tactics. At 15:00 o'clock we have Mathematics. At 16:30 it is Retreat. Dinner at18:00 o'clock. Indoors at 20:30 and "taps" at 22:00 o'clock. We still get up at 5:50 a.m. Breakfast at 6:20 a.m. It is a lot of fun here. Now that we are in the Squadrons we really have to toe the mark or get some "gigs."("Gigs" are demerits) For every gig one gets he has to walk an hour on the ramp in full dress with rifle, etc. Yesterday we got our rifles, gas masks, cartridge belts, bayonets and fatigue clothes. I have learned the Manual of Arms. I had some snapshots taken by a fellow. Will send some as soon as they are printed.

Today I went to church. The Chaplain is a very fine fellow. His sermon was on choosing the Lord as ones leader and cast off worldly things if they stand in the way of salvation.

Today being Sunday we were allowed to talk to each other at Mess and eat at leisure. Other days we sit erect, and don't talk unless we ask for food. Eat with one hand, keeping the other at our side. We have to finish in 30 minutes on weekdays. We are not allowed to "dive bomb" that is when you bend over and scoop the food into the oral cavity. I have ten Math problems to do tonight.

Thanks for all the news, but now that we are in the squadron we have newspapers and we also have radios to listen to. Thanks for the clipping about the Cadet. I'll put it on the Bulletin Board in Class as the instructor asked for items of interest. There are 55 men in our Flight, Six Flights in a Squadron and Six Squadron in a Wing. Yes, I like my hair cut as it is cool and I don't have to bother about combing it. In the Army you just about get time to wash your face and brush your teeth. We fall in formation 10 minutes after we awake. However, we can usually find time to take a shower every day. So far I have not gotten any gigs. I do my own sewing and my bed is good if I say so myself. We sweep and mop the floor every morning and Friday night we get down and scrub it. I think they are training me for the Navy. Or maybe the infantry with all the drilling we get.

That Red Cross course must be very interesting. Yesterday four Squadrons were in formation on the parade ground for a pep talk by our Physical director and Chaplain. The first speech we were told all about venereal diseases and what precautions to take before and after intercourse with a woman. The Chaplain then told us that it was wrong and not to do it. The greater percentage of the fellows here are of good character and sound minds. Most of the men are here because it is better than the draft.

Last Sunday I visited the Bowmen's in Mercedes, Texas. Did I write you about it? I also saw the Gulf of Mexico. I gathered a few seashells for souvenirs. Today we did not get off, but we do the next Sundays following. Terrible grammar. We have not been shot yet.

Where our camp is located it is all scrub trees. In San Antonio on the North side are the better homes with Palm trees, green grass and double lane streets, cacti plants, etc. It is real pretty. I think I would almost like to live down here, the only thing I don't think I could get used to is the Mexicans, negroes and specks…a cross between negro and Mexicans. The air is great, there is always a breeze and so far I have been bothered only a couple days with sinus headaches. The fellows are all so young they look like boys instead of men. We get more than enough to eat. Chicken dinner about three times a week, ice cream, cake... Dad should be here for all the chicken dinners. The food is perfect but I would like a few cookies. We can't take any food from the Mess Hall. If I pass my course here I will leave some time soon after the first of March.

Happy Landing,
Ed

June 6, 2016 - I just found a small bundle of letters all tied together with a blue ribbon and they are addressed to Miss Marjorie Irish from Aviation Cadet Randell, Edw. W., from the Pilot Replacement Training Center in San Antonio, Texas. Letters to me! **Oh! Happy Day!**

I have put them in with the ones to Edward's Mom according to dates.

March 1, 1942
Sunday P.M.
Cold.

Dear Marjory,

Tell your mother I received her card. Please thank her for me. I'm writing you, thinking you may write me in return. Am I the schemer? Seriously though, you don't have to bother if you don't have time or maybe you're engaged and your fiance wouldn't allow it.

Have you heard from Jack yet? This old world of ours is funny. One goes miles from home and meets a person who lived near you or knew a friend of yours and you get to talking and soon you travel all the way home. I met a Sergeant Whipple here at the Reception Center, who had been in the Philippine Islands 2 years and who knew Jack at Fort Sheridan. He refers to him as Lieutenant Howard Irish. I imagine he is about Jack's age. Most of the officers are so young they look like boys. The average age of the Air Corps officers is 22

1/2. I have heard by the grapevine that Mr. Whipple's parents and brothers and sisters were killed in an air raid somewhere in the Orient. His father was a pilot. You wouldn't think a fellow with memories like that would care to live. But he smiles and says we will lick 'm. He is a great fellow.

Today being Sunday I went to church. The sermon was good --- about choosing the Lord as our leader and not to let worldly things stand in the way.

We had chicken for noon mess and ice cream and cake for dessert. We have ice cream quite often. The food is perfect. Our tables are set with linen tablecloths and napkins. We even have waiters.

I am in Squadron 3, Flight C. Flight C barracks is the show or model barracks of the reception center. The downstairs floor is laid with linoleum with the Air Corps insignia set in the linoleum. The insignia is other pieces of linoleum raised 1/4 inch. The insignia is a wing with a propeller thru it. (He made a little drawing here of the insignia) The cots are double-deckers with springs and mattresses.

The barracks house 45 men, and are automatically gas heated. Excuse me while I laugh. A couple fellows were just having it out. We have more fun here. The men from the north are called Yankees and the men from the south are called Rebels. We are always arguing over the Civil War, and how the north won because of her good soldiers. The Rebels say they lost because they figured 1 southerner for 75 northerners but we sent 100 and they were outnumbered. We don't mean anything by the arguments as it's all in fun.

The two "misters" have now gone out for a walk so maybe I can finish this letter. Today has been the quietest in a long time. A lot of the fellows are out with their girl friends and to the movie on the post. The Pilot Reception Pool and Replacement Training Center is west of Kelly Field a couple miles. The sun is out today, and a strong wind is blowing. It is cold, too, also. Wonderful grammar I use isn't it? The first Sunday I was here it was nice and it has rained off and on ever since. After 5 weeks of school we leave for Primary training. I have not seen an airplane except those flying overhead. About 250 are in the air, coming from Kelly Field. The way we have to scrub our barrack floors I think they are training me for the Navy. Or maybe it's the infantry with all the drilling we do. We were told that we of the Air Corps would not be granted any more furloughs. However, we do get weekend passes to travel within a 200 mile radius of camp. Last week I went to Brownsville, Texas and drove out to see the Gulf of Mexico. Brownsville is the farthest tip of Texas. It was a pretty drive. I saw things I had never seen before. Things like orange, grapefruit and palm trees, green grass and cacti all over.

Yesterday we were issued our rifles, bayonets, gasmasks, cartridge belts and fatigue clothes.

We have a stiff course but I like it. It is a lot of fun. It is the men in the infantry that I admire.

We get up at 5:50 Reveille, fall out in formation at 6:00, Mess at 7:20, drill and calisthenics in the morning. We play volleyball, touch ball, do track and high jumping. 12:20 is noon mess. Our clock is the 24-hour airtime.

In the Marine Corps we called it 'Navy time."

In the afternoon we have Military science and tactics and Math. 16:30 is retreat, Mess 18:20, inside by 20:30 for study, 22:00 lights out, so we can do it all over again. This is the life. I'm very proud I'm in my country's uniform. I would not trade it for another. I

Edward in a trainer, learning to fly! Happy guy!

only hope this time we make the world safe for our children. Are you still working in G. R.? Lots of luck,

Happy Landing

Ed.

P.S. Tell your mother I knew Mr. Carson as we took flying lessons with the same teacher at Muskegon. Mr. Van Averill also took lessons there. Our heating system has been broken the last week. We almost freeze at night.

Ed

A post card dated March 19, 1942:

Dear Mom, Thanks for the letter. I have an awful time finding time to write. They say we will find less at Primary. We are due to leave for Primary school soon. I guess I write to Faye most. I may be sent to Primary up north. I hope. We are studying plane and ship identification. Hope the roads dry up. Happy Landing Ed

Wed. 9:30 a.m.
March 25, 1942

Dear Mom,

This morning at 8:30 a.m. we had our last class. We had the final exam in aircraft identification. Yesterday evening at 8:30 p.m. we had our final Math Exam. Mon. we had our third typhoid shot and second tetanus shot. Last week we were vaccinated for smallpox. After we have the shots we all talk in our sleep. (It is raining today so we aren't drilling - this mud is nice and sticky.) We got paid Mon. so some of the boys are playing poker. Thanks for all the advice. I'll try and be a nice little boy.

I'm looking out the front window of the barracks and it overlooks the parade ground. They are building a big Chapel and 6 more barracks on the North side of the grounds. They have a track in one corner and basketball & volleyball courts in another corner. They are building tennis courts on *either side. There is a little grandstand on the west side. To the north of our barracks they are building a large hospital and more barracks. Also a big P. X. (Post Exchange.) The rumors are flying around here thick and fast as to where we are going (nothing official yet) but I guess I'll be sent somewhere in Texas. Yes! The course at Armour helped me very much. I can see where the more education you have the farther you get. We are studying graphs & vectors in navigation like I had in Physics and machine stress & strain diagrams last summer. And the math is also right along the line I had at Armour. I still have my clothes. They say to keep something to wear home if we get washed out in Primary. As all they give us is our underwear and shoes (if we wash out.) No! We are not allowed to wear white shirts during war time. Our laundry is sent out to different laundries in San Antonio. After all the deductions were taken out I received $27.14 for the month of February. That sure is a lot of money, huh! I bought a canvas to cover the car for $15. I am sending you some more snapshots. I just got the money Mon. to get them printed. They are the ones I sent to Faye. Yes! I think I have gained some weight… 9 lbs. in the first three weeks. They are also toughening up our muscles, like steel. We have cross-country running, tug of war, volleyball, basketball and all kinds of field events. It is a lot of fun. It's like getting in condition for a big game that we are going to be in. Last week Thurs. the "Lassos" a group of girls from Jefferson H. S. came out to entertain us by formation marching and lariat twirling. They had on white cowboy hats, blue blouses, brown wide belts, red skirts and shoes and stockings. The girls aren't barefoot here like in the Ozarks. They carried the State flag of Texas and the U.S. Flag. Friday the boys R.O.T.C. from the same H. S. came out and drilled and paraded for us. They were perfection itself. I hear they have won State honors for three years. Our uniforms are better than the Regular army gets because we are supposed to use them for our officer uniforms when we get our "wings." The Cadet uniform was blue, but is now O.*

D. the same as the Officers. The hat has a blue band to show we are Cadets. It is to be taken off when we graduate. The O. D. band is under the blue one. Last Sunday I was introduced to a daughter of one of the Officers at Fort Sam. The four of us went to the Gunter Tea Dance and dinner. Then in the evening we went for a ride to a park north of San Antonio. There was a river there fed by springs. The place was very pretty. The young lady with me said she wanted to be a Cadet at Kelly if she could get such beautiful teeth as I had. So I told her I had them long before I got to Kelly. She was a very nice girl. I have invited her out to dinner Thursday… tomorrow. There is talk that we will have some time at the end of this week. There is also talk that we will leave some time at the end of next week. The gas masks are a little clumsy but not bad. The hard part is to get a deep breath. Because of that reason if you get excited you feel like you want to pull the mask off. Our rifles are 1917 & 1913 models. We use them only for drilling and Manual of Arms. No target practice. We do not fight (even amongst ourselves, or we get washed out.) I am in the Air Corps, which trains pilots, navigators, etc. The fighting force is separate. It is called the Air Combat Force and in that they do the fighting. We are chosen for flight by height. Sat. we had our Field day. We lost the cup to Squadron 2. Squadron 7 was in second place, Squadron 3 was in third place. I got six "gigs" one day for leaving my locker unlocked. They are the only gigs I've had so far; I have not had to walk the ramp yet. I guess I must get my letters mixed. As I write to Faye and think I have written the same to you. I write to Faye more than anyone else. No, I didn't see any of the Bowman children (all in their 20's.) They do not live at home and are married with children. Mercedes is about 400 miles from San Antonio. The Gulf is something over 200 miles. It is farther across Texas than it is from Chicago to San Antonio. It is a big state. It surprised me. None of the Bowman family is in the service. Yes, on some trees there is moss hanging. We have footlockers for our clothes that we do not hang up. Glad you

like the fruit. My young friend is now in another barracks. We got separated when we left the pool. I got a letter from Mrs. Randell, Cousin Lida. I met one of the boys from G. R. I finally got letters from brother Bud and Cousin Foster.
Happy Landings Ed

'Brother Bud' Edward refers to is his brother George. George was born in 1918 during WWI when they referred to the soldiers who went overseas to Europe as "buddies." There was even a song written entitled, "My Buddy." The dictionary defines "bud" as a form of address, usually to a boy or man. It was a nickname the family gave George.

Dear Dotty,

Thank you for all the letters. Our classes are over now so maybe I can catch up on my letters. Thank your friend for the note. But, you make me laugh. Here when we get in bed we find the sheets sewn together. Grape-Nuts and G. I. salt between the sheets. Also cartridge belts and bayonets in the bed, brooms between footlockers to trip us up. More darn fun.

You learn how to dance up at the school and then you can teach me. The temperature here is about 70 degrees. It is very nice. The trees have leaves on them and the farmers planted corn here two weeks ago. I don't remember hearing about Marie. That's too bad.

Don't write until you hear from me.
Ed

This boy wrote LONG letters to his mom!

April 7, 1942
Garner Field
Uvalde, Texas

Querida Mamae,

How do you like my Portuguese? In our spare time the foreign students teach us their language. The students are from Chile, Brazil and Argentina, most of the South American countries. They are being trained the same as us, thru the Good Neighbor Policy. They do not get commissions unless their country declares war. They hope to get jobs on the commercial airlines in their countries.

If I wash out and leave the Air Corps I am supposed to report to my local Draft Board in five days, but I am not going to "wash out." In Portuguese I am called a "Calours" or Bicho meaning "Dodo."

The dictionary definition of a dodo is ineffective, non-valid or uninteresting. Oh my!

We have to wear our goggles around our necks until we solo, and then we can wear them on our helmets. I have 5:37 hours Army flying time!

Saturday the flag was at half-mast for one of the students who stalled too close to the ground. It was the first accident at this field. The school was started Oct. 4, '41. It is privately owned but run by the government. Of our $105, we pay out $65 a month for room and board.

The instructor hollers and asks me where we are going and then after he sees the plane fly past he congratulates me on my quick thinking and says he is going to write that one down on my record. He is the best instructor in the world. He has not gotten angry once nor swore or raised his voice. He says some people say he is too easy. But he says he has found he gets better results by being human. He's "the tops." He is only 21 years old and just registered in February and has not gotten his questionnaire yet today. He acts just like a kid at times. His home is about 80 miles from here. He said he told his girlfriend he had four good-looking cadets for students, and now she wants to meet us, so some Sat. night we have off we are going to get together and be introduced. Aren't we silly? It's more fun every day. Yesterday we did stalls and spins and I felt like I was going to fly out of the ship, but I'll master it yet. When one is in a spin the controls seem a mile away. You are forced back in the seat and your feet feel like they're floating.

Flying is the safest thing in the world, our safety belts hold a load of 6000# and if that breaks we have our life preservers or parachutes, which are fool-proof. The parachute instructor says he has been folding "chutes" since the school opened and not one has failed yet. As a matter of fact no one has had to use one yet, he says with a smile. Seriously now, he exclaims, if we are in a spin and we have fallen to 2000 ft. and cannot get out of it, to leave the ship. He says a plane can be built in a day but it takes over 20 years to build one of us lads. He, too, is a wonderful man and knows "chutes" inside and out. At this school we get "gigs" for everything. In the morning the bugle blows and the O. D. says to rise and shine. And we really have to shine... our belt buckles, nameplates and shoes, our fingernails clean and our faces clean-shaven. We have loud speakers in the barracks, over which the orders come and also music when the O. D. feels like playing the recorder. The school has tennis courts, volleyball and basketball courts, a cadet lounge and officers mess hall. The airplanes are 175 H. P. Fairchild planes. We have 45 minutes of calisthenics and two hours of ground school. We are studying navigation and theory of flight. So far my average is about 95.

Two of the seven fellows in my bay are foreign students. They are swell fellows, real characters and lots of fun. I have met fellows from Lane down here. It's a small world. How do you like my stamp on the envelope? Novel. I expect to be here until June 15. We do not have a radio in our bay but we get the San Antonio newspaper. Last Sunday (Easter) I went to the Baptist Church. The people really welcome us. One fellow wants to take a couple of us to his ranch over the weekend. Had another tetanus shot here. The measles scare is over now and the boys are out flying. How is the chance of Faye and Dotty coming down to visit me this summer?

Keep 'm Flying. Happy Landings, Ed

P.S. Forgot to tell you we had a parade April 6. It was "Army Day," and the Captain said we were so good (both companies) that we would have Sat. off. I have also joined the Drum and Bugle Corps. They call me "Lucky" here because I have gotten out of marching off "gigs" by blowing the bugle.

Edward is answering every single one of his mother's questions!

Sat. May 2, 1942

Dear Folks,

It doesn't seem a bit different to be 22. It is 8:15 a.m. We just had a S. M .I. (Standard Military Inspection). We are really on the "beam" as we did not get any "gigs." Next week I will have to walk some "tours." I broke my goggles and so I was charged $5.00 and 5 "gigs." We have a new Officer in charge of the Cadets and is he tough. He won't allow us to have passes to go visit San Antonio. And he has changed our schedule. We now get up at 6:15 a.m. The "Dodos" got here this week. They look scared to death. I bet I looked the same way.

I had my Second School Check. This one was the 20-hour check. I also had the 90-degree accuracy spot landing check. I passed both. My teacher wants to solo me from the front seat next week. I was supposed to this week but it rained so we only got in a couple hours flying time. I have 6 hours of flying solo and 17 hours dual.

I received the cookies and also your other packages. I got a diary from Cousin Foster and a light indicator for taking pictures from Jim.

I got a very nice letter from Faye Thursday. She sent me a couple of snapshots, one of Dotty and Mary Jane. Gee! She is a swell young lady. I'm falling in love with her. As if you didn't know I liked her before. Maybe some day if I ever amount to something she will marry me, I hope.

That Red Cross Banquet must have been swell. The song Faye played the O. D. plays over the loudspeaker system for us boys. Last week the upper class had their Farewell Banquet. The mess hall was in some style. The week before they had their dance. The young ladies all wore formal dresses and the cadets had on their dress uniforms. The hall was decorated very pretty in blue and orange with blue lights. We all had a very nice time.

The weather here is fine. I have only been bothered once with my sinus trouble. They are awful strict here and if you have the slightest sinus trouble or ear trouble or hay fever they ground you right away. It seems that hay fever and sinus trouble makes one deaf in the high altitudes. I hope I never have to go to the hospital because if they discover my sinus trouble I'll get grounded. A few lads here have washed out with Medical Discharges. Out of my class of 120 twenty have washed out so far. Excuse me, as I have to go to school. Pause.

Well here I am again at 4 P.M. I have just gotten back from flying. I passed my 180 degree accuracy Spot Landing check. Gee, but flying is fun. Some fellows go up for the first time and the instructor puts the plane in a spin and after they land the student just asks to be washed. One student (a new dodo) went up for the first time yesterday and after he came down he was shaking and scared; he talked in his sleep last night and is afraid to go near the planes. The first couple times a person goes up they get sick. I almost did. It doesn't bother me now. I eat enough for a horse (a small horse). Because these planes are open cockpits, it really gives one a thrill doing aerobatics. When the plane comes out of a spin, you are just hanging by your belt or "girdle" across your lap.

It is quite a feeling hanging upside down…

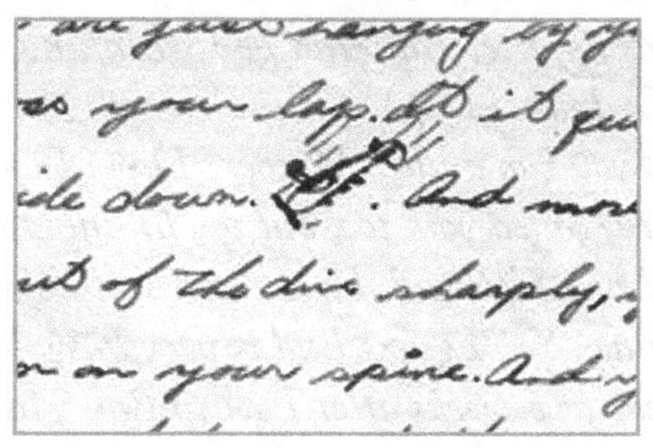
are just hanging by y
as your lap. If it qu
side down. And mov
out of the dive sharply,
on your spine. And y

Edward drew a tiny airplane plunging downward

This is to certify that №. 4327

EDWARD W. RANDELL

is a member in good standing of the

CADET CLUB

AIR CORPS REPLACEMENT TRAINING CENTER

(Aircrew)

KELLY FIELD, TEXAS

Lt. R. D. Kalb
Air Corps

SQUADRON COMMANDER

It is more fun if you pull out of the dive sharply. Your head pushes down on your spine and you feel like lead. My foot came off the pedal in a spin and it weighed so much I couldn't put it back on. We came out ok as we were spinning to the right. So I applied left rudder. Simple, isn't it?

I think we ought to move to Texas and sell milk to some Army camp as they sure buy and feed a lot of milk. We drink milk with every meal. Liquor is looked down on because one under the effects "blacks out" in a steep pull up.

I liked the card from Dotty. Thanks.
Happy Landings,
Your son and brother, Ed Reggie

P.S. We had a hail storm here… the largest hailstones I've ever seen. They were about 3/4"x1 3/4."

May 25, 1942

My Dearest Mother,

How are you? Well, I hope. I got a letter from Radda today. She is still in the hospital May 22. She said the draft board is chasing after Bud and he is thinking of getting in the Army Ordnance Dept.

Am glad you had a nice "Mother's Day." I would certainly like to have called you, too, but my finances are very limited. So, I'll write instead. Faye wrote and told about being over for dinner. Yes, I guess Bud is very busy, like I'm going to be the next five weeks after I get to Basic, as I will be an underclassman again. I think I will give Faye an engagement present for her birthday. What do you think of that? I had already thought of inherent diseases, and had a talk with our Flight Surgeon, and he said that there was nothing to it and not to let that stop me from getting married. Thank you much for the advice. The only one I have given encouragement to has been Faye. The young lady in San Antonio means nothing whatsoever to me. We just went out on "double dates" twice. We "potential Officer material" as we are called, have to keep up our Social Standing. In San A. we had a dance at the Cadet Club every Sunday evening, and it is not much fun going stag. I hope this explains things.

We had our Farewell Dance last Sat. night and had lots of fun. The underclass entertained us with a little program, which was very good. We all had a swell time. The underclass had the hall very nicely decorated with cartoons on the walls and the Air Cops Insignia. They used one of the "props" off a Fairchild and made the wings of Plywood. It was very good. The boy that painted the cartoons was a greeting card designer in civilian life.

We had our final test in Meteorology and Navigation and Theory of Flight. Tomorrow is our last test in Engines. And then 4 hours of Maintenance and our school days are over for a few days. In Basic we get the same subjects, but more advanced, plus a few more subjects including radio & code. Hot dog. Here are my marks: Meteorology 91, Navigation 77, Engines and Theory of Flight 89. These are the latest not the final. I have had Class "A" privileges. One gets those after he is an upperclassman and his marks are over

85. I'm ashamed of my last November marks.

Today I have 58:45 hours flying time. Today I passed my final school check. Tomorrow I have my final Army check. Boy! This flying is more fun every day. One day I went up to 7500 feet and did a 5 1/2 turn spin coming down, and then did a power off dive over 200 mph. It's great. Oh! Yes! Before I forget, I got a letter from Grandma.

As yet we don't know where we are to be sent, but the chances are 6 to 1 in favor of Randolph Field "West Point of the Air." Gee! I hope I am sent there. Don't worry I shan't get married during training. We are allowed to marry, but the Army won't take care of one's wife and family until they are officers. Then their doctor bills are free and they are taken care of royally. The Army & Navy is wonderful to its officers. I like all the social affairs. The girls wear formals and one is in the best of society. It's great. I hope you understand. Those pictures are nice but a little out of focus. Yes, you may wear my officer's insignias or would you rather have miniature ones?

The lilacs in those pictures looked very pretty, and I wish I could see all the flowers in the garden. Well, I went on my cross-country flight. It was from Uvalde to Eagle Pass, to Asherton, to Uvalde, making it a little over 150 miles. Please don't worry so much about Sabotage. Tell Dotty I would like to know what she would like for her birthday. Well, it is now near 10 P.M. Taps. Good night, Mom.

With love & Happy Landings,
Ed, Randy

May 28, 1942

Dear Dotty,

I am trying to get my correspondence up to date. We have finished flying and so I have a little spare time. I'm writing to all my girlfriends.

What would you like for a birthday present?

Am glad to hear you had a nice time at your Banquet.

From what I hear from all sides you must have been stunning.

So one of the teachers is joining the Navy. Well, that's great. You say his fiancee is a doll. I take it you mean pretty. Please tell me if my young lady friend Faye is still a doll.

Yes! Radda wrote me and said you were going to Chicago this summer. I hope you have a nice vacation.

So Willie has another girl friend. Who is she? Where does she live?

Not that I care, but you know how boys are. Don't know why, but girls always interest us.

Well, our stay in Uvalde is almost over. We have had a lot of fun. The girls down here are pretty and we have had a lot of fun with them. Our Underclass decorated the hall for the dance and besides putting up a big insignia and cartoons they had HAPPY LANDINGS 42-I in foot high letters.

*Tues. night at the Banquet the underclass put on another program that was a scream. One of the Dodos (underclassmen) walked in with a water pistol gunning for the upperclassmen Officers. He said he couldn't stand it any longer, for five weeks all he did was "pop to," "hit a brace," etc. and now he was after revenge. He was reloading his pistol out of a big bucket after each shot. The Master of Ceremonies told him to stop and throw the water away, so he picks up the bucket and swings it out over the tables. Some fellows ducked and others went under the table. What a climax as nothing but shreds of paper came out of the bucket. We roared laughing. They gave one of the instructors a bull snake ship to use on his students. Also the instructors changed helmets on the last flight and the students told them to *---- (?)*

We leave for Basic in a few days and it is not Randolph. Well, don't forget to Lux your undies.

Your loving brother,
Happy Landings Randy

June 12, 1942.

Dear Folks,

Did you receive the "Slipstream?" Our Primary School was written up in "Colliers" magazine, the June 13 issue. The foreign student pictured lived in my bay. We called him "Ceto." He is from Rio in Brazil. Poor fellow "washed." Did Dotty receive my letter and card? What would she like for her birthday?

It took your letter about 3 days to get here. This wildness is some more of God's country. The temperature was108 degrees yesterday and 105 degrees today, in the shade! I definitely do not like it here as well as Garner. Garner was like a Boy Scout camp or Country Club compared to this place. We are back to sleeping on army cots. They are very free here the way they hand out "gigs." I got one today because the blanket on my bed wasn't tight like a drum. We get a gig if there is any dust under our bed or on our locker. One cleans up and 20 minutes later it is all dust again. Boy is the dust here terrible. San Angelo has a population of 25,000 plus. My instructor had his training here. The school is about a year and a half old. They are tougher here on the cadets than at Randolph I hear because Randolph has a name and Goodfellow is trying to get one. Yes! It is a great climate down here… the heat will either cure or kill you.

You are indeed right. A lot of things have to be considered when getting married. But you know the old Army saying. Eat, drink, and be merry, for tomorrow no one knows.

Please don't worry as I am on the wagon and the beam. I don't smoke or drink. Yet! One of our pals washed out today because he was flying mechanically. And five others failed the eye test. I have had 150 hours training in the Link Instrument Trainer. More fun. Hope John is well again.

I saw an order in which I learned we leave here Aug. 8th and graduate from Advanced Oct. 9th, in about three and a half months. Well! I soloed the BT-13A Wednesday… more bounces. The ship weighs 2 tons. It is almost time for *taps so goodnight. Tomorrow is a big S .M. I. I joined the Bugle Corps here. Say Hi to Faye for me.*

Happy Landings, Ed

June 25, 1942

Dear John,

Am glad you are feeling better than previous conditions allowed. Our weather here is hot & hotter & dry 95 to 100. Last week I took 4 words a minute in code. We have to be able to do 15 words a min. I got 94 in the Radio exam and 89 in the Navigation exam. We are now studying meteorology and more code. The boy on Page 23 is from Arizona. H.H. Lee. Poor "Ceto" washed out so his picture is not in the Slipstream. He is pictured in the Colliers. The boy in the snapshot is McKinley. He washed too. He was from Argentina. Ceto was from Brazil. So Mr. Platt is in the R. C. A. F. I hope he gets all he expects, but don't let them fool you. There is nothing like the good old U.S.A. The pay is more, better treatment, living conditions, everything. We have some R C A F boys here. They sure are glad to get back with Uncle Sam.

We had our pictures taken here and am sending one to Dad. It's a serious expression type.

Life here seems tough at times but is fun. They, the tactical officers, are going to make the best flying officers out of us or kill us trying. During personal inspection we have to be immaculate to the nth degree. Hair cut & combed, clean clothes with the military tuck in our shirts, teeth & finger nails cleaned, shoes polished. We get gigs for everything not perfect and they add up in a hurry. Well! So far I haven't lowered myself to drinking, smoking or wild women. Say Hi to the Bartholomew's if you see them and especially Faye. I received a nice letter from Faye's mom.

Sunday we are invited to a picnic given by the Lions Club. Swimming, etc. If you folks move to the city and you wish to join the Army, the Air Corps is best of them all. My instructor says if I keep at it, I will make a good instrument

pilot and bomber pilot. Here's hoping.
Happy Landing.
Tailspin Randy

July 2, 1942.

Dear Mom,

Thanks for all the letters. Am dead tired tonight, but have a few minutes, so am writing this lying on my cot. Today I went on my first solo X-country. Gee! Was it fun! It was about 200 miles. It took me 1:50 hours. On the return leg I drifted off my course 8 miles in 50 miles. I found my position and got back just ahead of a big cumulonimbus "thunderhead" (my meteorology cropping out.) One of the boys went around the storm, as we were told to do if we meet one, and got lost 70 miles west of San Angelo. He is now back home. He lives in my house and every so often someone comes in to hear his story. The night before last I did my first night flying and soloed. We did floodlight landings. If we made a boner concerning our flying we get stars and each star cost 15 cents. It cost me 60 cents on my first night flying. More beauty! The moon came up a little after midnight and shone on the ship and the ground. Part of the time during my X-C I flew on instruments in the overcast. Some boys had a big 4 engine B-17 pass them in flight. I have done spins and stalls under the hood instrument flying.

I am trying to answer your letters. I have a few blisters on my dogs as the first week here I had to walk three tours on the ramp, the same as 200 other cadets. Yes! We had a parade at the post in honor of our new Commanding Officer. No! Cadets do not get a raise in pay. Oh yes! We are upperclassmen today. We have 3 more months to go before we finish. San Angelo has a population of 25,000. They had an air raid in town yesterday and the Wasps drive the cars and motorcycles. Women with bars! Can you imagine that? I am the third from the left in the Bugle Corps in the Slipstream. (Slipstream is the name of a newspaper-like magazine for the Military.) The slipstream is the portion of the air that is drawn back by the prop. The boys have a lot of funny names for things in the Air Corps.

What advanced school is Nick going to? The way it sounds the farm is still the old hard grind. Why don't you sell the place and move back to the city? John & Dotty would then meet some decent young people. I got a letter from Betty telling about the Westrate boys.

I have a good chance of going to Kelly Field for advanced, but I'm not counting on it.

Weather is interesting when we study it in Meteorology.

Yes! I suggested to Faye she go with other fellows. So who knows what the future holds.

Army life so far hasn't changed me. No, I don't drink, smoke or swear, and I don't hate anybody nor do I want to kill anybody. It is not for me to know the reason why, but rather for me to do or die.

I had a very nice letter from Faye's mom. I hope Faye has thanked you for the present you gave her by now. She is probably disgusted with me.

We get open post every Wed. and Sat. night & Sun. I have rented a garage for $5.00 a month day & night. Yes! I am getting the feel of these ships finally. I took 8 words a minute in code today. Tell Dad I'm trying for the Commander-in-Chief seat, but a fellow has to keep up his morale by going out with the gals once in a while.

The last two classes didn't get furloughs on graduating, but I am trying hard for one. Am also sending a picture to Dad next week. The serious type with my mouth closed.

It is light here until late. We buy our Officer Uniforms in a few weeks. They say when one gets into Advance it takes an act of Congress (almost) to wash us out. So far Uncle Sam has spent over $5,000 on me.

Why is Violette moving to Idaho?

There is a lake and river near here where we go swimming. One of the enlisted men drowned the other day so they are getting strict with us. You can see we are valuable fellows.

Yes! The Link Trainer does almost everything but leave the ground. Well! I hope this finds you all well. Tomorrow being the 4th we hope to get off at noon Sat. until Sun. night.

Happy Landings
(Hot Pilot) H. P. Ed

July 25, 1942

Dear Mom,

Thanks for all the letters and stuff. I have been busy as a beaver so

I have not written anyone the last week. We expect to leave here by the first of August. As yet we do not know where we will be sent. I hope I get sent to a twin-engine school.

I think it a very good idea to leave the farm. It has always been a lot of grief and hard work. John wrote and said he would like to get in the Air Corps, which I think is a very good idea. This flying game is the coming thing and it is the safest of all employments. I think it would be best if the Randell family moved back to the city where they belong.

As the days go by I wish I had a college education, the man with the education has the advantage. Even the work I'm doing here would be made a lot easier. That extra Math I took at Coopersville Post Grad and the Course at Illinois Institute of Technology helped me a lot.

No! John is wrong. We do not get any increase in pay as we progress. And this new increase in wages did not affect the Cadets. It is still $75.

My feet are almost healed now. Yes! The doctors take good care of us. They gave me some kind of a salve. It is very potent.

Being in the Bugle Corp I don't carry a gun. We have been issued gas masks but have not had to drill in them yet. Did you folks get my portrait? No! I don't know all the Bugle calls. I got a very nice letter from Mrs. Irish telling about the Sunday Service and flag.

The garage I rented is in town. We are on the city limits

of the town about five miles to the business district.

The graduates can choose after graduating one of the following: Ferry Command, Instructor, or overseas duty. And then the Army sends you where they want you. Good joke.

The other night I flew X-C to Abilene, Big Springs and home. Gee! Was it pretty! Abilene looked like a big Christmas tree with all the different colored lights. If we fly up to midnight we get up at 6 a.m. If we fly until 2 a.m. we get up at 8:30 a.m. the next morning. Yesterday I forgot to enter my flying time in the dispatch sheet and it cost me $1.50.

Our planes we fly have greenhouses on them, or in other words, are closed over by a glass covering.

We are now on instrument flying. Flying the beam. We have a covered hood over us in the rear cockpit. Observer rides in front.

I too heard a locust for the first time last Sunday. Fall is almost here.

It is 95 degrees here all the time. We do not notice it as it is so dry.

Down here all the army seems to be getting promotions.

Naturally I'll take my car with me when I finish training. What did you think? Those who have signed up in the Air Force and want to be called, get $21. a month, private's pay. I was sent to Texas the same day I was sworn in. Savvy? Also if those men wash out they are made privates in the Regular Army immediately, unless they go in for Navigation or Bombardier. We are having a little sprinkle right now. Two weeks ago I went canoe riding with some cadets and a young lady. More fun.

Oh yes! I want Dotty to come to my graduation this fall.

I met this fellow Bruce Kilborn at Uvalde. We lived in the same bay there. He is a swell lad, doesn't drink or smoke so we get along fine. He is from Conn. and is quite a dancer. He is a quiet type of fellow and a very good swimmer. Swam all his life in the ocean.

Last week a lad jumped from a spinning plane and still

later an instructor and student crashed in a plane. The student was from Joliet, Ill. Both were killed.

Next Sunday we hope to have a big party.

Am buying a $25 bond every 3 months and am sending them to Dotty as beneficiary.

In a half hour I have to go to "Link." We are now on radio flying the beam.

Please write soon and lets hear what is happening to you all.

I got a nice letter from Betty Westrate.

Hope Hitler doesn't get Egypt or the Suez.

Cousin Foster has been sending me letters and keeping me posted. He says they are going to train Cadets in the Stevens Hotel.

Happy Landing, Ed

P.S. Are there any Army men or Navy men in my ancestors of past generations? They would like the information for the publicity office.

Chapter Three

August 7, 1942

Dear Mom,

Well, here I am at Advance. I bet you will never be able to guess where I am! I am at Moore Field, Mission, Texas. It is about 26 miles north of the Rio Grande and Mexico and about 75 miles west of the Gulf. The Field is 30 miles from Mercedes, Texas, where father's cousin lives. Will have to go see and visit her again I guess.

All furloughs for the two classes ahead of me have been canceled. Some boys have been sent straight into Foreign Service. I'm afraid now I'll have to cancel my invitation to Dotty about coming to my Graduation as it will cost more than I expected and I may not get home again very soon. Some boys of the last class were sent to the state of Washington.

Now I shall answer your letters. The way you write I must be an old man. The portrait is exactly the way I am… a young child with no worries. (Don't I wish it) I have a new class book for you.

Have worn out only 1 pair of shoes. Yes! I have met lots of boys here I was with at the replacement center. The boy landed safe when he jumped from the spinning plane.

So Jack is in Chicago, isn't that news! What are you and Dad going to do with the farm?

Our 'star' money goes for a big party every four weeks.

Please don't worry so much about my auto. Being a Cadet I may keep it and all the tires. And when I'm sent overseas I let my wife take care of it. Bet you didn't know I'd gotten married.

Seriously, though, we are told the war is getting serious and that is why the furloughs are being canceled. Here we get our first gunnery practice. I have been sent to a pursuit school. They have P-39s & P-40s here. We have to learn how to take machine guns and cannons apart and put them together.

For our tow-target practice we are sent to Matagorda Island in the Gulf. It is N.E. of Corpus Christi.

Went motorboat riding at San Angelo last week... more fun. Also met a fine young lady there. Very interesting. And she didn't smoke or drink which is something now days.

Well, I must study now on how to kill Japs & Jerry's, so...

Happy Landings, Ed

Next is another letter to Marjorie.

Aug. 10, 1942

Dear Marjorie,

I bet you must think me impossible, after I ask you to write me and then I never answer your swell letter.

Truly I like to get letters but find little time to answer them. We fly half a day and have ground school the other half. And when we get a day off or an "open post" we all sail into town for some entertainment. I had lots of fun at Goodfellow just riding around the countryside going on picnics or swimming. There are still some nice people in the world even with all this war. The people treat the Cadets swell.

I am now stationed in the Rio Grande Valley, beautiful place, palm trees and all that sort of thing, you know, tropical vegetation.

Moore Field, Mission Texas, about 70 miles from the Gulf.

For our aerial gunnery we are sent to an island in the Gulf.

I have been sent to Pursuit School.. All the fellows are shorter in height than I. I wanted to go to a Bomber School, but I may still be sent to one. We have a P-40 to fly. Today I soloed the AT-6A, almost as much thrill as the Primary trainer. These new ships have retractable landing gear and of course machine guns. We learn how to machine gun tow-targets and ground targets. We are also taught skeet.

We will not get furloughs on graduating as they say the war is too serious.

I am going to volunteer for Foreign Service to get even with those Yellow Japs.

Have you heard of Jack's whereabouts? If you haven't I'll go get him for you. Wish me luck. Will write more later. I have to study some more about my machine guns.

Good luck and Happy Landings,
Ed. Randy

P. S. Thank your Mom for the swell letter.

August 15, 1942
3 p.m.

Dear Mom,

Conditions are the best. Hope you have my new address by this time. Here it is again in case you didn't get my other letter.

Moore Field, Mission, Texas

I did not know Tony B. was inducted. I feel sorry for the boys in the regular army. As Cadets we are not allowed to go to the U. S. O. 's. but we have our fun.

Down here the cadets have the McAllen Country Club

reserved for them on Sat. evening, dancing, etc. It is formal or informal depending on the occasion. Tomorrow... Sunday... we are invited to a big tea dance at the Casa DePalmo Hotel in McAllen. It is the wish of the C.O. that all attend.

Am writing this from the flight line and I see I have to fly again in 15 minutes. I'll write more tomorrow.

Sunday, August 16, 1942, 9 P.M. Almost bedtime. Well, the big tea dance is over. They had a dance orchestra, and the ballroom was very pretty, so were the girls! The people down here treat the Cadets swell. A lot of the girls are out to get themselves a Lieutenant.

Who is the Webber you speak of? I have found a town named Webb. Will keep lookgvbing for Webbersville. I finally found Titus County on the map in the N.E. corner of Texas. The AT-6 planes we fly are the tops. Tricky to land but fly beautiful. I can't think of much to write of and I'm tired so will quit. Want all to know I'm always thinking of you even if I don't write often.

With Love and Happy Landings, Ed.

September 4, 1942

Dear Dad & Mom,

Here is to your health and hope you are both well and enjoying your vacation. Boy, I wish I could be with you all.

I went on a navigation flight today about 300 miles. More fun. We ran into a "front" and the ceiling dropped to about four hundred feet. So we just about hedgehopped across the brush at 150 to160 miles per hour.

While we are cadets we have to go to certain controlled (specified) airports on our cross-countries. After we become officers we can plan our own cross-countries up to 800 miles and go anywhere.

During night flying this week we had five airplane accidents (all minor accidents.) One boy forgot to put his wheels down when he landed, so the ship skidded in on its "stomach." The Cadet (Gadget) was not hurt, just surprised.

The damage was about $1400 worth.

I wouldn't mind living in the Park Place Hotel like those Navy boys, sounds like a real setup. Most of the Bomber schools are in the north. Am still hoping I get sent to one. The bombsight the Army has now will work up in the stratosphere (8 miles high.)

Thanks for the clipping, but I hardly believe I'll get to the Berlin Fair this year unless it's in Germany.

Gee! I hope Bud doesn't have any aftereffects from the blow he received. This army life is safer.

Thanks for the ancestral information. Have not gotten to Mercedes yet. Please excuse me for not writing more, I want to answer about 8 other letters. We have finished our ground school and now shoot skeet at the range and do extra flying. Was up until two A.M. this morning. I was supposed to fly but didn't as my plane caught on fire when I started it. Other than cutting my hand getting out, turning off a dozen switches and gas line and getting the fire extinguisher into action, I'm okay. This life is full of adventure. Whew!

Happy Landings,
Ed.

Have Dotty send my letters to you all.

Sat. night
(Some time in 1942)

Dear Mother,

Please excuse the paper. Would you please send me a large envelope so I could send you a map of Texas? I hope you like the pictures I am sending Dotty. The young lady I met at San Angelo. She is originally from Houston, Texas. She is a very sensible girl and doesn't smoke or drink, and I haven't taken to it either. The pictures we took of each other. Her aunt took the ones of us together. We went on a picnic one Sunday to a small park west of San Angelo. They had the river dammed up so we could go swimming. She likes to swim most of anything. She put up a lunch for us and I ate most of it, being a big boy. Lois is one girl I don't think is out for a Lieutenant, like most of the girls down here are.

Well! I have ordered my new uniforms. They look very military.

I got Dad's card. Tell him I'm going to see if I can find the old Webber estate. I must be very near it, as I am near all the towns mentioned in the letters.

No! It is against the law to fly over the Rio or Mexico. Our date of Graduation is still Oct. 9. Some of the boys' parents are driving down from Chicago.

We have found that it doesn't make any difference what we fly in Advanced.

If they need bomber pilots we go to bomber school. If they need pursuit pilots we leave here immediately for overseas. They pick us at random. We are given a choice and then are sent where we are needed.

I got a letter from Mrs. Johanson. She said Mr. Moffatt announced in church I'd like to receive some letters from the church members. I wrote her since I've been here.

Today we had a hurricane warning including the coast of Texas. The bays were all evacuated from the gunnery island. And we were to stand by and fly planes inland. But it didn't get bad, as we all were given open post. The wind did shift from the prevailing SE to N. and the temperature dropped to 80 degrees.

Sunday.

So today is Sunday. It is nice and cool. The temp is usually around 105 degrees so 80 degrees is cold.

That Sunday school picnic sounds like a lot of fun. Today I've been invited to a gentleman's home here for a big outdoor steak fry. About 50 Cadets are invited.

The house would look like something if it were all painted, you're right. What are you folks going to do with the farm now that Dotty is back? Are you going to stay there all winter? I'd sure like to get home for one of your Sunday dinners.

I guess Bud might just as well get married. He won't be

any better situated by putting it off.

42-G finally left here with sealed orders for overseas duty. Everyone had long faces. They had to go by government transportation and were not given any furloughs. The Major read us letters from the other men at the Bomber schools and they say they are flying 7 days a week and a Cadet's life is like heaven in comparison to their officer's life.

We get all the important information on the war now in class. It is pretty serious. We are studying all about the actual fighting.

We hear the Class 43-A or B are not to be commissioned 2nd Lieutenants but Flight Officers.

I have been up on one high altitude flight so far. One has to use oxygen about 10,000. I was only up about 4 miles. One can see for miles. The clouds, you know, reach as high as 8 miles and some fighter planes fly just about that high. I have also completed my first navigation flight. And had a few hours of combat and formation flying. It is all hard work but fun. I got 84 in my armament course. Our ground school is over next week. And then we get extra flying.

I finally wrote Mrs. Irish.

Love and Happy Landings,
Ed

Sept. (1942)

Dear Folks,

The Greyhound Bus goes to McAllen, Texas, which is the best and largest town to stay.

Will send you my government map showing Moore Field & McAllen, Texas, which you may return to me when you come out to the field. Yes! Texas is the land of Tourist Courts. The reason I would like to know if you are coming is so I can make reservations for you as everything is taken during graduation time.

And... I don't expect to be here from Oct. 1 to 7 as that is the week my flight goes to Matagorda Island. Also there is some talk of the Graduation being Wed. the 7th. I think it would be best to come on the bus or train and then you can use my car while you are down here. And the payments are all up to date, too!

Will send the Texas map. Plan it so you can get here a day before the graduation so you can rest up a day. The Graduation starts at 9 A.M. until 12:00 noon. The guests are then invited to Lunch at the Cadet Mess Hall. After graduation we have to live in town until we receive our orders stating to which station we will be sent.

If possible I might get a "delay on route" pass and drive you home.

The last graduation was held at the field in one of the hangars.

Yesterday it dropped to 60 degrees F. The wind was from the north. So one would have to bring a few heavier clothes or a sweater. It is warm enough in the sun, but cool at night. We will graduate in khaki. October 20 we change to Olive Drab.

No. We do not practice jumping. Parachutes, like life preservers, are used only in case of an emergency.

No! It will not be necessary for Dotty to buy a formal… although I thought she had one.

Will write again soon. Happy Landings

Boy! Wait until you see my new clothes—whistle —and me in them!

Ed

.

Edward was so proud of his uniform. He *did* look great in it.

Sept. 28, 1942.

Dear Folks,

Received your letter today and am answering per immediately.

We're going to do this the Army way. You telegraph me not later than Thursday morning, so I will get it Thursday morning.

Just say, "proceed with plan ___" Then add any pertinent or important suggestions, if any.

Plan Z. Reserve rooms for five at the Hotel ($2.50 - $3.50 a night)

Plan Y. Reserve rooms for three at the Hotel (same price)

Plan X. Reserve room for Dotty at Hotel

Plan W. Reserve rooms for five at Tourist Court ($1.00 a night cabins)

Plan V. Reserve rooms for three at Tourist Court

Yes, I believe I can get two extra guests in; all I have to do is initial (EWR) your ticket. The Graduation is Oct. the 9th, Friday. I may get my orders Sat. and I may get them Mon. I do not know. Yes! I have a room reserved at the Hotel where I can stay until I receive my orders. I really don't think we will get furloughs so it would be best to buy the round trip. The graduation will start about 9:30 a.m.

Oh! Mrs. Irish wrote Marjorie was going to Texas to visit a friend if you folks don't go maybe Dotty could come down with her as far as she goes, that is if she was coming about this time.

You folks would have to leave about Mon. to get down here Thursday night.

Oh yes, thanks for the snapshots. And you may keep my class book from Goodfellow. My time is very limited but will see if I can get to the courthouse. I hear there is a Webber living in Edinburg.

Am almost through flying here at Moore. An Instrument (blind flying) check and some spot landings and that is all. Will write again after I receive your telegram.

Happy Landings,
"Wings, Randy"

When I was at Kelly the boys nicknamed me "Randy" and it has stuck ever since.

Ed.

Oct. 6, 1942
9 P.M.

Dear Mom,

You ought to see your son now when he walks down the flight line, wearing a life preserver, a parachute, a helmet and with 400 rounds of ammunition around his neck.

It is swell here, cool, mosquitos, flies, sand and wind and sun, like a desert and tropics in one. There is even sand in my bed. I am in bed writing this letter as the only place I can get away from the mosquitos is under this netting over my bed.

We wear life preservers as we do all our aerial gunnery out over the Gulf. We may return home tomorrow if we finish. We have to shoot 1500 rounds. The picture I enclosed in the Goodfellow Book was taken at Moore Field, to be sent to our hometown newspaper when we graduate. You may keep the book. I got your cookies. Thanks a million.

Also received your telegram. Gee! It's too bad you couldn't all get down. Yes, Dotty should have her tonsils out. According to your letter Bud is having a hard time of it. I hope he gets along okay so he can get married.

I wish John could go to College and become an Engineer instead of a cattle raiser. When I get to my new station I'm going to ask for a furlough. I won't count on it but I do hope I get it.

Thank you for writing the news of Faye's doings.

No! The thought of Mary Lee coming down to my graduation doesn't bother me in the least. I'd rather have my own family come than her. Yes! I'll admit I did discourage her about coming.

Yes! I guess Radda will be living alone as soon as Bud gets married. She wrote me that she didn't fancy the idea of living by herself. Maybe she will move in with Mae Trenbeth. I wrote and told her to hook some guy. Hope you are over the poison ivy by this time and Dad's teeth have stopped aching.

One of the boys just mentioned that our group hasn't had any accidents during our stay here, of which we can be proud. The last group had 3 crackups. One boy from Foster Field spun in. Yes, he was killed. We dive at the round targets and pull up at about 50 ft. or less… more fun and thrills. The cause of accidents is getting into another ship's prop wash and losing control of your ship. Other than this, low turns are not dangerous.

Tell Dad there is an article about Johnson's milk business at Detroit in the Readers' Digest (Sept. '42 issue)

Your loving son,
Happy Landings Ed

"Faye's doings" turned out to be Faye *getting married.* Edward made no comment other than the one above but he must have been profoundly affected at the time.

Faye had no idea what she was missing! What a handsome fellow he was the first time I saw him in uniform!

Edward came home to Coopersville after graduation. Am not sure if he had reported in to his new duty station of Romulus, Michigan, near Detroit before he came home or not.

2nd Lt. Edward W Randell–Home

Edward and his Mom. You can see she was proud of him.–Home

One afternoon he came over to my parents' farm to visit them. I was at work in Grand Rapids. My parents must have been impressed as my mother said several times, "I wish Marjorie was here." "I wish Marjorie could see you."

Edward came back that evening! He asked if I would like to ride with him to Muskegon to pick up his brother John from work. Of course, I told him I would. I was impressed with this "new" Edward Randell, too.

Chapter Four

It was the beginning of a whole new life for me. I had been dating an older fellow, a Canadian who had been drafted and did nothing but bitch and complain about it. *My brother was a prisoner of war of the Japanese!* What in the world was the matter with this man… a Canadian who had lived in the United States for ten years and still had not filed citizenship papers? Why was he complaining? When I saw Edward ready, willing and eager to serve his country proudly, I was smitten. Our very first evening together was the beginning of a romance, before long turning into a courtship.

Edward's first letter to me sent from Romulus:

October 23, 1942

Dear Marjorie,

We both seemed to have missed each other. Wed. night I went to your house to see you but no one was home.

According to your letter you were at the movies in G. R. I bet you had more fun without me boring you. Seriously, I wanted to see you.

Yes! I would like to have gone hunting Thursday. But you know how an Officer's life is (or do you?) Here today... gone tomorrow.

We work 7 days a week, 8 A.M. to 5 P.M.

How do you like this for an idea? You pick out some big State Football game you would like to see and I will endeavor to get a pass and we can go and shout our lungs out and forget the war for a while. I hear Ann Arbor has some lively games.

Yes! You did look surprised when I walked in on you Wed. I promise I won't do it again.

No! John is still in Coopersville. (Darn this pen.)

The first month here we go to the transition school to learn to fly multi-engine ships.

After we start ferrying we will be gone 20 days out of the month and no time off between flights. Well, so far you have not asked anything I can't answer.

Today I went up in an AT-6 like I flew at Moore. So I will get my flight pay for this month. We flew until 7:30 P.M. and it was dark on our last landing.

The first night here I stayed at a Hotel in Ann Arbor. Am now rooming in Romulus (Darn this pen!) and get my meals at the Club. I love the Air Force more each day. Please write, hope you can read this letter. Yes, and Happy Landings to you.

Ed.

Edward's letter showed that his pen was obviously acting up as often times his writing was almost invisible, other times it was a dark black.

Friday
Oct. 30,1942.

Dear Marjorie,

Thanks for the nice long letter. Also, thank you for the information on the football games. Yes! I think the best date would be Nov. 7.

I would like to get home for Thanksgiving Day, too, but if gasoline is rationed. Well! The future holds the answers.

Being an Officer I am on 24 hr. duty and may be called to use my car at any time, so I am told, but it doesn't seem to sway the tire board. We will also have gasoline rationed to us the same as anyone (civilian.) As of yet there has been no mention of it. I buy Ethyl gas on the Field for 15 cents a gallon. Swell! Huh?

I hope to have my car repaired the first of next week. All I can get out of the tire board is a "recap." Oh well! I won't complain as a lot of fellows like you mentioned are working harder than we are and don't get any rest or entertainment.

I hope the Schmidt boy is just missing and not dead.

Yes! The war does seem closer when it affects someone you know or someone <u>close</u> to you. I also hope the stars on the Service Flag at Church do not change to gold.

When I see you soon I'll tell you how afraid of flying I am. No! I'm not afraid now, but I still get a thrill out of aerobatics. You know how it is... to be hanging on ones safety belt upside down... your heart begins to beat just a little faster and after the maneuver is completed you sigh and feel a new confidence in yourself. It's a great feeling.

Yes! I think you had a very busy afternoon, what with all the sewing and shopping. Next time I see you I'll bring all my socks to be darned and buttons to sew on. Believe me, I'm only teasing.

I think your idea of visiting Eloise and Howard is a "good deal." I'm using Air Corps slang.

I will try to get off Fri. at 5 P.M. and visit my folks Fri. night and come to your house Sat. morning. We will be in Lansing Sat. afternoon, Northville Sat. night. If you would care to attend you may be my guest at the Grosse Point Country Club Sat. night for a big dance.

You can plan something for Sunday and Sunday evening I'll see you home. It sounds like a big weekend. If you don't like any of my ideas or wish to change them it will be okay with me.

Wish me luck on getting my pass as I have asked for one for this Sunday to visit my Cousin in Detroit. I'll have to be a very good pilot this week.

If there is any doubt about my getting the pass I'll let you know in time.

My cousin asked me to go to the Methodist Church with him and Mrs. Pratt this Sunday.

Have been visiting Bob Wilcox in Detroit every night to keep up his morale. I have not seen my sister's snapshots as yet. Nor has Bud answered my letter yet, but don't worry, it may have been a false alarm.

Well, Marj, the top of the day to you &
Happy Landings.
Ed

Nov. 4, 1942

Dear Marjorie,

Darn! I guess we are both in a muddle. However, I am still planning on coming home Friday night. If you cannot get off Sat., I guess we will have to call off the football game. I hope you won't be too disappointed, but I think it means a lot more to the young lady to see her hubby than for us to see a football game. Do you agree? Swell! If you aren't disappointed I shan't be either.

Yes! The dances at the Country Club are formal, but maybe we best forget it this time, as I'm afraid we would not be able to get there at the proper time. Some time later you can come see me and then we will go to the Country Club. As for you getting to Detroit and home this time, let's just say that I'll drive.

I don't imagine I will get to Coopersville much before 10:30 P.M. Fri. night and if you are up I'll stop and "chin." And then you can tell me what you decided. Sure I'd like to go with you and your pals Sat. night and Sun. So you decide, if you want to visit Eloise. Write or let her know and then tell me all Fri. night. Okay? Am sorry this seems so hurried but I want to get this note mailed tonight.

Today I was informed the fender for my car has not come yet, so I have to wait another week. No peace for the wicked. No rest for the weary. Well, be good to yourself and I'll see you Fri. night and show you the beautiful moon.

Happy Landings,
Ed

Next is a post card to sister Dotty with the return address of:

Edward W. Randell, 2nd Lt.
Student Training Detachment
AAFCCS
Smyrna, Tenn.
Class 42-4-O

Nov. 16, 1942

Dear Dotty,

We arrived safe Saturday. Hope you all got home safe. I slept most of today. We start our course tomorrow. It is swell here. Thanks a million for helping me and driving all over. Will see you soon.

Happy Landings
Ed, Randy

Nov. 16, 1942.

Dear Marjorie,

First I shall give you my new address and then hope you will write me.

2nd Lt. Edward W. Randell
Student Training Detachment
A. A. F. CC. S. Smyrna, Tenn.
Class 42-4-0

Marjorie! How did you make out with the pay roll Friday? Golly Gumdrops, I'd hate to think you made a lot of mistakes on account of my keeping you out so "early."

My Mom asked me what I did so late. Mothers are so awful inquisitive don't you agree, but I wouldn't want her to be any different. I told her we watched the blackout. So she says… well it didn't last all night did it?

I got to Romulus Friday afternoon and was checked out by 5 P.M. After leaving my bags at the airport I stayed all night with my cousins.

I arrived here Sat. noon. We took the Airline down here. It was a great trip. Every airport we landed at or factory district we flew over the stewardess would close the curtains so we didn't see a thing but clouds. More fun. Saturday afternoon we checked in at the new station and Sunday I took the rest cure and slept almost the whole day. Today, Monday, we meet our flight and ground school instructors.

My Pilot is a Capt. Proctor from Romulus Air Base. He is a swell fellow. He looks like my older brother Jim, tall, but he has blonde hair. He said after our training here we would be sent back to Detroit. What do you think of that idea? He has asked for the South Atlantic foreign ferrying and asked me today, if I would like to be his Co-pilot. So, you know me, I said yes! Sir! If I am accepted it means I'll leave the Detroit Base. Maybe I'm getting a little ahead of myself. I guess I'll wait until I finish the course and then decide where to go. Don't you agree?

Today we got in a few hours of cockpit time familiarizing ourselves with the cockpit controls, instruments and switches.

If you would like I'll explain the duties of the Pilots. The Pilot handles the controls and does the actual flying and watching of the flight instruments. The Co-pilot relieves the pilot during flight and operates the engines at all times and watches all the engine instruments and during his spare time acts as radioman and navigator and is the pilot's valet. It really isn't as bad as it sounds for the Copilot. Our pilots kid us and say that we also have to have some good telephone numbers at the different towns where we stop on

Edward with five of his pilot buddies . . . all ferry pilots, I presume. Can you tell which one is Edward? They all have big smiles.

flights. Capt. Proctor said he would like to go to Brownsville or Mission Texas. He has a brother living there.

I am sitting on my bed writing, as there are no tables in our rooms. I am lounging in my P. J.' s. Now to tell you a secret...s-s-h-h-h...the weather down here is a perfect 62 degrees F. during the day. Now don't tell a soul I told you that.

I am reading your last letter over. Am glad you liked the candy and maybe some day we may even get to see a football game. Who knows?

I don't get it about the colors on your knees! Please explain. Did you fall or something?

I think your penmanship is very good. So do as your boss says but don't let him get you down.

No! I did not get the opportunity to see "Ten Men From W. P."

It is now 8:30 P.M. I must get to sleep soon as I have to be up at 5 and on the line at 6:30 A.M.

Am glad you didn't mind my taking my brother & sister skating. Some girls wouldn't have liked my being so thoughtful to someone else. Did you hear the News tonight? Swell, huh? Thanks for the swell week. Happy Landings.

Your pal,
Ed Randy.

Comment in an aside here…he signed his letter, "Your pal." H-m-m-m-m. I thought I was *more* than a pal. Oh dear! Could the tall fellow on Edward's right (left, to you readers) be Capt. Proctor? Maybe. We will never know for sure.

Mon. Nov.23, 2 P.M.

Dear Marjorie,

Capt. Proctor and I didn't fly this afternoon, so am writing letters. We came in and found one of our pals asleep, so Capt. Proctor set his clock 4 hours ahead and wakes poor Lt. McManus. The Lt. jumps up and thinks he has missed his Link period. I tell him its 6 P.M. and time for dinner. The Lt. then gets dressed and calls up to make an appointment for a Link period this evening. So they tell him its only 2 P.M. Well! I have just finished drying myself off. Lt. Mac came back from telephoning and threw a bottle of water at both of his antagonists. Aren't we the little devils? Don't answer that.

Today I had the honor of receiving a letter from you. Thank you very much for the long letter. Yes! Smyrna is some 20 miles from Nashville. Southeast of Nashville, you might say. Lebanon is to the east of Nashville.

My mother always told me to be truthful and never say anything to a young lady I didn't mean. But, seriously, Marjorie! I like you, especially the way you tease me. At least I hope you are teasing me and not angry with me. My face is red. Sure I remember taking you skating and your falling down. But for the life of me I couldn't understand your letter when I read it. (Marjorie's remark concerning her knees) I read your letter on the airplane between Detroit and Toledo and so many things had happened during the week that I didn't know which way was "up." Please forgive me.

I hope you will come to Romulus to visit me some time. Do you have any time off near Christmas?

Marjorie! You tickle me. To the best of my knowledge I don't believe I know anyone at either Brownsville or Mission, unless of course you meant my cousins, who live in Mercedes.

I'm sorry to hear you are getting a cold. I have beaten mine off at last. I wonder where you got your cold. Hm. Now I didn't say anything, so don't hit me. That is terrible when the whole office has colds. I noticed a lot of the boys down here have colds or coughs. I'll bet you look cute with a little red nose.

Yes! We live in barracks. One man to a room, it is very nice as we have it very private. We have a closet for our clothes and personal things. A nice soft steel cot with springs. Oh yes, and the room is steam-heated, when someone builds a fire. Sunday our orderly was "off" for the day so we acted as our own firemen.

I have a system of strings "rigged" up whereby I can turn out the lite when I'm in bed. Clever, aye what? I write such stuff and nonsense to make you think I'm a smart fellow. Oh! I forgot. We also have a chair in our little room.

I'm glad my kid sister is a good driver. So she showed you my card and you say it was very nice. What do you mean was nice... her, the card, or me, or the idea of the thing? Silly, aren't I?

The next time I need a wash job I'll come to you. I'll bet you are cute in slacks and a sweater.

Some time when I visit you I'll explain how the knowledge of our weather can help the enemy. If it won't put you to sleep to listen to one of my orations or dissertations.

Yes! I remember that ride very well with Jean and Jack. Jack was in a quandary over his girl friends.

I saw the picture "Sir Eileen" with LaVerne. I really enjoyed it. Bud saw it as a play in Chicago and said it was even funnier.

Golly! It's too bad Howard Bush has to leave for the Army so soon. They weren't together very long. But such is life, and I love it. There is something new each day. This year will be my first Thanksgiving away from home. But I'll be thinking of my folks and you also, when I thank our God for the many blessing I have received.

Miss! I think you're right. You should get more sleep and not stay up so late. 11 P.M.! Terrible! It is almost two weeks ago since I was at your home. Just think 3 more weeks and maybe I'll be back again. Isn't that a gruesome "thought"?

Some folks say every day it gets closer to winter and then they feel miserable, but you know what I say… you don't… well, I'll tell you. I say every day brings the spring closer. Isn't that a much better outlook?

I wish it was me and not M. J. that was walking with you on the moonlight night. Some mornings when we go to breakfast the moon is shining and is yellow in appearance.

You asked for it, so I'm sending you a snapshot of 'yours truly.' It's not very good but you can at least see the dimple in my chin if nothing else.

No! Your chatter doesn't bore me. As a matter of fact, I like it.

Now, Marjorie, I'm really going to give it to you. It's swell here… I love it, even if I do have to fly tonight from 7 to 11 P.M. It's lots of fun and very pretty to see all the lights twinkling some thousand feet below. At night, I mean. Of course, I like anything that has to do with the Army and this Field is strictly Army, more so than Wayne County.

We sure get the exercise here, as we have to walk to the ground school and the flight line, which is an estimated 3 miles a day. Oh yes, and then we have an hour of calisthenics per day to keep our tummies flat.

Excuse me a minute . . .

Okay, I'm back again. The orderly polished all my shoes and has just brought them back to my room. Some service. Oh boy!

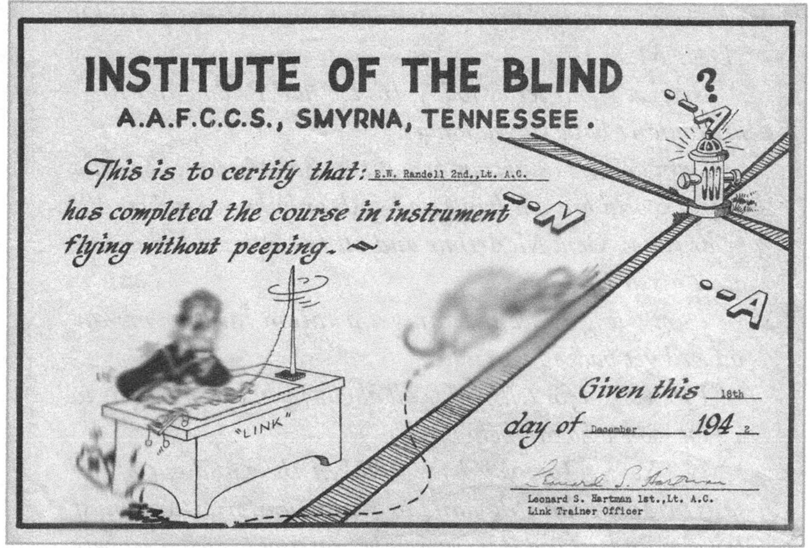

INSTITUTE OF THE BLIND

A.A.F.C.C.S., SMYRNA, TENNESSEE.

This is to certify that: E.W. Randell 2nd.,Lt. A.C.

has completed the course in instrument flying without peeping.

Given this 18th day of December 194 2

Leonard S. Hartman 1st.,Lt. A.C.
Link Trainer Officer

Institute of the Blind (Comic) Smyrna, Tennessee

Let's see, where was I? I have 8 hours and 15 min. of Co-pilot time and have flown the ship by myself. It is truly work, but fun.

My Pilot has made his first landing without the instructors help. Soon, I hope to occupy the co-pilots seat in the landings. This ship has a few new controls, which I have never used before including a "supercharger" and "intercooler shutter." The co-pilot job is to run the engines while the pilot flies the ship. Take offs and landings are tense moments you may be sure. The ship weighs 15 ton and has 16 ply tires and a 200 ft. wingspan. Compare it to your barn. Huge isn't it?

Marjorie, write soon and Happy
Landings
Ed Randy

The above was a three-page-written-on-both-sides letter! See Institute of the Blind (Comic) Smyrna, Tennessee above.

Nov. 25, 1942.

Dear Mom,

Received your letter today. It's too bad Radda and Jimmy couldn't have stayed longer.

I am going to start an account in San Antonio, because it is a world known bank and gosh only knows where I'll be at times. Gen. McArthur and all the Officers have their accounts at Ft. Sam.

I am going to see if I can get a ration card for my car when I get back to Romulus.

I thank you for telling me all about Jack. I hope he gets to a Doc soon who can help him.

No! Young Top, you haven't taken the wind out of my sails because I am still going to get my uniforms. You must try and understand it is very embarrassing to go somewhere improperly dressed for the occasion.

However, if you wish I will apply for an allowance for my dependents. Please advise me on this subject. Please don't get the idea I have a lot of money as I haven't and I have a few unpaid bills. If you gave up on or sold the farm then we could live together thus cutting down expense. Depending, of course, on my having permission to live off the post which I think could be arranged.

Gee! That's great news about the Schmidt boy and Capt. Eddie Rickenbacker and party. Monday we had a two hour lecture on what to do after a "crack up," how to repair or help the wounded. And also what to do if forced down over the sea. It was very serious but humorous at times. It's a great Army. There is always some guy that has a sense of humor and saves the day.

There is to be a Band Concert tonight and a trumpet duet and I have to miss it as I am scheduled to fly tonight.

Sometimes Bud is a little hard to figure out, but I guess we are all the same to each other.

I am thinking of asking for a transfer south after I get back to Romulus. Yesterday we flew to Chattanooga, Tenn.

in a 3 bomber V formation. We had ice on the wings and windows. It was a lot of fun.

I was Co-pilot on the trip.

Happy Landings, Wings

Nov. 30, 1942

Dear Marjorie,

Gee! Was I surprised today! An Air Mail letter! For some unknown reason my old heart did a couple extra beats.

Did you see Walt Disney's "Bambi"? I guess I must be "twitter-pated" like Thumper, the rabbit. You must see it if you haven't.

Yours surely must have been a wonderful Thanksgiving, as mine was also. Here's what I did. Got up at six, had breakfast and then went to school at 7:45 A.M. After school and at 11:30 A.M., I went to dinner. It was "magnanimous," complete with turkey and all the trimmings, cranberry jelly, everything. I sat there thinking of my folks and all the many things I was thankful for. I was also wondering what you were doing about then.

At 12:30 Capt. Proctor and I reported to the flight line and our instructor Capt. Cory had a nice little cross-country all planned for us. It was to Montgomery, Alabama (Maxwell Field) Headquarters for the Southeast Training Area. Capt. Proctor acted as Pilot and I as Co-pilot. Our instructor was the radio operator. Capt. Proctor flew on instruments (radio range) and under the "hood" so he didn't see much, but I got a big kick out of all the scenery. We passed over the T. V. A. dams and reservoirs... that wasn't a swear word... and on over the Birmingham jail and steel mills. We stopped at Maxwell only a short time, when I got back to the ship the Captains were waiting for me with Col. Weiss who was to fly back with us. I had been to visit Gen. Royce, who wasn't there. Darn it. Sat. I got a letter from him so do I feel good. He is from Michigan. We got back to Smyrna in the dark and landed without any bounces.

On our way back our heaters burned out and it got a little chilly. At first we wondered what the smoke was and sent the engineer to investigate. Well! He tells us the heaters are burning up so off go a few switches and that's that.

Here it is 11:30 P.M. We just got back from "Local" night flying. For your information, dear! I have to be up tomorrow at 6 A.M. for school at 7:45 A.M. This finishes our ground school. Wed. we are to have an examination to see what we forgot. Wish me all kinds of luck please. Thanks.

Today I was told we leave for Romulus Nov. 18. Now is that a good deal or is it? Yes, it is.

Tonight my instructor said maybe we could make a cross-country flight to Chicago or Detroit, so I'm going to see just how close I can get to Coopersville. I'll write again later and tell you what he decides to do. Maybe I'll fly over your house. Tomorrow night I guess I'll have to cram for the exam. Speaking about mail delivery. We get mail every day including Sunday. We don't seem to have holidays.

Here's hoping you got your gas tank filled tonight.

Please excuse me this time if my letter seems all mixed up. It's the way I'm thinking of things tonight.

Tonight Tennessee had a blackout from 8:45 to 9 P.M. We were flying at the time and didn't know of it beforehand and we thought we were seeing things. We then woke up to the fact that it was a black out. All the lights at the Air Base were out also. It was very effective; the whole countryside was dark except for a few automobiles on the highways.

No! Marjorie, I'm not teasing. My permanent station is Romulus until I get an idea that I want a transfer. And to be real truthful with you, I've got an idea buzzing inside me for adventure in Africa and to get it I would have to be stationed in Tennessee or Texas. Believe me I'm in a muddle. I feel I'm not helping our side until I get in the scrap.

If anything did happen to me, I'd be happy, and no one would miss me except my Mom, as I'm the kind of a fellow only a mother can love.

Say! Your record beats mine. I think you are entitled to a day off. I'm going to be looking forward to the day on which you can come to visit me.

Marjorie, remember those fingernails you commented on once - well I only have three left. I broke the others off on the flap and landing gear controls. I guess I let them grow too long.

Today has been most beautiful, cool but sunny. So you like my light putter-outer? I wouldn't say it's being lazy, but rather darn smart, aye what?

My grandfather Randell (Milton Paul) always told us to use our heads and save our feet. Good idea, don't you agree?

I wish I could be there to rub or massage the lameness out of you. I'll bet you didn't know we were taught how to massage each other for pilot fatigue. You ought to see us during calisthenics, some show.

Yes, I knew Miss Gray had a projector, but have never been fortunate enough to see any pictures.

I guess it's a sign I'm getting old saying I'd rather be in the south during the winter. Don't misunderstand me nor let me change you. You're perfectly right. There is nothing wrong with the winter. I, too, like the snow and skating. Believe me some day I'm even going to go on a Hayride. I have never been on one. I'll bet they're lots of fun.

I've always been too serious during my young life and so now I'm going to make up for lost moments.

It just seems like every one is getting married. It must be war hysteria. I'm only joking as I'm all for it. Except where I'm concerned.

I'll bet you sat home alone last week Friday. I probably won't have a chance when I get back.

I have heard Holiday Inn was very good. Do you like the song "There Are Such Things?"

I'm not sure but I think we are on Chicago time.

Thank your Mom for the news flashes. Gee! Married 26 years! Now that's what I call swell.

Well, Marjorie I must close as it is past midnight. Think of me once in a while and write again soon. I'm glad you beat off the flu.

Happy Landings
Your Pal Randy

Below is the letterhead showing a B-25 in flight on the writing paper Edward uses while he is in school at Smyrna, Tennessee.

ROSECRANS FIELD
ST. JOSEPH, MISSOURI

Aug 8th
Sun Nite.

Dear Dad,
Received your letter to day.

Wednesday
Dec. 2, 1942

Dear Dad,

How is everything including your health? As for me, I am in the "pink" of condition.

Above is a print of the ship I fly. It is 110 feet in span, 64' in length and 18' high. Its gas tanks hold some 2000 + gallons of gas. We fly all day on one loading of gas.

I must tell you what I did on Thanksgiving Day. In the morning we had ground school 7:45 a.m. to 10:45 a.m.. Then after our dinner, at which we had turkey with all the trimmings, we reported to the flight line at 12:30 noon. My instructor had a cross-country trip all planned for us to Montgomery, Alabama. (Maxwell Field Headquarters for this Area) and back. I acted as co-pilot and while I wasn't looking at the instruments I enjoyed the beautiful scenery.

We passed over the TVA dams and reservoirs. We also flew over the mountain ranges. The evergreen trees were the only ones in leaf, very pretty. My Pilot, Capt. Proctor, was flying on instruments and using the radio range. He was under the "hood" so he didn't see anything until we landed at the airport.

While I was at Maxwell I went to visit General Ralph Royce, Commander of this Area. He was not in his office but I got a letter from him the other day. He is a friend of Mr. Sinclair, my old instructor at Muskegon. He is from Michigan.

On the way home our Stewart Warner heater started to burn up. We sent the flight engineer down into the nose to find the trouble. He couldn't locate it so we had to turn off the heaters. We got home about 8 p.m.

Monday night we flew again and while we were up Tenn. had a blackout, even the airport. It was very effective… all was dark except for a few auto lights.

Next week we have a few daylight cross-country flights. Capt. Cory says we can go to Detroit or Chicago. I am working on him to let us fly to Muskegon. If we do I'll dip down and roar the engines when we pass over the house. We are also going on an overnight X-C to Texas next week. We had our final exam in school today. This week ends our ground school. Must quit so I can get some sleep.

Happy Landings,
Ed.

NORTH AMERICAN B-25-C

PILOTS CHECK LIST

1. CHECK FORM #1.
2. ENGINES TURNED OVER BY HAND
3. GAS AND OIL TANK CAPS — SECURED
4. PITOT HEAD COVER — REMOVED
5. WHEEL CHOCKS — IN PLACE
   PARKING BRAKE — ON
6. NOSE WHEEL TOWING PIN — IN PLACE
7. ENGINEER HAVE SCREWDRIVER
   PLIERS, ADJUSTABLE WRENCH.
8. CHECK HYDRAULIC FLUID LEVEL
   AND SPARE FLUID CAN.
9. DRIFT METER CAGED
10. CHECK CREW & "CHUTES" — ABOARD
11. " EMERGENCY AIR BRAKE
    400-600 lb control & SAFTIED
12. CHECK EMERGENCY NOSEWHEEL
    PAWL — OFF

Pilot's checklist

Dec. 2, 1942

Dear Mom,

Thank you very much for the advice on the fair sex, and please don't think I'm as wild as I wrote. After all I was teasing a little. I don't go around kissing all the girls in the first place as Bud says it's unhealthy.

You're right and I am thinking it over.

Now! I must answer your questions. Yes! We have window defrosters, wing deicers, and propeller deicers... all the latest protection.

Yes! On our cross-country flight to Texas, we will land and stay over night. Now! What makes you think it takes me so long to pack my clothes. Maybe you better not answer that. I'll just take my toothbrush and nightshirt and anyway they couldn't leave without the co-pilot.

Our room rent is $45.00 a month and our board is $35.00 and $3.00 for Officers Club dues. And $5.00 for valet service. He makes our beds, cleans our rooms and shines our shoes.

The way your letter sounds maybe I should find me a wife and an apartment.

Yes! I agree Jack should have a different environment.

I'm glad to hear Bud and Radda could get home and drive Jack to the sanatorium.

Can't John give you a better description of the place where he bought the gun?

I have been informed that Officers are not given any allowances except for their immediate family (wife and children). I was also advised that being an officer I should have some money to help my family. So please have Dotty get her teeth repaired and let me know the cost.

In my own personal opinion Bill Ball would pay the least for the gun of anyone.

Yes! Bud is right. Jack has a brilliant mind.

I have heard you had 6 inches of snow. Must be very pretty. It is getting colder here with frost again tonight.

That's the best news yet about Bud and I hope he gets a

good job. He looked underweight when I saw him.

What would each of you like in the way of Christmas gifts? And what shall I send Jack? Please write soon.

Your loving son,
Happy Landings
Ed Wings

Wednesday
Dec. 2, 1942

Dear Dotty,

Was told that we leave for home on the 18th of Dec. Boy! I'll get home just in time for the festivities of the Christmas season.

Have decided on the San Antonio bank, as it is known worldwide. Yes! The form was signed correct.

I do hope you have the recapped tire by this time. I wouldn't want to lose it. Did you get the gas tank filled up before the first of Dec.? I hope.

Yes! I may be an officer but I hope you didn't offend the man by correcting him. If he is the one I am thinking of, he took good care of my tire.

Am glad you understand the tire situation (use the recap and save the tire on the car for the spare.) Maybe when I get to Detroit I can get another tube as the one in that rear has over 15 patches. I believe the car should have a winter overhaul, but let me tend to it when I get home. The operating instructions are in the glove compartment. It tells in there when the wheels need repacking, etc.

I hope Jack will not be angry that I have a new co-owner. I don't think he will and we can explain to him. Have you been driving the car to school? I am reading your letter as I write this one. Thank you for taking such good care of my car. So you got a gas ration card? Well good! About getting the dent "bumped" out and fender put on, go see the man that works in Lemmen's Garage (the repair shop part) and see what he charges and ask him if he can do the job without taking it to G. R.

I haven't the faintest idea what hit the speedometer cable hose.

I hope you got my canvas dry after using it. Any water left in it may cause it to mildew.

I hope your cold is better by this time. Am thinking very seriously about getting myself some flannels (red) as it has been really cold here lately.

Marie does get very silly at times. I know she thought a lot of Bud in a friendly way. Will do your little favor for you. You, rascals, you!

Glad to hear Kit may have a little vacation. And Willie is coming home, too! My! My! Only wish I could be home at the same time.

I think you girls are too silly about the marriage situation. I know you're joking but maybe other people don't understand that. After all, marriage is serious and you just don't go out and "hook" some guy. Please believe me, I'm not scolding.

Happy Landings,
Randy

P.S. Will you please sign the enclosed blanks in the upper half at the proper spaces I have marked and send me the old license identification card? It is in the holder on the steering post. Thank You. H.L.

Randy

Edward sent a clever Hallmark card with a Russian theme,

"Sorry you're sick **COMRADE** *Can't* **BEAR** *to be thinking that you're feeling sickski,* **VODKA** *be ailing you?* **STEPPE** *on it quickski, Quit* **STALIN** *around And start* **RUSSIAN** *instead-- Get better and* **TROTSKY RIGHT OUT OF THAT BED***"*

On the back of the card he wrote:

Dec. 8, 1942

Dear Marjorie,

Here is hoping this card helps you to get over your cold. I would write a letter to you tonight, but we were just notified we are to leave for New Mexico tomorrow. Will have to get up early tomorrow and have all my things to pack yet tonight. I'll answer your letter when I get to my new station. As always,

Happy Landings,
73-Roger. Ed.

The picture postcard below is postmarked Albuquerque, N.M. but Edward writes his return address as A. A. B. Tarrant Field, Fort Worth, Texas.

Aren't the flowers pretty? Am staying here overnight on my way west. This is a very nice town; I like it. Well! Cheerio! Happy Landings, Ed

There was another postcard with the Albuquerque postmark of December 10.

Dear Marjorie, Hope to get to my destination tomorrow. We are staying here overnight. Will not get the chance to fly to Muskegan.

Happy Landing,
Ed

Albuquerque, New Mexico
Dec. 12, 1942
2:30 A.M.

Dear Marjorie,

As soon as we fly back to Smyrna and finish this cross-country trip our course will be completed.

The reason I am keeping such early hours is because I never went to bed last night. We are to leave for Smyrna in a few hours so that we can get "home" by noon. We are to put on a show there for General Arnold. He is visiting at Smyrna.

Did you get my card I sent from Fort Worth? We had a little trouble with the supercharger regulator on engine #1, so landed at Fort Worth and stayed there all night. Our crew chief got it repaired by midnight. Capt. Proctor and I got a room in a hotel. It was tops. I liked Fort Worth. It is a clean neat town, but then I like Chicago and Detroit and now I like the open spaces of Albuquerque. I guess I just like the whole U.S. I mean the parts of it I've seen, although I even think I'd like the places I haven't seen, too. Easy to get along with - that's me.

I suppose I can't tell you anything about the mountains, the one who has climbed them, but I will say they are majestic and beautiful. I liked their cumulus clouds in a dark blue sky.

Last night I was looking at the stars and the moon and they looked so near as if you could reach out and touch them. The air is so pure and clear, not like Chicago.

The sunsets are beautiful, too. The sun seems to drop behind the mountain and then it starts to get cool.

Albuquerque is situated in a valley on the Rio Grande River between two mountain ranges some 60 miles apart. These snowcapped mountains fascinate me. Every time I step outdoors I find myself gazing at them. Because the air is thinner one breathes faster. Boy, the air smells fresh. One just feels good all over - slaphappy, maybe - huh. Ones breath comes in short pants - hmm. Corny! Because of this thin air it takes more power to fly the airplanes and longer runways to take off and land on. The runways here are 2 1/4 miles long and in my estimation that is some strip. And of course the air speed (true) is higher. The planes land about 130 mph (ground speed.) Near sea level, the air being heavier the plane lands slower. 115 mph air speed (indicated.)

Must close for now, as it is time to leave for "home."

Dec. 13, 1942

Hello again Marjorie, Well, I'm back "home" safe and

sound. I did not have time to finish this letter so I brought it airmail from AQ. I think you will get it sooner if I mail from Smyrna. I expect to be sent to Romulus Dec. 18 (not Nov. 18 - my mistake) so please write me care of my Romulus address (s'il vous plait.) Emily Post says one isn't correct in using foreign phrases in writing letters. So I hope you won't object to my lack or wrong use of intellectual knowledge.

This afternoon the sun is shining for the first time in a week (at Smyrna). We had beautiful sunny weather while at Albuquerque. They claim they have only 10 non-flying days in a whole year.

Yesterday when we got home it was freezing cold. We all said, "Take us back to AQ."

When I got home I saw they were building some new B. O. Q.'s and upon inquiring I found out they are for the W. A. A. C.'s due to arrive soon. Speaking of W. A. A. C. s did you read of the WAC that went AWOL and was found doing a "strip tease" at some theater? Oh! Boy! I think I'm going to like the W. A. A. C.'s. Aren't I a "devil"? Don't answer that last question, please.

Speaking of B. O. Q.'s the ones at Albuquerque for the visiting officers were the tops. There were drapes on the windows, rugs on the floor, big heavenly mattresses on the beds, a desk and chair and clothes closet. The bed (head piece) had the Air Corps wing and propeller insignia carved on it. The barracks were really, positively, and absolutely... military and Air Force thru out. The barracks were, as well as the whole Base.

In answer to your letter Major Ralph Rogers is Commanding Officer of the Southeast Air Corps Training Center.

Capt. Proctor is a blond, has a cute mustache. He reminds me of my brother Jim. I'd rather tell you about him than write - okay - swell.

I got an 87 in my exam. Capt. Proctor got 92. Aren't I the ignorant one?

I'm sorry we couldn't have made a cross-country trip to

Coopersville, but the weather was against us. So, I guess you can stop looking now every time you hear a "plane." I liked the way you finished your last letter, "I'll be watching the skies for you."

Gee! Christmas is near isn't it? And I haven't done any shopping as yet. Isn't that terrible?

You know, Marjorie, you answered my letter just the way I wanted you to, when you wrote about my wanting to get into some action. Thank you for your lucky charm and good wishes. I'm ashamed to admit I've forgotten how you answered me. You'll have to tell me again when I see you.

Seeing as you are such a good typist, would you like to be my secretary and take some dictation from me? That is if you like to type and I wouldn't bore you. Before I get myself involved any deeper do you have a typewriter?

Am glad you're living the life of "Riley." 9 to 5 sounds like swell working hours, but I hate to hear you have to sacrifice your afternoon off to get them.

Am crossing my fingers so Madelyn will get extra gasoline ration cards. I'm sure she will.

That farewell party sounded like a lot of fun. The Officers had a big dance here last night but I was too sick to attend. Will tell you about it later.

Say! When your Mom wants to spank you some time I'd love to help her. I'm a vicious spanker.

Marjorie, how would you like to celebrate New Year's "Eve" in Chicago? I'll ask for a pass and visit my folks and then we can go to Chicago and visit all my relatives and, of course, hit the "Hot Spots." If you have a better idea for celebrating the New Year "in" please write and tell me.

"I'll be flying in the skies for you."

Happy Landings
Ed.

Dec. 14, 1942

Dear Mom,

My legal and permanent address on all my Army records is Chicago. So therefore, I am going to continue to buy my license in Illinois. Savvy? For all I know I may be sent to Tennessee or Texas as soon as I get back to Romulus. And also I'll want to use my car as soon as I get back to Romulus.

I am going to ask for a furlough as soon as I get back home. And during this furlough I hope to get, I want to spend part of it in Chicago. I've even asked Marjorie Irish if she would like to go to Chicago with me.

We are to go home Dec. 18 so write your next letter in care of my Romulus address.

Please say Hi and Happy Landings to Bob Wilcox, as I won't be able to see him during his furlough.

We are to return to Romulus "by the fastest means of travel" so our orders read.

It is now 10:00 P.M. I have just returned from the U. S. O. show at the theater. It was very good. They had acrobatic dancers, a marionette show, clown and singers.

You may stop craning your neck now, as I won't be flying over very soon. Because the weather was bad up north we took our cross-country trip to Albuquerque, New Mexico. It was lots of fun. I'll tell you about it when I get my furlough.

Am glad you got the retread tire. I think the man charged a fair price. As soon as I get the car back to Romulus I shall ask for a spare tire and tube. I hope you had the new tube put in the retread tire and you are riding on it. Okay.

Good Lord! Mother, I would like to help Dotty but I am not made of money. According to your figures her doctoring will come to #$30.00.

No! I did not get October flight pay nor did I get November's flight pay. So you see I am having a time of it to make ends meet. Don't worry about my Christmas spending. I have nothing to spend.

I would like to get Dotty the ski outfit is she wants it.

Please advise me as to size, etc.

Have written to John but have not received any reply. Has he written you?

Yes! I've read about the gremlins, cute little devils. The spade-nose gremlin, you know, digs holes in the runways when you come in for a landing.

Oh say, my car insurance ran out on the 10th of Dec., so I don't think you should drive the car until I have it renewed, which I will try to do this week. I am writing to Mr. Meerman tonight.

Will LaVerne Kettle be drafted?

Did I understand you to say Kit was in Chicago now?

During my short stay here I have learned quite a little, like how to take care of myself when forced down at sea, what effects oxygen and high altitudes have on a pilot. At 40,000 feet a person will die in 1 minute with 100% oxygen. Pressure cabins are needed at that altitude. Happy thought. Oh well!

"There are bold pilots,
And there are old pilots,
But there are no old bold pilots."

Happy Landings,
Your loving son, Ed

Edward sent a Christmas greeting to "Miss Marjorie Irish" with a note inside.

Dec 20, 1942

My Dear Marjorie,

You know I never thought until I had mailed that letter --- maybe you would think I was moving to Albuquerque, New Mexico.

I found your letter waiting here when I returned from Smyrna.

So my Mom is even helping you get over your cold. Swell! She always has liked you.

Am very happy to hear about Jack. Your "charms" really do work.

Yes! We all have much to be thankful for.

When I got back "home" and was told I had to live in the B. O. Q. I thought I ought to complain, as one could get a furnished apartment for $45 a mo. but have since been thinking of our boys in foreign lands, and what they may have for Quarters. So you shan't hear me complain--ever.

I talked to my C. O. yesterday and I am to see him again Mon. He said he thought I could get the leave.

We get Thurs. afternoon & Friday (Christmas) off.

Am going to ask for a leave from Sat. Dec. 26 to Jan. 3, 1943. We could go to Chicago Thurs. and home again Sunday. What do you think of that plan?

Wish me luck and I'll wish you the same.

Must close as I am in a serious mood and I might write something I shouldn't.

While in Tenn. I learned of a bunk buddy of mine that was killed in a plane accident.

Well! Marjorie, Merry Christmas to you and yours,

Happy Landings Ed "Randy"

EDWARD W. RANDELL

LIEUTENANT, AIR FORCES
ARMY OF THE UNITED STATES

Edward enclosed one of his new cards. I was impressed.

Jan. 2, 1943

Dear Marjorie,

It is now 2200 o'clock and I have just returned from the Officers Club after "catching up" on all my "reading."

And I just have to write you and thank you again for your company, which I so thoroughly enjoyed the past week.

Marjorie! I found your boots in my car and am mailing them to you. Also enclosed is a Christmas gift for you, which I hope you like.

(For the life of me I can't remember what it was!!)

Today has been a rather sad day as one of our aircraft crashed with death to one and injury to two others.

It was almost your last "so long" to me as another lad and I were going to go up in the doomed ship -- but by a quirk of fate decided to play chess. Maybe it wasn't my time as your mother puts it. When I bought that little "chess" game I had no idea that some day I would owe my life to it.

Please do not mention this accident, as it has not been released "officially" and please don't let my mother hear of it as she worries about my flying as it is.

I don't even know why I wrote it. I imagine it would be defined vanity. It is a great life, Marjorie, and I'd rather lose anything than to give up flying. Even if I do have nightmares and talk in my sleep - and roll out of bed.

I was scheduled for a trip just as I got leave. The lad that took my trip said he had a swell time. He went west and then south. Was gone a week. So, I informed him I had just as nice a trip, if not better. I think your idea to see Sonja was swell. She is to be in Detroit this week.

That leave sure did me wonders. I'm all set to settle down for another year of duty.

I arrived here safely after an awful night of driving. I kept falling asleep. Please write - it is my wish.

Happy Landings, Ed

Postcards this time: one to the folks and one to Marjorie (me!).

Jan. 6, 1943

Dear Folks,

I got home very tired but I made it with 3 gallons and two coupons to the good. This is a beautiful country. The more I see the better I like it. Am back at work. Thank you for the nice Christmas. H. L. Ed

Jan. 6, 1943

Dear Marjorie,

Am writing on the Airline. This is a wonderful state. (Kansas) The more of our country I see the more I like it. It seems like ages since I was home. Say Hello to your folks for me. Happy Landings,

Ed Randy

Jan. 10, 1943

Dear Marjorie, I found your letter when I was home (Romulus) the first of the week. Thank you. This is a nice part of the country. What I've seen of it.

Happy Landings, Ed. (The card was postmarked St. Paul, Minn.)

Jan. 11, 1943

Dear Mother,

Yes! Let's hope that this year will see the end of the War.

I am on a trip, other than that I won't say what I'm doing. We are as usual, flying from A to B.

I arrived home with some gas in the car and two coupons. Great, aye what? The snow did catch up with me and I got sleepy but I made it okay. Thanks to Marjorie's "Good Luck" charm.

A special note here: I spent a great deal of time selecting a very special gift for Edward that Christmas and the small (about an inch and a quarter in diameter) round, "gold" penknife with a raised center of clear plastic covering a four-leaf clover seemed perfect. I was so excited to give it to him. When he gave me a box of candy I could hardly believe it. I was so-o-o disappointed. I don't know what in the world I was expecting, but it was not a box of candy! I learned years and years later that the box of candy had been one someone had given the Randell family. He had appropriated it to give to me! I also learned many, many, many years later… now in 2016 as I copy these letters into Edward's story… he had no money to buy anything! Poor guy. That Christmas vacation, however, he took me to Chicago in his car! We stayed with his Aunt Isabelle. It was on this trip that I learned the family called her Radda and how they happened to. It was the most wonderful trip as we talked, talked, talked all the way and I really got to know this young man. On New Year's Eve he took me to see Sonja Henie ice skate in person.

Sonja Henie was a Norwegian figure skater, a three-time Olympic Champion. It was an exciting evening.

We came home on the streetcar and it was exactly midnight on the trip home, but did Edward kiss me? No! I was so disappointed. I had always thought on the stroke of midnight on New Years Eve one kissed whoever one was with at that very moment.

Where he got the money for all of the New Years celebration after not having any money for a Christmas gift I still, to this day, do not know. I forgot to ask!

Thanks, Mom for all your sound advice and wisdom. But where on earth did you get those ideas about marriage. We have never even mentioned the word love to each other, much less marriage. Please don't rush me.

Here is hope for father's quick recovery.

Happy Landings,
Lucky Randy

Jan. 18, 1943

Dear Mom,

"73" stands for Good Luck, so there! No! I did not see any

of Minneapolis, as we stayed in St. Paul. We were not there on a vacation, so I didn't get to see very much of the town.

I was over to Cousin Mildred & Hazen's for Sunday dinner January 17. Mildred said I should have taken her with me to Minnesota. Gee! Has "Curt" grown! He was six months old Sunday. We celebrated his half-year birthday. The Pratt family is lots of fun.

I have been taken off Operational Orders for a while. Until I get checked out in the AT-1, (twin engine trainer) I have been assigned to the transition school so will stay here in Romulus until further notice. Yes! I would like to have shown Marjorie more of the interesting spots of Chicago, but we did not have the time. That was very kind of Marjorie. I did not know she loaned Dotty her housecoat.

Why not see if you can find a room in town for Dotty? She could then get to school and I believe she would have less colds and her health would improve. Norma B. is boarding at Mary Jane's. I'll pay her room and board if you will consent to the idea. Did I also tell you Dr. Greenwood said Dotty must have her teeth fixed?

Minnesota had some two feet of snow and was 15 degrees below zero. But one does not notice the cold as much as here in Detroit.

No! I did not see Nick. You know that was the funniest thing. I was returning from the west on a commercial airline. We had just landed at CG (Chicago) and we heard of the accident. The fellows we talked to didn't recall the crew's names but it wasn't any of our boys so we never thought anymore of it. So! I didn't get to see Nick. The accident happened just before we landed. We did not take the time to view it, as we had to continue on to DT.

I got a letter from Bud and he tells me Marjorie is a nice girl. Cousin Foster even told me many reasons why he thought she was nice. Every one I introduced her to seemed to like her. Hm. I wonder.

Last weekend I had an opportunity to stay overnight

in Chicago. Bud came over and we had a swell talk. He is leading a more normal life now and says he is finding time to write a few letters. He designed a new tool for Buick last week so was feeling pretty good.

Also saw Jim & family. Every time I go to Chicago I like it more all the time. Maybe it's because of the fuss they make over me. I hate it's weather though. Radda was in fine health. Said she was expecting me to drop in when I did.

I would like to send Dotty to College this fall. I think Northwestern would be a nice place to start. Cousin Hazen says M. I. T. is co-educational.

Well, let's hear the latest scandal.

Happy Landings,
Ed.

P.S. Happy Birthday! It's late I know, but the thoughts and wishes are sincere. Your loving son, Ed

Jan. 18, 1943

Dear Sugarfoot,

Thank you for the very nice letter. Oh yes! That towel you sent my aunt was perfect. She let me use it so I could tell you how swell it was. And I like big towels. So the gift was tops and she liked it and thinks you're a "peach."

In case you're wondering I was in C.G. last weekend and stayed overnight at my aunt's. She said she was expecting me. Mental telepathy.

Bud came over and we went to Jim's for a little while then he brought me back to my aunt's. We talked until 2 A.M.

He said Vilolette and her mother had a little party waiting for me on New Years Eve. When we didn't get back by12 they thought we had gone downtown. So they went on home. He wants us to come to visit at his home. Bud tells me you're a swell girl, as if I didn't know it already.

They liked their Christmas present.

Poor Bud has the worst luck. He has his car running again, however. We had a long talk and he told of the weird-

est things that have happened to him this last year. He says he found out he was mistaken about Howard, it was someone who looked just like him. His stories make your spine tingle. Small wonder my little brother broke down. Please, if you like me even a little bit don't mention anything you may have heard us talk about.

Am glad you liked the "hankies" but they don't begin to compare to the good luck I have been having all because of your "lucky" piece.

Yes! I meant I was catching up on my reading. Do you really think I'm so deep you can't understand writings?

So you are becoming an accomplished Chess player. Well! Good for you. It was very polite letting your cousin win. You "took" me once, young lady, but it won't be so easy next time. I'll fight to the finish.

Marjorie, I think that was very nice of you to loan my sister your housecoat. My cousin thinks you are nice because you remember the little things. I hope I can be just as thoughtful.

We are given two days leave a month. Not bad, aye what? It is twenty-four days vacation a year with pay. Plus, getting paid $70. each week and I'm only a kid of 22. Do you see now why I like the Air Force?

I think you were a tired little girl that night going home so I'll forgive your impoliteness. H-m-m-m!

Don't wear yourself out at work. I like that A. E. 'after Ed' business, but then you were also doing things to help, Marjorie. Yes, you get an E for effort.

Your talk of teaching Sunday school reminds me of my Scoutmaster days. Miss, you are 'k-e-e-r-e-c-t' about keeping a jump ahead of them — maybe two jumps. For all the trouble they caused me, I liked them.

I arrived at the C.G. Airport right after Nick's accident. We heard about it after we landed but I didn't know Nick was in the crew.

Well, "Bless Bess," here it is 1 A.M. and I'm still up. I hope you're getting your beauty sleep, howsoever.

Do, or have you ever, collected post cards, sugar wrappers or matchbox covers? I have some I'll send you if you would care for them. Please write and tell me the latest scandal.
Happy Landings,

Ed.

Edward sent Marjorie a beautiful birthday card (early as it is postmarked Yuma, Arizona, Jan. 20, 1943.)

"On the Birthday of a Friend!

The years go by and you and I
Have watched a few go past,
But time and tide can never change
A friendship holding fast;
And so with sweet remembrance
As your Birthday comes anew,
I wish a world of happiness
With all my heart for you."

Feb. 11, 1943

"Happy Landings" Ed "Randy"

Postcard postmarked Yuma, Arizona. Edward was with the Ferrying Group at Yuma Army Air Field there:

Dear Dad,

Today, Jan. 28, '43, marks my first year in the Army Air Forces. And I love it. My new address is on this card. Arrived in Tucson Tues. and spent the day there. Arizona is a very interesting state.

Happy Landings.

Jan. 28, 1943

Dear Marjorie,

Today at 4:05 P.M. marked the first year of my Army life. I am celebrating tonight by writing letters.

My temporary address, <u>in case</u> you care to write me is:

Ferrying Group,
Yuma Army Air Field
Yuma, Arizona.

I am writing lying in bed and wondering what you are doing about now. Having a great time, I hope.

If I had only known at the time I could have stayed at home another day. Next time I shall know better.

Oh! Marjorie, remember you said something about joining the

W. A. F. S.? Were you serious? Or joking? Do you think you would like to fly?

Today we went thru the usual procedure of signing forms

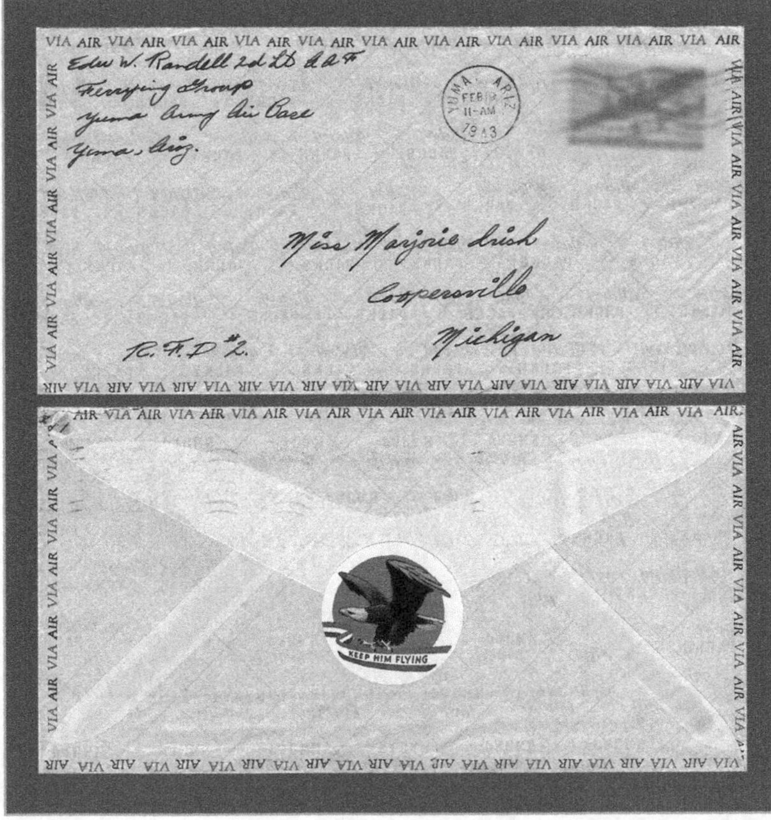

and stating the lucky one who is to be notified in case of accident.

This country is somewhat barren, but is also very beautiful. There are mountains to the north and west of us. The days are very warm. The boys were all sun bathing today. Howsoever, the nights are very cool.

I can just see you shivering from the cold. I'm in my shirtsleeves. You have my deepest sympathies.

Say, how would you like to come home and find me asleep in your living room again in the future? And please next time you wake me, don't say a word. Savvy? Hmmm.

I hope you thanked your Mom for Sunday supper. I always feel so guilty when I forget to thank someone for something.

Happy Landing,
Randy

The envelope of Edward's letter contained a number of "Keep Him Flying" stickers like this, except this one is greatly enlarged. They are actually a bit larger than an inch in diameter.

Edward sent a postcard from California picturing the Ambassador Hotel in L. A. The postmark is Feb. 1, 1943.

Jan. 31

Dear Marjorie,

Greetings from L.A.! This sure is a beautiful spot. Have been to Santa Monica and a few interesting places, including the Ambassador Hotel. We had our dinner there.

Happy Landings,
Ed.

Feb. 1, 1943.

Dear Mom,

Would you please mail the enclosed letter in Coopersville and don't tell Marjorie about it? Thank you very kindly.

It was a Valentine with the signature of "Guess Who?" He should have known I would recognize the handwriting! :-)

Yes! The towels are for you.

Did you have another snowstorm? Is Dotty staying in town? Have they started work on the car? Has John written again?

I think I will get my new license and auto title in Michigan. Could Sister pick up a couple blanks at Lemmens? One would be for the title and one for the license. She could then sign them like she has done before and send them to me here..My address:

Yuma Army Air Field,
Yuma, Arizona
A. T. C. Ferrying Group

What will Mrs. Bowser charge Dotty to stay in town?

Yes! It would be wonderful if Dad could move to Chicago this winter. There are a lot of people living in Arizona that have asthma. It does seem to help one. I even feel better.

Some of the fellows at the base here are wearing their "sun tans." It is very warm and pleasant weather... very cool at night, however. The main street is three blocks long. The scenery is beautiful. One can see for hundreds of miles.

I got a card from "Bob" today. They seem to be forwarding my mail from Romulus.

Happy Landings Randy, your loving son.

Feb. 6, 1943.
Sat. night.

Dear Dotty,

For the present, why not forget about getting a job and work on your studies and build up your health? I think it would be nice if you could get your teeth "repaired" & cleaned.

If you will do it I'll send you the money. Forget about you owing me anything. However, if you would like to, you could "Simonize" my car. I have some Simonize cleaner in the car trunk. And I'll send you some polish to polish the trim and bumpers. It's a big job as Lois (Texas girl) and I cleaned the car last summer. I'll send you a check for $50. You can cash it at the bank and then pay Mulder. You can use the remainder for your board and to have your teeth fixed.

Am glad to hear the car looks so fine. I don't quite understand about the trim, but you can explain it to me when I see you.

I'm envious of your sleeping hours. I get to bed by midnight or after and am up at 7:30.

I am drawing a copy of the fuel system of the P-40 for the ground school class. It is on Bristol board, the same size we used to draw maps on at school.

My instructor is a graduate of "Lane" Class '41. He is very good. We get along like a couple of old peas in a pod. He took an Aviation course at Lane and he had the same instructor I had.

Please keep the statement from the bank, as I would like to see it.

Our flying is going rather slow so we may be here until April 1st.

How is the gasoline situation holding out?

Do you keep the car in town?

Some enlisted men came down with scarlet fever this week so the whole post has been quarantined. Thus, I don't expect to go to town tonight.

I thought the clipping was pretty "sharp."

Have you heard any more from "Jack?" I, too, got a card from Willie and believe it or not I could read every word.

No! I have not heard anything about Tony's doings or where he is stationed.

The Lord only knows how long it will take to get the Bonds, but don't worry as Uncle Sam always comes thru.

Last week I was in Los Angeles. While we didn't see any movie stars we did have a swell time. We saw the beautiful blue Pacific.

I took the plane from Chicago to Tucson, Arizona. I met a very nice gentleman (Mr. Ellegood) and spent the day in Tucson. He drove me around the countryside and invited me to dinner. I hope you can some day see this country. It's beautiful. One can see for hundreds of miles.

Yes, Yuma is noted for its famous $5.00 weddings and as the town time forgot. The surrounding country is desert. But the government is doing wonders in its irrigation.

Group Commander Donaldson was here yesterday and put on a little air show for us. Slow rolls 100 feet off the ground, etc.

Well! It is late and I must take a shower and prepare for bed. Oh! Yes! I have to Lux my undies.

It sure is fun here. We sleep between wool blankets and do they itch. What do sheets cost? I may start housekeeping. And I live in a one- room barracks with 50 men. The noise and confusion! Whew!

I'm silly maybe, but I still love the Air Force.

Happy Landings
Randy

Feb. 7, 1943
Sun. 8 P.M.

Dear Marjorie,

Thanks for the swell letter. I received it Saturday.

How's this for snappy stationary?

Yuma Army Air Field, Yuma, Arizona' in red below a large dark blue circle containing yellow wings over a white star with yet another circle within it in red this time. At the very top of the page are the letters 'VIA AIR VIA AIR VIA AIR,' alternating red and blue and running all the way across the paper. Edward numbered the pages of his letter 'Uno, Duo, Tres.'

Marjorie! Would you please tell me what it is that you are worrying about? Did I do or say something that has hurt you or is it what you wrote about, changing your work. I don't want you to worry as it will put wrinkles in your brow and gray your hair! So, please, Marjorie, promise me you won't do any more worrying. Remember going to Grand Rapids Sunday night and you told me not to worry. Well, you were right, as I made the train.

I remember a Sunday school lesson of your mothers in which she said how some problem seems so large to us today and tomorrow when it was solved you wondered why you ever worried over it. I have always remembered and try not to worry.

In your letter you asked me for some advice. Well! I'm honored as only a very few people have ever asked me for advice. I feel like I'd rather talk to you in person so that you wouldn't misunderstand something I say, and I could explain better what I mean. In giving advice I'm afraid I would try to impress you with my idea of life. So, if I write something you don't understand don't feel hurt, because that is the last thing I would want to do to you. Gee! I wish you were a boy, as that would make it a lot easier.

Yes! I think the W. A. A. C. okay. I was joking when I said I wouldn't like to see you join them. I said I didn't like to see you join the W. A. A. C. because I wouldn't get to see you when I came home, but don't let my selfish ideas stop you from doing something you want to do. I probably won't get home very often anymore anyway.

I know how you feel about getting a job that has some-

thing to do with the war work. I think it is a swell idea, but don't think for a minute that the work you're doing now isn't helping, maybe not directly, but those Bonds all help. If you do get a job in a factory, why not try to get a clerical or secretarial position. I think it would better suit you. Of course I think the W. A. F. S. is the best of them all. I understand your position when it comes to flying lessons. However, if one wanted something "an awful lot," I don't think anything would stop one from getting it. Why don't you ask Emily Porter what the requirements are to join the W. A. F. S.? I don't know what they are. I'll have to ask her, too, sometime. I think if you got a job in a Defense plant that you could save enough money in a short time to do flying lessons. If you so desire when I get back to Detroit I'll inquire about lessons. The more I write about this idea the better I like it.

Well, I've rambled on and not said much of anything, but I do hope I have helped you in some small way.

I hope you receive this letter in time for your birthday. I want to be the first to offer my congratulations on your attaining your 21st birthday. I bet you wish you were 18 still. Just think, I'll be 23 in July (I had to put in 2 cents for ego.)

You know, Marjorie, I remember the summer you were 16 and that trip back from Traverse City.

When I write what I'm thinking I hope you won't want to slap my face for being "impudent" (as my great Aunt always said) and also hope that you would wish you were 100 years old. Now to tell you what I'm thinking. If we were together for your birthday anniversary, I'd make you a present of a kiss for every year of your young life. One for good luck and one to grow on too, as the saying goes. But seeing as how I won't see you on your birthday I want to wish you the best of everything—luck, health and happiness, and may you have a lot of children. Say! How did that silly phrase get in here?

I know it's none of my business, so you needn't answer if you wish not (silly sentence). Does your boy friend in Texas write to you as often as he used to?

I'm not asking you to marry me and please don't misunderstand, but Marjorie! Please don't marry someone you don't love. Life is too short to live it otherwise… without love, I mean. But then again it is none of my business what you do. I hope I haven't offended you.

Tonight I wanted to see a movie, but decided to write to you instead. Aren't you impressed?

Do you remember the picture "China Girl," and the poem the fellow read to the girl? I liked it so much when I heard it I wanted to remember it but alas! I have forgotten it. It was pretty anyway. I hope some day I can meet and fall in love with the right girl so I can say things just as nice. You know, Marjorie, I meet pretty girls and have lots of fun going out with them, but I don't love them. It's just that I like the opposite sex's company. . . the same as you or any other human being. Tell me how can a fellow know if he is in "love?" When I'm lonesome and I go out with a girl and she is nice to me, well I think maybe she is the one. In other words do I like the girl or is it just that I'm lonesome.

You know, Marjorie, I like you because I feel I can talk so easy to you. Most girls are just out after a "man" and lie like the "devil" to build themselves up in his eyes.

Let's hope Clare gets a furlough soon so M.J. and he can get married and two more people can be happy. I'll probably be an old man with gray hair before I can find someone brave enough to marry me.

Gee! I hope poor Nick gets his promotion okay and has some good luck from now on.

Say, Marjorie, what is this I hear about Horace Walcott? Dotty said he passed on to our God. You know I always liked to hear him sing. But that's life, isn't it, the bad with the good.

No! I did not know Dotty was staying at your grandmothers' house until I got a letter on Sat. the same day yours came. I'm glad because now she will be able to keep up with her studies and build her health up. I think your grandmothers are swell for bothering to let her stay at their home.

And I know she really appreciates it, too.

Tell me, how does our car look with the new fender and the bumps taken out of the door?

So all you could say to Dotty going home was "Hm! Hm!"? I think I better promise here and now that I shan't keep you up so late again. My Mom scolds me every time I come home late. You'd think I was a little kid, but I love it.

As yet I have not flown the P-40. I hope to tomorrow. I have been flying the AT-6 to get back in shape. We are on a sevens day a week schedule so are kept very busy what with our ground school and flying. And this last weekend we (the Air Field) have been quarantined to remain on the field as some men have broken out with scarlet fever and we have all been exposed. The men were mechanics working on our ships. Even the ships in that squadron have been grounded.

Being rated pilots we can take up passengers, so Sat. I took my first passenger for a flight. He said he liked it and thanked me. Then I told him he was the first person I ever took up as a passenger. All the mechanics joked with him about it, but he laughed. I let him fly the "ship" when we were in the air and he got a big kick out of that.

Sat. Group Commander Donaldson of Great Britain visited Yuma Air Field and put on an air show for us. Slow rolls 10 feet off the ground, etc. He is touring the U.S. teaching gunnery and keeping up morale. He is some 5'4" tall with a huge mustache. Oh! Yes, he's a blond. Was in the battle of Dunkirk and has been shot down 9 times. He swears like a trooper when he gives a speech. He hates the Germans. Goodnight and pleasant dreams.

Happy Landings,
Randy.

P.S. Because of the mood I'm in tonight, I feel I love the world and could write forever, but I really do need some sleep. Next time I'll try to describe my trip, if you wish. Again, be "sweet" and Happy Birthday. Randy.

There is a lovely Valentine card to his Mom among the letters he sent her. This one is entitled "Mom is my Valentine"

"Who was it brushed my tousled head,
And sent me drowsily to bed? Mom!
Who sent me off to School each day
And warned 'gainst "Hooky" on the way? Mom!
Who is it still waits up for me
When I'm out late? Who could it be? Mom!
And whom do you suppose I choose
To be my Valentine? Can't lose!
It's YOU, Mom!"
Wasn't he a sweet thoughtful son?

I have scanned one of his letters to his mom with a little drawing of the area in Yuma, Arizona showing the Air Field. It is difficult to scan as he used sheer lightweight paper on which to write. See the next page. I've transcribed the writing below.

Feb. 12, 1943
Lincoln's birthday

My Dear Mom,

The local "Arid-zoners" say the last big rain was a year ago last March. There have been three dust storms since I have been here. It never rains it just blows dust. Yuma is situated in the middle of the desert with mountains around all sides. The Colorado River runs thru the town. The river has two dams in it just north of Yuma. So where the fields near Yuma are irrigated they are green and fertile.

This is, as you see, a very crude drawing of the countryside. Drawn by an old Indian Guide years ago. It happened to be on this piece of paper. It has been wonderful here, the sun shining all the time, not too hot or too cold. Just right.

Yes! There are many Indian Reservations in Arizona. As soon as one steps off the train you are greeted by Indian

Squaws trying to sell all kinds of fancy beadwork and trinkets, which are very pretty.

I visited while in Tucson what is supposed to be the oldest Indian Mission in America. It was most interesting from a standpoint of Art and Architecture. The Indians still use the Mission for worship.

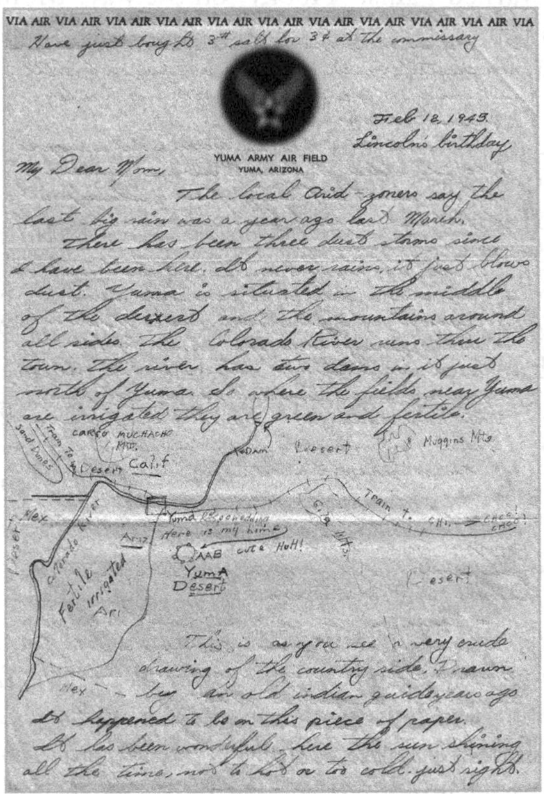

VIA AIR VIA AIR VIA AIR VIA AIR VIA AIR VIA AIR VIA AIR VIA AIR VIA AIR VIA AIR VIA

Have just bought 3rd salt for 3¢ at the commissary

YUMA ARMY AIR FIELD
YUMA, ARIZONA

Feb 12, 1943.
Lincoln's birthday

My Dear Mom,

The local Arid-zoners say the last big rain was a year ago last March.

there has been three dust storms since I have been here. It never rains, it just blows dust. Yuma is situated in the middle of the desert and the mountains around all sides. the Colorado River runs thru the town. the river has two dams in it just north of Yuma. So where the fields near Yuma are irrigated they are green and fertile.

This is as you see a very crude drawing of the country side. Drawn by an old indian guide years ago It happened to be on this piece of paper.

It has been wonderful here the sun shining all the time, not to hot or too cold. just right.

Letter to Mom

What are Dotty's measurements, or size? I'd like to bring her a dress or something from Hollywood if I get back there. While there I met a young lady that knew Capt. Proctor when he was stationed there. So we all got acquainted in no time and had a great time. They sure serve good liquor out here. Hum.

No, It isn't necessary to send my socks here. Thank you.

Has Marjorie got a birthday? I didn't know. Yes! We had a terrible quarrel! Grr.... grr.

I don't remember a quarrel. I think he was just making up an answer to keep his mom from asking more questions.

Well, March 1st is almost here and I'm supposed to be home by then. So. I'll be seeing you soon. I hope you get this letter and write soon.

I have not checked out in the P-40 as yet but hope to soon. I'm doing a lot of Hangar Flying. Have heard my income tax will amount to $125.

Will mail this and write more later,

Happy Landings "Randy"

Feb. 17, '43
Wednesday P.M.

Dear Twinkle Eyes,

Received your letter today. I was sick in bed all last week and did not receive any mail, so I thought everyone had forgotten me out here in the middle of the Yuma dessert.

I feel "lots" better now after getting your swell letter and all's right with the world again.

I wasn't very sick. I just had a headache along with chills a sore throat and I lost my voice. When I spoke I had to whisper so everyone I spoke to would whisper back. More fun!

Because I was sick I was grounded all last week so am behind in my flying time.

How would you like to be married to a fellow that couldn't talk? Then you could have the last word. (Joke!)

I wish I could have seen you personally on your birthday but am glad you received so many swell gifts and cards. Yes! I too get the same feeling as you. And when I'm extra happy I want to cry. Silly, isn't it?

Yes! I think your stationery "snappy." I thought I'd tell you as soon as I saw the envelope, before I even opened it.

More power to you, sleepy head, I wish you could sleep until noon every day.

You know that is the way it is in Brazil. People sleep late and have supper about 9 or10 P.M. It seems like a most fascinating life.

Am glad to hear Dotty is so well. I think I lost over 5 pounds last week. Isn't it funny how weak one is after sickness?

So I make you laugh. Well, Good! No! My birthday isn't in July, its January.

Why was this man telling me his birthday was in January? It was actually the 28th of April! Full of deviltry, that man!

Good luck. Our quarantine is over as of yesterday noon, but the Ferry Pilots are still confined to the limits of the Air Field. Hard luck! I won't be able to meet any of these suntanned Yuma lassies.

We have been behind schedule, but by flying 7 days a week we hope to be back to Romulus by March first.

I flew 3 hours today and honestly I'm tired.

Monday was the day of days. I soloed the P-40. I was complimented on my fine landing. Oh! It is the sweetest ship. I love it. It handles and responds so beautifully. One gains 1500 - 2000 feet doing a Chandelle. Gee! Twinkle Eyes, I just love flying, even if the noise makes one deaf and the vibration makes one sterile, and the lack of oxygen damages ones lungs and heart. And when I'm sick like last week I want to quit flying.

Golly! I'm worried. Please tell me your Mom doesn't dislike me for putting those ideas in your mind about flying.

Really, flying isn't so bad and its fatality rate is lower than for automobiles. See how much safer it is for me to fly than it is to ride in an auto. And the terrible things I mentioned above don't affect one unless he has been flying 8 hours a day for years.

I still can't believe you're 21. Every time I see you I think you're 18.

I think your answer to my question on "love" was perfect. You see, I really do think you are very wise.

Thank you very much for the clipping about General Ralph Royce.

Marjorie! Did you ever have a dream so real that it woke you up? Well, I did. The other night I was over to your house when someone drove in the yard. You and I went out to see who it was and there stood Lt. Irish as big as life and twice as natural. It startled me so I sat straight up in bed and looked around. But, alas! I had only been dreaming. Wasn't that silly? Have you heard any news from Jack?

Maybe you would like to call me Randy. Marjorie seems so impersonal, but I wouldn't want to call you by any other name if you like me to call you Marjorie.

Muggins, I want to thank you for the swell Valentine card. The verse was very nice. Of course, Valentines are never signed, and I have no idea who is sending you Valentines. Ha! Maybe I have competition in another admirer of yours. You say it looks like my handwriting. Hm-m-m.

Maybe if you're real nice to me I'll help you track down the mysterious "Casanova."

When I was a freshman in H. S. I too had some "beauty" spots. Our family Doc made a serum or antitoxin of the germs in one of my "beauty spots." She would give me a shot every week with the serum. It helped, I think, but she also told me to stop eating too many sweets. Guess she thought I was sweet enough. (Joke)

Sweetness, it is near my bedtime and I am awful tired tonight. I flew 3 hours today to try to catch up with my class, so—I'll wish you sweet dreams and Happy Landings,

Randy.

March 2, '43

Dear Dad,

Thank you for your letter and advice.

I have been on a trip for the past week, which took me again to the South and Southwest. We had wonderful flying weather out west as usual.

I have changed my insurance from a 5-year level premium plan, or term, to a 20-year payment plan (life). My insurance company is our "Uncle Sam" so I don't worry about being "taken." The other insurance was only good for a five-year term. And I felt I would rather have something which my heirs could take advantage of. The sooner one changes policies the cheaper the premium is, as you know.

On my last trip I was made both a Flight Leader and Flight Commander, who's duty is to see the planes are delivered safely from A to B. and am very proud to say I got my flight thru a 1,000 mile trip without a scratch. I was told before I left that I was made Flight Commander because of my serious, quiet and unassuming attitude.

We had lots of fun and I was with a swell bunch of fellow pilots. We took turns navigating, which gave us all good experience.

Today I went to dinner with the Pratt's. They certainly are swell. We took "Curt" with us and he was very good. Am learning how to bring up children. Oh yes... we had Tea and Crumpets.

Today has been nice, but with an overcast. However, the sun did break thru once in awhile, so we took some pictures of "Curt."

Happy Landings
Ed.

March 21, 1943.
Spring

Dearest Dotty,

Am returning the gas Ration Book to you. As yet I have not gotten the new title. Am also sending you the little trinket I got in Yuma and forgot to give you.

Am enclosing $5.00 to help out on your room or board in town. How much more do you need to finish having your teeth fixed? I thought your teeth were very pretty the last time I saw you. Just keep brushing them. Am glad to hear you have gained so much weight. Keep up the good work. Your voice sounded very natural over the phone. Thanks for all the news.

So! Marjorie is a Pvt. in the Marines. Isn't that swell? I hope she becomes a General. I feel very proud of her. I only wish she could have joined the W. A. F. S. Of course my reason is very selfish being that now the Lord only knows when I'll see her again.

Have you picked out a formal for your graduation as yet? You pick it out and I'll buy it for you. Oh yes! And you must tell me when your graduation is going to be as I want to be sure of getting a leave at the same time.

I have just returned from a trip, which took me once again to the sunny Southwest. It was beautiful weather.

Today I went to church with the Pratts and then was their guest for dinner. We had a swell dinner and then they drove me home.

Well, drop me a line on all the latest scandal.

Happy Landings with love, Ed

March 26, '43

Dear Mom,

Received your letter today. On every flight or trip in which there is more than one airplane being flown, someone in the flight is made a Flight Leader and if there is more than one flight someone is designated as Flight Commander.

Three or four planes make a flight. I had the care of 2 flights or 7 planes. The title is only held for the trip. Have I now thoroughly confused you? I hope not.

Beginning April 1st we start making foreign deliveries. So maybe I'll get to Africa or England, etc.

On my last trip I strained my back lifting my luggage into the ship and it felt like I had an attack. So, I have been taking it easy the last week.

Will Dotty have to get a bridge for the teeth she is having pulled?

Hope you make out OK with the chicks.

Have not heard from Bud or Radda since my return.

Edward is back in Romulus as he writes.

Curt is not yet creeping all over the floor. Yes! He has lots of hair and 6 teeth.

My insurance is a paid up policy in 20 years. Thanks for all the local news and more power to M. J. Arnold.

Unfortunately I did not see you in the yard, but I did see Coopersville. I didn't get my bearings quick enough (on my trip from Muskegon to Detroit.)

How many handkerchiefs did I leave? Will try and drop in some weekend and get them.

Love and Happy Landings
Ed Randy

March 26, 43

Dearest Dotty,

Long time no hear from you. No, I am not in Yuma as this writing suggests (the stationery I mean.)

Gee, kid—do you know what? I am attending the transition school at Romulus to learn to fly the At-9 and the P -39 and if I ever get two periods together to fly the 39 you may be sure of being "buzzed." It will take me about 40 minutes to get from here to Coopersville. You better burn this letter, as I wouldn't want my superiors to know of my wild ideas. We are only authorized to fly about as far as Lansing.

Have you decided what you would like to study in school? (College)

What kind of a job were you thinking of getting this sum-

mer? After you graduate from College you may then start thinking of paying me back for whatever your education costs.

After you are 21 you can start taking flying lessons and then if there is still a war "on" you may want to join the W. A. F. S.

As soon as I am relieved of my duties in 1947 I would like to go to college and learn to be an Aeronautical Engineer, which I've always wanted to be.

Happy Landings
Ed Randy

Believe it or not…from March 26th until April 14th there is a big gap in correspondence from Edward to either his mother or his sister. I shall try to fill in the gap.

On the evening of March 27th Edward brought me home from wherever we had gone together and we sat in the car outside the house for a bit. He started talking and talking about his great love of airplanes and flying, on and on, *finally* coming to the point of all of that to ask me… not to be his wife, but to be his co-pilot! I was dumbfounded. I had told him earlier in February how I felt about him, that I had fallen in love with him, but he never told me how he felt about me! I gave up on him and went ahead with my original plan to join the Marines. I was sworn into the United States Marine Corps on March 9th. I guess he thought things over after that, came to a decision and proposed on the 27th. Much as I wanted to I couldn't say yes right away, as there were so many things to consider. We talked quite awhile as I explained my predicament. At last I said, "Yes." He was over the moon with joy and presented me with a miniature of his beautiful wings. I put them under my pillow that night but forgot to take them out in the morning before going to church as we were 'running late' and in a great hurry.

After church Edward and I came to my home together for Edward to ask my Dad's permission to marry me. Daddy said, "I'm sure glad it's you, Ed." Of course he said yes to Edward's question. Unbeknown to me Mother had found the wings under my pillow when she made up the bed before we got there, so Daddy was prepared. All of us were happy and smiling together! After telling my parents Edward and I decided we had better go to see Edward's folks and tell them of our engagement.

Mr. and Mrs. Howard H. Irish
announce the marriage of their daughter
Marjorie Jean
to
Edward W. Randell
Lieutenant, Air Forces, Army of the United States
on Sunday, April the eleventh
Nineteen hundred and forty-three
Coopersville, Michigan

The wedding announcement

Wedding snapshot

The following weekend I went to Detroit where Edward and I found my engagement diamond and wedding rings. They were platinum with three diamonds on the engagement ring and nine tiny diamonds on the wedding band. I had always thought my wedding ring, if I ever had one, would be a plain gold band similar to my mother's and my grandmother's. The platinum ones were Edward's choice. I was so happy it didn't matter to me. Edward was what mattered and these were his choice. It could be gold, silver, platinum or whatever… if it is what he chose.

The same weekend we talked a lot more and decided that we would like to be married the *next* weekend so that we might have some time together before I was called for active duty. Our decision caused some excitement and a lot of rushing around to get ready as we were going to be married at my parent's home on the farm. Plus! I must have a wedding dress… and a veil, too? Mom and I went shopping in Grand Rapids and found a simple long, white formal. Veil? I borrowed my best friend Eloise's veil, which she had worn at her own wedding just six months earlier. Mom said later she never had her "spring cleaning" done so early and so fast before!

Marine Recruit May 6- '43

Mrs. Marjorie J. Irish Randell left Sunday evening for Hunter college, New York, to start her basic training in the United States marine corps women's reserve.

Mrs. Randell is a graduate of Coopersville High school and attended Grand Rapids Junior college. She has been employed in the office of the Capital Lumber & Wrecking Co. for the last year and a half.

On April 11 she was married to Lt. Edward Randell, with the transport command at Wayne county airport, Romulus. Her brother, Lt. Howard H. Irish, jr., is a prisoner of the Japanese in the Philippines.

Miss Marjorie Irish Joins U. S. Marines Women's Reserves

Miss Marjorie Irish, daughter of Mr. and Mrs. Howard Irish of Coopersville, became a Private in the United States Marine Corps Women's Reserves when she was sworn in at Detroit Tuesday by Captain J. K. Strubing, Jr., U. S. Marine Corps.

Miss Irish is waiting call to active duty. She is to receive basic training at Hunter College, New York City. A graduate of Coopersville high school in 1940, she attended Grand Rapids Junior College one year before being employed by the Capitol Lumber and Wrecking Co. in Grand Rapids.

Her brother, First Lieutenant Howard Irish, Jr., is a prisoner of war somewhere in the Philippine Islands.

Pvt. Marjorie Irish Randell, who recently completed her preliminary training at Hunter College, New York, in the Women's Reserve of the United States Marine Corps has been transferred to Bloomington, Ind., where is taking a twelve weeks' course in aviation storekeeping at the University of Indiana. Her address is: Marine Training Detachment, USNTS (SK-W) Bn 4, Company 24, Bloomington, Ind.

Miss Marjorie Irish Became Bride of Lieut. Randell

In a ceremony taking place at eight o'clock Sunday evening at the home of Mr. and Mrs. Howard Irish, their daughter, Marjorie Jean, became the bride of Lieutenant Edward R. Randell, son of Mr. and Mrs. James P. Randell of Coopersville.

An improvised altar of palms, candelabra, large baskets of white snapdragons, calla lilies and and sweet scented stock formed the setting for the ceremony, performed by Rev. Victor B. Niles.

The bride, given in marriage by her father, wore a white silk marquiseite and taffeta gown with fingertip veil, and carried an arm bouquet of calla lilies.

Mrs. Howard Bush, matron of honor, wore a soft blue gown of lace and net. Dorothy I. Randell, sister of the groom, as bridesmaid, wore pale blue chiffon. Each carried a bouquet of pink rosebuds and sweet peas. James P. Randell of Chicago acted as best man. Miss Jean Lietzke of East Lansing, played the traditional wedding marches.

The Misses Mary Jane Arnold and Madelyn Hastings were ushers, and Mr. and Mrs. Hazen C. Pratt of Detroit completed the wedding party as master and mistress of ceremonies.

Mrs. Irish chose a two-piece navy blue sheer dress for her daughter's wedding, with corsage of red rosebuds and sweet peas. Mrs. Randell, mother of the groom, wore a blue silk print dress with corsage of red rosebuds and white sweet peas.

A buffet lunch was served the guests. The lovely three-tier decorated wedding cake graced the table. Floral decoration in pink and yellow, with lighted candles, were used in the room.

Other out-of-town guests were Mr. and Mrs. Orin Irish and daughters Beverly and Shirley, of Delta, Ohio, and Dwight F. Pitkin of Chicago.

The couple left upon a short wedding trip Mrs. Randell's going away outfit was a two-piece light crepe dress trimmed with same color lace with hat to match. Accessories were dark brown.

Lieut. Randell will return to the Wayne County Airport at Romulus the latter part of the week where he is serving with the Transport Command. Mrs. Randell is waiting orders for active service in the Marines.

Sister of War Prisoner Joins Marine Corps

Coopersville—Miss Marjorie Irish, daughter of Mr. and Mrs. Howard H. Irish, sr., has become a private in the marine corps women's reserves. She will receive basic training at Hunter college, New York city.

A graduate of Coopersville High school in 1940, she attended Grand Rapids Junior college one year before being employed by the Capitol Lumber & Wrecking Co. in Grand Rapids.

Her brother, 1st Lt. Howard H. Irish, jr., recently was reported to be a prisoner of war in the Philippine islands.

ANNOUNCE ENGAGEMENT OF MISS MARJORIE IRISH

Mr. and Mrs. Howard Irish of Coopersville announce the engagement and approaching marriage of their daughter, Marjorie Jean, to Lieutenant Edward W. Randell, son of Mr. and Mrs. James P. Randell of Coopersville.

Miss Irish is a graduate of Coopersville High School, attended Grand Rapids Junior College, and has been employed in the office of the Capitol Lumber and Wrecking Co., Grand Rapids, for the past year and a half.

Lieutenant Randell graduated from Lane Technical School in Chicago and received his wings at Mission Field, Texas, in October, 1942. At present he is stationed at the Wayne County Airport, Romulus, Michigan, and serves with the Air Transport Command.

MISS ARLENE PARISH JOINS MARINE CORPS RESERVES

Miss Arlene Parish, daughter of Mr. and Mrs. Erwin W. Parish, has been sworn into the United States Marine Corps Women's Reserves. She is the third young lady from this community to enter the service of her country. The others are Miss Charlotte Ter Avest and Mrs. Edward Randell (Marjorie Irish).

Miss Parish is a graduate of the Coopersville high school, class of 1940, and attended Heaney's Commercial College in Grand Rapids. For the past year she has been employed in the office of the Air Control Products, Inc.

Newspaper clippings

The only evidence of all of this found among Edward's letters to his mother is a large cream colored envelope within an envelope, which when opened reveals a cream colored card announcing the marriage of Marjorie Jean Irish to Lt. Edward W. Randell on April 11th, 1943.

As most Honeymooners did in those days, we went to Niagara Falls! We flew the short distance from Detroit to Buffalo, New York for our very short three-day Honeymoon. We *did* see the falls! Edward had to be back at the Base reporting for duty on Friday, so we came back to Coopersville on Thursday, then went to Grand Rapids to have formal wedding pictures taken.

I was expecting to be called to active duty at any time. Edward came back Friday night and stayed until Sunday, then back to Romulus. We had a few weeks together before I was called for active duty on the 5th of May. Edward saw me off on a train leaving Detroit for New York City on that date. We were together less than a month.

Side note here:

Another "Unbeknown" to me… at the same time Edward was dating me he was also dating Cleo Reynolds, daughter of our rural mail carrier! Many years later I found a letter Father Randell wrote his sister (Radda) in Chicago in March of 1943. He wrote, "Well, the Marine won out!"

I heard later after we were married, Cleo said, "He was supposed to marry *me!*"

I never talked to Edward about it. I wonder though, on what he based his final decision? I'll never know.

What difference does it make now? We had more than sixty-seven wonderful years together. I loved and still love that man! *I am so happy he decided on me!*

I have found clippings my mother saved telling of my enlistment in the Marine Corps, along with the news of several of my friends joining various branches of the service. They are copied here on the previous page. I hope you can read the fine print.

Back to more of Edward's letters with a couple of postcards first.

4-14-43

Dear Dotty, How's conditions? Isn't this a beautiful scene? We did not take the ride on the "whirligig" as it was too cold for my better half. It has been snowing all day. Happy Laings and love,

Marjorie & Ed.

The "whirligig" was an aero cable over Whirlpool Rapids, Niagara Falls. It was pictured on the card he sent Dotty. The other card was one picturing the Hotel Tuller in Detroit and was my writing, although the "Ed" at the end was Edward's own signature. Mailed April 20, 1943.

Dear Folks, I arrived safely and found Ed in the best of spirits. Expect to call Cousin Mildred tomorrow. Hello to Herbie. Love and Happy Landings,

Marjorie and Ed

Chapter Five

May 19, 1943.

Dear Folks,

Would you kindly let me know how much money was deposited in my account for April? Thank you.

I have a notice from Prudential to pay my insurance, so I would like to know where my account stands. Also I received a notice to pay the interest on a loan on my premium, is that correct, is there such a loan?

I do not believe I will be able to get home May 23, or is it May 21st the day of Dotty's School Banquet.

Last week my "day" started at 6:30 A.M. and lasted until 9 P.M. and this week I am living the life of Reilly with "Bankers Hours" 10 A.M. until 9 P.M.

We have finished our course on radios, in which I got a mark of 95, and passed a ten words a minute code test (sending and receiving.)

Have not heard from you folks for some two weeks. I might add that Bachelors Hall is rather lonesome without Marjorie.

She is swell to me. I get a letter from her every day. :-)

We had some more rain this morn. I'll bet the farmers wish it would hold off for a while.

How is Herbie getting along? Does he still call horses cows? Tell him Hi for me.

I received Vi and Bud's clock. It is a "beauty." Also received a nice letter from Radda and one from Cousin Foster, plus another from Mary Lee.

Hope you have a nice trip to Chicago, Dotty, and I am hoping to be home for your graduation.

In instrument school we fly the Link trainer 2 hours a day, fly the airplane (under the hood) 2 hours, have 1 hour of code and 2 hours of ground school. This continues until we have some 30 hours of each.

Must close, as it is my turn at the Link. Please write.

Love and Happy Landings,
Ed.

May 26, 1943.

Dear Folks,

Enclosed is my new "Will" and new insurance paper, would you please send the old one to Washington D.C. And also do you have the receipt (blue color I believe) from the permit I used to get my old tire recapped and to obtain the new tube. It seems I have to have them before I can send in my application for a new tire.

Dotty, I hope you have a high old time on your skip day.

Today has been very nice, sunny all day. I am due for an instrument flight in a half hour. My hours this week are from 2 p.m. to 11 p.m. Not so bad, aye?

Hope Herbie is behaving himself. Will enclose a piece of gum for him.

Yes! I have changed the beneficiary on my insurance and then wrote and told Marjorie I hoped she wouldn't collect it.

No! My address will not be changed. Yesterday I learned I would be paid as a single officer as of the time Marjorie was called to duty. No one can say I ever married for money.

Today there is a gloom cloud over the Air Field as a Lt. Ruelle was killed this morning at 7 a.m. when a P-39 in which he was flying crashed after the take off. They think the ship went into a flat spin.

Will try and get off for Dotty's graduation but won't know for a while.

Am holding open house as my roommate Lt. Peter Buck is on a trip.

Must run to school.

Love and Happy Landings,

Ed.

Postcards:

June 6

Dear Folks,

Happy Birthday, Dotty! Arrived here at 2 p.m. I went up for a check flight with a different instructor, who helped me a lot by telling me what I was doing wrong and how to correct my mistakes. I then flew again with my old instructor, Lt. Edwards. We are getting along swell together. We did not get today off. So I have to fly in a little while. H.L. Ed

June 17

Dear Folks Here is my new address and station. Classes are in 10 minutes so I must run. It is beautiful here. Happy Landings,

Ed.

His new address: Rosecrans Field, St. Joseph, Mo.

June 14, 1943.

Dear Dad,

How much money do you need and by what date? By Marjorie joining the service I only get paid as a single Officer, so I am not making very much money. Nor do I have a cent in the bank, but I could probably borrow the money, as I hate to see you lose the Traverse place.

My phone is Wayne 9106. If you call, make it 8:30 my time and 7:30 your time. Or any time after midnight. Some evenings I fly from 8:30 P.M. to midnight.

After you get the Traverse place back please rent it, so you can pay me back.

I have learned that I can not name a trust company as my beneficiary for my insurance, so in that case will there be any papers for Marjorie to sign to turn the money over to the Trust Company?

Can Jim or Bud help you on the mortgage?

Oh! Would you please send me my car title?

Have Dotty and Herbie left for Chicago?

We have had nice weather this week. Today is rather warm. I had my local instrument check yesterday and failed it. So will try again next Tuesday and Lord willing and my trying I hope to be finished by Wednesday.

Hope you get my letter in time to do some good.

Happy Landings
Ed.

June 15

Dear Dad,

I am leaving the car keys at the Officers Club.

How is this for an idea? You take the bus to Detroit and get in touch with the Pratts and ask them to take you out to the field. I feel sure they would do that.

The Officers Club hours are from 8 a.m. to 5 p.m. so you would have to get the keys sometime during those hours. The car is in the parking lot beside the club. It is full of gas.

The Pratt's address is:

760 Campbell Ave.

Phone: Vinewood 2-5367

All the bank will loan me on my signature is $100. Will that help?

How's about selling me the Traverse place?

Will send my new address as soon as I learn what it is. Will be gone until July 25 or August 1st.

Enclosed are some papers and a gas ration book. Please keep them until I return. The gas coupons have to be used by July 21st.

Happy Landings
Ed

June 16

Dear Folks, Am almost to my new school. It is nice and cool here after a rain. We flew here last night, and ran into a storm over Kansas City. More fun. Will send my address soon. Happy Landings

Ed.

June 24

Dear Dad,

I am sending you a copy of my new "Will" and Personal Order, which Marjorie will need to collect my insurance and pensions in the event of my death. They also advised me to make you my Power of Attorney, because I may see Foreign Service. I was also informed that the Gov. does not pay out the insurance to beneficiaries in lump sums but pay them so much a month according to their age at the death of the insured. What with the pension it amounts to quite a "good deal." So, I guess we had better forget the "trust." It was a good idea, though.

I'm getting along great in school. Start my Link tonight at 8 p.m. Soon I hope to start flying. My, the time passes fast here, because we are so busy, I guess.

After checking my finances I can only send you $100. I hope you can save the place. Please let me know what "cooks." I have to run to a Navigation Class. Yours in haste,

Ed.

P.S. Due to a misunderstanding I will mail my "Will" to you tomorrow. Please put them in the safe deposit box. Ed.

June 28, 1943.

Dear Dad,

This last idea of yours is a brainstorm. I think it is fair, however I would advise you to sell the truck and don't mortgage the car. In the first place interest on car loans is too high and in the second place you may lose the car.

I have sent you $100. The car is $1200. That makes $900. I owe you, which I shall start paying you Sept. 1st. Is that correct so far?

Next I would advise you to sell the farm and go back to the city. I will try to pay you the $100. a month. Man. That is real money.

The tires on my car I beg to tell you are <u>not</u> about gone. There is still quite a few thousand miles in them. The car, however, does need a grease job and the brakes checked. The insurance is paid until 1944. Please take as good care of it as I did. It should have a bath.

Has the cottage been plastered? How is the roof? And is there any bathroom plumbing in it? I have not been there for years so do not know what the score is.

The banks did not say they would not loan me any money. They said they would not loan without security. Boy! How you get things mixed up.

I think it would be best to have the Deed to the Cottage made out in both Marjorie's and my name. I have sent the title to Dotty for <u>quick</u> action.

Would there be any chance for you to go to Traverse and see about getting the house plastered and decorated, also plumbing put in? Let me know what these would cost. I would like very much to rent it to some Officer.

I don't think seeing Jack helps him any. I think it will be a matter of years before he is normal again. All we can do is pray for his recovery. The Lord does some wonderful things.

I'll appreciate anything you can do in getting the cottage finished.

Happy Landings
Ed.

Enclosed in this letter from Edward is a copy of the land contract drawn up between Edward and his parents for the purchase of the Traverse City property. I believe it was later redrawn to include 'Marjorie' with Edward. However, this one Edward has signed and it was notarized in Missouri.

The letterhead is Rosecrans Field, St. Joseph, Missouri on this next letter to his dad.

July 4th, '43

Dear Dad,

Thanks for the latest "dope." The tire record is in Detroit. I'll send it to you as soon as I get back to DT.

You may destroy the old "Wills" as I will have no need for them.

Marjorie and I have a joint checking account and in the event that I am out of the country, she will send you the payment. Okay.

Likewise if I am out of the country please consult her on anything that you may have to do in my name. Roger.

That knotty pine interior sounds like a good idea. But do you think anyone would rent such a place for a home?

I hope you can sell the farm and get back into the Real Estate business again or maybe a renting agency.

On the other side of the paper is a letter to his mom:

Dear Mom,

Hi and stuff. At first I was wondering who Mercury (HG) was. I will have to write to Bud... does he still live in Evanston?

When John is allowed to come home I do not believe the farm is the place for him. I think he should have a change of environment.

Am getting along just perfect in my flying. No trouble on the "gauges" at all.

Am reading over your old letters. And for goodness sake... you don't give me much credit. I failed my local check at DT... <u>but</u> I did not flunk the course. I passed my XC check at DT. Am a qualified instrument pilot with an "A" card. Please don't make everything look so bad. My instructors in DT were <u>very</u> good and taught me many helpful ideas on "gauge" flying. Being sent here is an honor <u>not</u> an alternative. I volunteered because it is what I want. The more education I get the further I'll get in this world.

I do hope John gets well soon. I'm sure that he will.

Love and Happy Landings,
Ed.

Below is a copy of the paper given Edward saying he is a well-qualified pilot who can fly anywhere any time. It should have made him a proud guy, I would think.

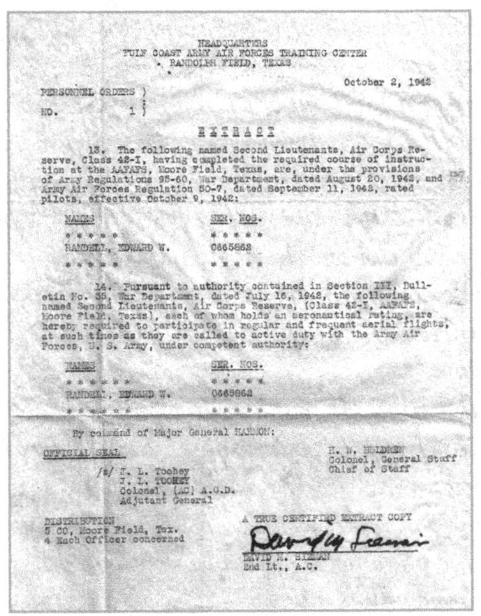

HEADQUARTERS
GULF COAST ARMY AIR FORCES TRAINING CENTER
RANDOLPH FIELD, TEXAS

October 2, 1942

PERSONNEL ORDERS)
NO. 1)

E X T R A C T

13. The following named Second Lieutenants, Air Corps Reserve, Class 42-I, having completed the required course of instruction at the AAFAFS, Moore Field, Texas, are, under the provisions of Army Regulations 95-60, War Department, dated August 20, 1942, and Army Air Forces Regulation 50-7, dated September 11, 1942, rated pilots, effective October 9, 1942:

NAMES — SER. NOS.
* * * * * — * * * * *
RANDELL, EDWARD W. — 0665862
* * * * * — * * * * *

14. Pursuant to authority contained in Section III, Bulletin No. 35, War Department, dated July 16, 1942, the following named Second Lieutenants, Air Corps Reserve, (Class 42-I, AAFAFS, Moore Field, Texas), each of whom holds an aeronautical rating, are hereby required to participate in regular and frequent aerial flights, at such times as they are called to active duty with the Army Air Forces, U. S. Army, under competent authority:

NAMES — SER. NOS.
* * * * * * — * * * * *
RANDELL, EDWARD W. — 0665862
* * * * * * — * * * * *

By command of Major General HARMON:

H. W. HOLDREN
Colonel, General Staff
Chief of Staff

OFFICIAL SEAL

/s/ J. L. Toohey
J. L. TOOHEY
Colonel, (AC) A.G.D.
Adjutant General

DISTRIBUTION
5 CO, Moore Field, Tex.
4 Each Officer concerned

A TRUE CERTIFIED EXTRACT COPY
DAVID M. [illegible]
2nd Lt., A.C.

Paper saying Edward is a competent pilot

I was proud of him! I am still proud of him today, seventy-four years later!

August 8th, '43.
Sunday night.

Dear Dad,

Received your letter today. What we need to do is predict the future and our problems are solved. Thank you for your advising letter.

Today the Doctor told me he didn't think I had fractured my knee, but that I had just bruised it. They took some more x-rays today.

Most of the soreness and swelling is gone. This noon the Doc took the bandage off and I was able to bend my knee a bit. They have not told me how long I am to be in bed. They are treating me swell.

The nurses scold me when they catch me out of bed. The patient in the room next to mine is a nurse. She too, has a sore knee. She fell in the kitchen.

The Chaplain has been to see me, and other fellows have brought me reading material.

According to the papers both "Mussie" and Hitler have resigned. I wonder how much longer the war will continue.

The ships we fly here are twin engine B-25's. They fly like a feather. I have made a couple landings and they land easily. They fly and land faster than a B-24.

One of the men in my Ward is related to a Samuel Randall and is a descendant of Robert Richard Randall of Sheffield, England. Do we "hail" from the same R. R. Randall?

Will close for now as the heat has got me.

Happy Landings
Ed.

August 11, 1943

Dear Folks,

Yesterday the Doctor told me I had not broken my leg, so I was released from the hospital today. I now have to wait to be crewed again. I may be here yet another 2 weeks. I hope I can make Marjorie's Gradation.

Well! Cheerio! And Happy Landings
Ed.

EWR & MIR at Indiana University

Edward *did* make it to my Graduation from Navy Storekeeper's School at Indiana University in Bloomington. It was the first time we had seen each other since he put me on the train for New York City.

Guess what? I just found another small letter tucked in this box of letters Edward's mother saved! It is a lined page torn from a notebook and was written April 6, 1943 to his sister Dotty. It was folded into a tiny square. Edward *did* mention our wedding plans in a letter home after all.

April 6, 1943.

Dear Dotty,

Please excuse the writing paper. Received your letter last week.

Yes! I am a very busy boy.

So the Busman's are proud parents. Swell. Marjorie told me of it, too. Got your note and Jim Luther's but did not get to see him. What is the name of Tony and Kit's boy?

Well the weekend has come and gone and Marjorie and I had a wonderful time. We went to church with the Pratts, had dinner with them and went for a ride.

We have decided to get married Sunday, the 11th. 8 P.M. I have asked Cousin Foster and Radda to try and come. I am asking Jim to be my best man and have asked Reverend Moffatt to perform the nuptials.

I'm as excited as a cadet on his first check ride.

Cousin Mildred says she would like to come, as she just loves weddings.

Am not planning on flying any planes until after I'm married. So I feel safe.

No! I don't think a permanent would be nice, but if you like them, go ahead.

Am enclosing $10.00. Would you try and get the car license and then don't use it. Aren't I terrible the way I write and the things I say! I want to have enough gas for the wedding, etc. and honeymoon.

I wish you would let me know how you stand financially. Do you need more for your teeth or school?

No! We have decided against a military wedding. Because of the war we have laid aside our dress suits and sabers.

Cousin Mildred said she wished Marjorie would be staying in Detroit as she likes her very much.

Chicken is $1.00 a pound wholesale in Detroit.

Oh! Has the statement of deposit come from the bank for this month?

Your loving brother,

Happy Landings,

Ed

"I'm as excited as a cadet on his first check ride." Bless him. I was pretty excited myself. *It was all happening so fast!*

Edward had no formal pictures of himself in uniform, thus when he and I went into Grand Rapids after our honeymoon to have our formal wedding photographs made he posed for the above. Oh my! What a handsome man I had married! I had a little travel clock given to me as a gift, when I went into the Marine Corp, from the people I worked with at Capitol Lumber. It had spaces for pictures on either side of the clock face itself. It was a perfect fit for those two pictures.

I was the envy of all the Marine girls in my barracks when I had it set up and open in my locker!

Now back to 'letters to the folks'. From here on the letters are intermittent and mostly written by me as Edward was very busy at work and had no spare time for letter writing. I was busy, too, but my schedule was more flexible.

I had been sworn into the USMCWR (United States Marine Corps Women's Reserve) on March 9th and was called to active duty on May 5, 1943. Edward saw me off on the train headed for New York City.

Boot camp was certainly nothing like the male Marine's boot camp. We were housed in apartment buildings adjacent to Hunter College. Classes, classes, classes. We learned the basics of being a Marine, learned about companies and platoons, marching, times to salute our superiors… history of the Marine Corps. The learning seemed to go on and on.

At roll call each time they called out "Irish" I would yell back, "Randell." Another girl in my platoon would hear "Tarnofsky" and yell back "Fox." We soon became friends and learned that both of us had been married between the time we were sworn in and the time we reported for duty. We were not supposed to do that, but it was already a done thing. We were not penalized at least. I still keep in touch with Betty Fox after all these years. She lives in Las Vegas, Nevada and I live in Seal Beach, California. She and her husband Al had three children, two boys and a girl. Edward and I had four boys. Those early years didn't leave us much time to get together. She lived in Santa Monica, California then and we lived in Westwood, not too far apart.

After boot camp I was sent to Navy Storekeepers School at Indiana University in Bloomington, Indiana. (The Marine Corps is a part of the Navy.) After that I was sent back to Cherry Point to await assignment. Assignment turned out to be orders to report to Jacksonville, Florida. Only twelve girls were chosen to go there. It was a "hand's on" duty assignment to learn the ins and outs of actual "Shop Stores." We worked in a huge aircraft hangar on the base. The time period for us to be there was supposed to be 30 days. I don't know if they forgot about us, if it was intentional or if they didn't know what to do with us, but the time turned out to be three months. We became publicity figures for the USMCWR and were cautioned as such to always be on our best behavior. It was a memorable and enjoyable period of my service. Edward made it several times to see me while we were there and I was allowed "off base" to spend time with him.

We girls marched in parades, were invited out to Civilian homes for parties, behaved ourselves, worked in the A & R Hangar (Aviation and Repair) and eventually were sent back to Cherry Point to await a further duty assignment. In the meantime we worked in the A & R hangar there at Cherry Point. The "shop store" consisted of a caged in supply center for parts to repair the planes. I could look at a screw or a bolt and tell you the size of the thing immediately without checking the box. Screws, bolts, fabric, etc...everything needed to repair an airplane was available from our little cage. I was later chosen to work in an office in the hangar ordering supplies, taking dictation and typing which was general office work. It was a good thing I was married for some of those Marines were great fellows in addition to being handsome...and I was attracted!! In retrospect I think Edward knew this might be a possibility if I joined the Marine Corps and that is why he suddenly decided to ask me to be his co-pilot. In spite of being attracted I behaved myself and remembered my marital status.

Edward did make it to Cherry Point to see me several times causing a flurry of attention on the flight line as to why in the world an Army Air Corp plane was landing at a Marine Base !! Among his papers I found that he had qualified to be a single pilot, flying by himself, which is what he wanted so he could then ask for trips near where I was stationed without having to consult the rest of his crew.

Edward writes, "I sure am lonesome for Marjorie"

I felt the same way about him!

Edward is writing now from St. Joseph, Missouri where he is going to yet another flying school. He writes on such thin lightweight paper and on both sides, it is hard to read. I have copied his next letter below.

Fri., Aug. 13th,'43.

Dear Folks,

I received today the letter you sent to DT.

Yes! Marjorie had written me about Mr. Reed.

Where have you thought of moving after you sell the farm? Am glad to hear about Jack's improved condition, but don't think he should live on the farm again.

I don't intend to be leaving the good old U.S.A., not at present anyway.

Am sorry I can't pay you any money on the contract this month as my money for this month is spent. I had figured on $2.50 a day while training, but have learned that Uncle Sam stopped Temporary Duty and "TD per diem" as of June 1st.

About the taxes... do I pay the $18.53 for the year '42 and $7.50 for '43, and do I pay them in my name?

I also received a bill from John Meerman for $34.65. Is that Fire Insurance for one year? Right.

On the car insurance transfer... why do you need Marjorie's name on it? He name was never on the title. Savvy? Also, I do not know the policy number. Yes! I have some extra car keys.

I have read an article in the Colliers magazine of how they give the patient a drug to relax their muscles before they give them shock treatments, this keeps them from hurting themselves.

My knee is healing fine. I am a wee bit wobbly but okay. No fracture.

I'm glad Uncle Sam takes such an interest in his nephews.

I am still a 2nd Lt. I have been crewed up again as a 1st Pilot. The Major said he would not put me at the bottom of the list again... so I should be flying in a day or so.

So help me, I injured my knee playing softball. Yes! The Army has a few games we play during calisthenics. Baseball is one of them. They have now told us to play - "not so hard."

Am glad Jimmy and family were able to visit you folks. Say Hi to Radda for me. Must write my dear Marjorie.

Glad to hear Jack is better.

Love and Happy Landings
Ed.

An aside note here: Edward wrote in his last letter that he was still a second Lieutenant. I well remember his coming to see me at Cherry Point, N.C. after his promotion to First Lieutenant. He never said a word about it. I hadn't noticed until we were getting off a bus that was taking us into town. He got off ahead of me and I looked down at him. Those gold bars were no longer gold… they were *silver!* He had been promoted!

First Lieutenant! *We celebrated!*

Another remembrance… Whenever Edward came to visit me I would obtain permission to leave the base overnight and we would go into town. Later, in town, when we asked for a room in one lady's home she doubted that we were married! Edward learned from her expressed doubts. From then on he always carried a copy of our marriage license/certificate with him. *What a special guy he was.*

Several times the Navy Shore Patrol stopped him to question his being out with an enlisted person when he was an officer. In the Navy and Marine Corps officers and enlisted personnel were not allowed to fraternize. Edward always had an answer for them… the marriage license again.

The following two pictures were taken during a leave both Edward and I had, spending some of it in Chicago with our Randell relatives.

1943

A couple of happy people!

Newlyweds finally get to see each other after six months apart!

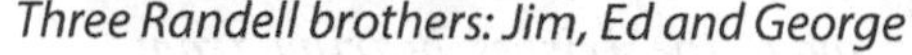

Three Randell brothers: Jim, Ed and George

EWR & MIR on pier at Chicago

Now, another postcard:

9-6-43

Dear Folks,

Arrived on time and am attending transition school to check out in different types of ships. Happy Landings

Ed.

Sept. 11, 1943

Dear Folks,

How's the Hay Fever, etc. I am in fine health myself.

This week has been a very eventful one.

I was assigned to transition school as soon as I arrived to check out in the B-25. I have been attending ground school all week and today I got my recheck.

Next week I am to attend Pursuit School and check out in the P-39 and P-40. I also want to check out in the B-25 if they can squeeze me in. These assignments are quite full for next week.

Last Wednesday I had a Co-Pilot trip to St. Paul. I flew right over the farm about noon at 4,000 feet. While in St. Paul I called up both Cousins Mildred and Hazen. Boy did I surprise them.

A letter from Marjorie today says she is on her way to Jacksonville, Fla. She sure gets around.

It has turned very cold here this last week. Thursday we had a Review during a rainstorm. Some fun.

As near as I can figure I have 4 days leave coming to me before Oct. 9.

Oh say, they are finishing the lounge in our barracks in knotty pine and does it look swell. They have covered the walls and ceiling. They shellac or varnish it so it has a light color to it. Beautiful.

That was great news about the Irishes hearing from Jack. (My brother.)

Also, it is good news about Italy.

Had a letter from Dotty this week.

I have been very busy attending ground school and studying and writing Marjorie in the evening

Well, it is time I get some shut-eye so I'll say goodnight.

Love and Happy Landings
Ed.

Postcard:

Dear Folks, 9-21 Am back home after a trip to Niagara.

Love and Happy Landings
Ed.

Sept. 28, '43

Dear Dad,

Enclosed is my check. The tax receipts were sent to me at Romulus.

Had a fine visit in Chicago and visited all my relatives.

Arrived here this morn. and am continuing my Pursuit

Training.

Happy Landings Ed

Oct. 23, 1943.

Dear Folks,

Arrived home okay.

Am on orders again to deliver a P-39 to Great Falls. We hope to get out this afternoon or tomorrow.

At present we are waiting on the weather to break, it is down to the minimums, poor visibility and low ceilings.

Thank you for the account of your expenses. I will let you know what I learn and maybe I can send you a little money each month.

Yes! You may be sure if I get to the coast I shall look up Grandma Pratt. I also hope I get a trip to Florida. Am going to work on that after this trip. On this trip I hope to be checked as a "fly alone." Then I'll recheck in the P-40 and then hope for a trip to the south.

Marjorie's pen disappeared when she was at Cherry Point so I got her a new one. Simple, huh! It also makes a nice anniversary present, don't you think?

(It must have been a six-month anniversary)

Have not heard from Marge but I do hope she gets home for Christmas. According to my figures she has 10 days due her.

Well, I must go check the weather so I'll write again. Love and Happy Landings,

Ed

Oct. 29, '43

Dear Mom,

Thank you for all the "Local" gossip. Hm!

It is almost Halloween again.

I have just gotten back from another trip and expect to leave again tomorrow on another one.

I am a "fly alone" pilot now so am hoping for a trip to

the South to see my better half.

Was visiting Radda last Tuesday. Had dinner with Cousin Foster and spent the evening with Radda. Expected to, but didn't find Dotty in Chicago. Radda says you folks are going to Chicago the first. Well! Good for our side. I hope you have a nice trip. Who knows I may see you there.

I hope Dotty's cold is gone by now.

I wanted to go visit Grandma Irish. Am sorry I didn't. I shall have to write her now.

I spent a couple days this week in South Bend waiting on weather.

Yes! I got the marriage license and Uncle Sam has made the copies for me, so I'm all "set." Thank you.

My last trip was without incident. The speed indicator on my ship went out, so my Flight leader and I changed ships. One boy in our Flight nicked his prop blades so we had to go on without him.

There was snow on the ground in Montana.

I'm enclosing $100.00 on account.

Must close, as it is midnight.

Happy Landings,
Ed.

The next postcard was mailed from Tulsa, Oklahoma:

11-28-'43

Dear Folks,

Welcome from Tulsa. It is a pretty and clean town.

The weather is perfect.

Love and Happy Landings,
Ed.

Postcard to his folks

This time Edward's letterhead paper was from Hotel Niagara, Niagara Falls, New York.

Dec. 7, 1943.

Dear Folks,

Well! This date two years ago was very important. Let's hope we have all our enemies in hand before another two years pass.

I read an article where some Professor says the war with Germany will be over July 1, 1944 and the war with Japan will be over April 1st, 1945.

His estimates were pretty close!

I was able to get an early bus, which left Grand Rapids at 4 A.M. and arrived home okay. Because it was foggy here we did not do any flying Sunday. Am still attending ground school and learning something new each day.

Am glad you folks got home safely. That was some fog. Yes, I was able to get some sleep on the bus. The clerk at the Hotel desk was a school boy friend of Mert Wilcox. So we had a long talk about the good old days. The man had not seen

Mert since he joined the Army in World War One and the past 20 years has lived in Grand Rapids and didn't know Mert lived in Coopersville. He said I made him homesick.

Say... Am I to pay this tax bill... is that the idea?

Must close and write my best half.

Love and Happy Landings,
Ed.

These post cards from El Paso, Texas:

12-25-43

Dear Folks,

Merry Christmas! Hoping it is a nice day up north. Am spending my Christmas on the Airliners. Love and Happy Landings, Ed.

Dear Folks,

I have been hearing of your cold weather and snow. It is very nice here in the southwest. Spent Christmas with Mr. Ellegood and friends in their desert home. It is very pretty. Love and Happy Landings,
Ed.

Jan. 27, '44

Dear Folks,

Now! Shame on you! Don't you know me well enough to know that if I ever leave the country you shall be the first to know? My, goodness!

I have been in the good old U. S. flying both east and west and south, too. My last trip took me to my loved one at Cherry Point.

They have kept me very busy on deliveries, so I have not done any too much letter writing.

Maybe I can get a day off when Marjorie is home to see the pictures of "usuns."

Oh, yes, I had breakfast with Radda at her apartment

and last Sat. we stayed over night. Bud & Vi. and Jim & Mary Lee all came to visit. More fun!

The gloves I spoke of are leather. I do not need shoe stamps.

No, I am alone. No roommate. I have not heard from Pete as yet. I shall let you know when I want you to come to Detroit.

Nothing has been said about raising my rank. Tonight it is raining. Hope to leave on another trip tomorrow.

Love and Happy Landings,

Ed.

Oh! I received your and Radda's Christmas gifts. Thank you.

March 6, 1944

Dear Folks,

Am glad to hear you received the fruit okay!

No, Lt. Jeff did not go with me on my next trip.

The Aerial Engineer, Frank, (Schreckengast) has been on at least ten deliveries. We are together on this one. We have been very busy. We are In one day and out the next. We have been flying nights; the landscape is very pretty at night, plus the air is smooth.

I hope you have good luck with your "chicken hatcher."

Today the weather to the west of us has been "low," so we are waiting until tomorrow. I have not been on this route before, so we decided to wait a day, rather than to run into a hard mountain.

We are in "Shy Ann." It is a nice town. I like it. I like the west because of its clean air and sunshine. It's cold here today with a little snow in the air. I seem to like the wide-open spaces. I think I'll be a rancher after the war.

It is near time for supper so I'll close,

Love and Happy Landings,

Ed.

P. S. Mom, will you put $20.00 of your check in the Coopersville bank in Marjorie's and my savings account.

Thank you. Ed.

This next letter has the letterhead of Hotel Boise, Boise, Idaho:

March 28

Dear Folks,

Have been busy this past week. Delivering South and West. I am writing this at 3,000 feet as we fly to Montreal, Canada. We have another hour to fly before we get there. We are out over Lake Ontario.

The outside temperature up here is 32 degrees +F. Freezing. Hm!

The ship is flying on the Auto Pilot, nickname "George." Frank is acting as observer in the Pilot's seat and I am writing at the Radio operator's desk. Lt. Fisher is acting as Pilot and Navigator.

We started on our trip from Louisville, Ky. this noon. It is now 3:15. We are hungry, as we have not had any lunch.

Thank you for all the letters. I am doing my best to write Marjorie more often. She writes she spent the last weekend in Raleigh, N.C.

The air is getting so rough I can't write—until later ____

The air is a little smoother now. I'll check on material if and when I get to Mexico again.

No, those of us on flying status are not to be given leaves or days off—indefinitely.

I saw my first Robin today, this morning in Louisville. It was in the yard outside my barracks.

Everyone is talking about Henry Ford's statement. I certainly hope he is correct.

Last week I was assigned to foreign operations. My first trip will be as co-pilot.

I am enclosing my two checks. Will mail this when I get back to the States.

Love and Happy Landings,
Ed.

At Cherry Point I had a bunkmate named Hazel Waddock who was a staunch Catholic. She knew Edward wanted me to become pregnant and be mustered out of the Corps. She also knew I felt I owed it to the Marine Corps, who had spent *beaucoup* dollars on my education, to work at my job as I agreed to do until the war was over. Well, as you can imagine, Hazel kept bugging me and bugging me, telling me *I owed it to my husband to do as he wanted me to do*. I finally gave in to the two of them, and after more visits from Edward, I became pregnant. On June 17, 1944 I was released from the Marine Corps. It was a sad/happy day. All the rest of the twelve girls sent to Jacksonville were subsequently sent to a Marine Base in Southern California. I hated to miss going to California, but I must admit as long as I could be with Edward it was *much better.* Plus… a big plus here, I had so much to look forward to with a young Edward on the way! We had agreed on a name for our firstborn. Of course the baby would be a boy. Where we got the impression we could predict the sex of our child I have no idea! We tried it years later and it never worked again.

June 7

Dear Folks,

I tried to phone you last evening about 1900 and was told your phone was out of order.

Happy Birthday, Dotty! It's really a famous date now, with the invasion.

How is my nephew Herbie? Say Hello to him for me. I flew over the house yesterday evening on our way to Minneapolis. We stayed overnight at MP and are now on our way home.

No, I did not get to see the Pratts as we didn't get to MP until midnight.

Marjorie and I figured up the roof area again and found we had made a mistake of one square of roofing too much.

Monday Marjorie got the P. C. A. Airline to Washington.

(I was headed home to Edward!)
Maybe I could hire Mr. Westrate to paint the cottage.
What kind and how long is the insurance on the cottage?
I am attending an advanced instrument school at Romulus.
More later. Love and Happy Landings
Ed.

I came back to Michigan; Edward and I rented a tiny house close to Romulus, Edward's home base. We bought a few maple furnishings… a bedroom set, a drop-leaf table with four chairs and a small Welsh cabinet. I made curtains for the windows and we were feeling quite happy with ourselves.

Edward had a few trips away while we lived in the little house on Cambria Ct. in Romulus. One of them took him to South America, crossing the equator to do that. There is a custom in the Air Corps, perhaps not just the Air Corps, but when one has flown over the equator one is supposed to grow a mustache. Guess what? Edward followed tradition and had grown a mustache! *It was a big bushy almost red mustache!* And it tickled! Kissing a man with a mustache was a daunting experience for me. I am ashamed now as I write, to say that I insisted he shave that thing off! Edward was a bit crestfallen, but bless his heart, he shaved it off… just for me.

It was not long before Edward received orders to report to Nashville, Tennessee to await further orders for overseas duty! I went home to Coopersville to be with my parents. Daddy and a good friend and neighbor took the neighbor's pickup truck down to Romulus and loaded all of our newly purchased furniture into it and brought it back to my parent's home. Mother told me I could use the very largest bedroom upstairs and everything fit into it nicely. It became my 'home' at home. Mother and Daddy even wallpapered one wall *and the ceiling* in a beautiful floral paper I chose. We *all* giggled a lot while they papered that ceiling while I looked on. Back to Edward…

Edward had flown down to Nashville. He soon phoned

to say it would be several weeks for him down there, could I come? I checked with my doctor who said it would be all right providing I flew.

I flew.

We had a motel room not far from the gate at the Base and a number of other wives were there in the same motel. The husbands weren't supposed to but they sneaked out under the fence each night to join their wives. When the time came closer to Edward's leaving he put me back on the airplane headed for Michigan. A few days after I came home he phoned me from New York.

"Do you remember where I thought I was going to be sent?" he asked.

"Yes, of course."

"Well, that's where I'm going."

It was India.

The photo on the previous page was taken of Edward, just before he left for India, in his new tropical summer uniform and cap without the reinforcement along the top edges.

Handsome guy I married!

Edward sent this postcard to his parents from Homestead, Florida:

Sun. Aug. 20th

Dear Folks,

Received your letter last week. I have not been able to get to Homestead, Florida. I had a day off last week and went to Miami to see the sights, including Al Capones' home. Hm!

I am now busy flying 4 hours a day. It has been very interesting and instructive. Love & Happy Landings Ed.

I believe this next letter was written before Edward left for India, but he hasn't given his location or the complete date.

Aug. 27
Sunday.

Dear Folks,

Today is not much of a rest day. The C.O. has everyone on the Post on a work detail, beautifying the base. They must be expecting the President himself. The only reason I'm not on the detail is because I'm flying nights this week. This week will end our stay here. I should be back in Romulus next week. And where we go from Romulus the Lord only knows.

If you folks don't need it Marj and I would like to buy the kerosene stove you have at Traverse.

Say, Mom, my address is 2nd Operational Training Unit. (A. T. U.)

Yes, my ground school average was 90%. However I only made 86 on my flying. They have done away with the top10% idea. I guess they need pilots bad. Hm!

The C-54 is a dream to fly—it's nicer than the B-24 I

think.

Must run to code class.

Love and Happy Landings
Ed.

P.S. Met Bruce Kilborn in Georgia last June. Did I tell you?

There is quite a gap in letters here. Where are they? Maybe they were never written. Who knows? He did send his mother a picture postcard folder of 'Florida Flowers,' but with no message.

This next letter was the first one I've found Edward wrote home to his folks after arriving in India, obviously not his first as he is answering his mother's questions again.

Dec. 12, 1944

Dear Folks,

We are enjoying nice weather, however the days are getting a little cooler so that one has to wear a light coat.

No, as yet I have not seen the northern lights. I haven't been looking for them. I'll let you know if I see them.

Yes, we have enough soap, and everything else.

We have all kinds of plumbing, hot and cold running water… all the comforts of home. We have a theater with a movie or stageshow every night.

In the club we have a game room, a bar, a snack bar, a lounge and writing booths, with pretty girls painted on the walls for atmosphere. Hm!

Yes, I, like Richard Halliburton, had a desire to see the pyramids. So another friend and I hired a Dragoman (guide). He took us inside the pyramid of Kheops. We all carried candles (very eerie.) We saw the niche in which both Mr. and Mrs. Kheops were buried. We also saw where the High Priest worshipped. The guide told us how the pyramids were built, very simple. During the flood season the stones were put on barges and floated to the site where they were put in place. You should see them some day. In the temple the floor is made of marble, the walls granite and the roof sandstone. The finish on the stones is as smooth as glass.

As we sat in the bottom of the pyramid in the candlelight I could imagine seeing the priest reading the stars. The guide said the priest foretold the future by reading the stars.

We only saw southern Palestine and then not too much of it. Yes, we see the U.S. papers. The "theater" also puts out the C .B. I. Roundup_a summary of the news.

Thanks for the clipping. I too feel that flying seems to help my sinus trouble.

Some of the mountains we fly over have snow on them. A few have snow the year round.

Your V-Mail letter took 13 days to reach me. I think Air Mail is faster.

Lt. Fenwick has informed me that he has written seven letters while I wrote just this one. I have had a route check so that Lt. Fenwick and I are flying together again.

I will keep an eye open for the packages. I have been getting an abundance of mail. Will try and write a more informative letter next time.

Love and Happy Landings
Ed.

P.S. I wish you both a Merry Christmas and a Happy New year. I have an addition to my address_Squadron B. Ed

The India-China airlift delivered approximately 650,000 tons of materiel to China at great cost in men and aircraft during its 42-month history. For its efforts and sacrifices, the India-China Wing of the ATC was awarded the Presidential Unit Citation on 29 January 1944 at the personal direction of President Franklin D. Roosevelt, the first such award made to a non-combat organization.

The next two letters I've found that Edward sent home were the tiny V-Mail letters used in WWII. Is it a bit hard to read? See the following page

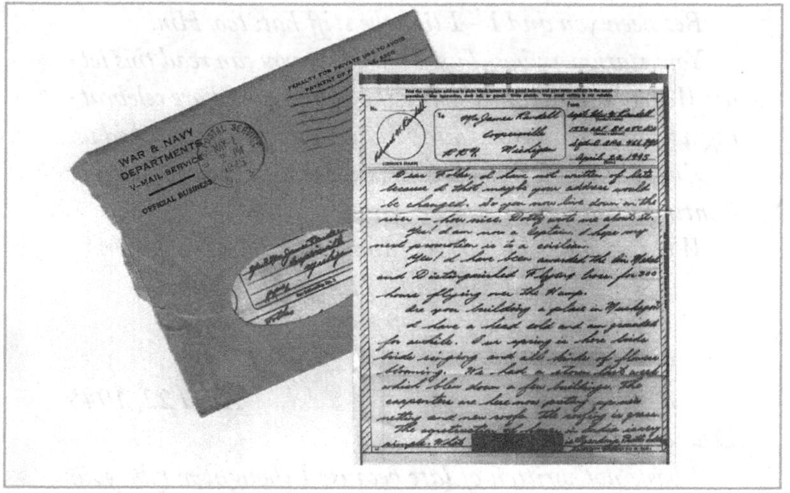

V-Mail to folks with envelope

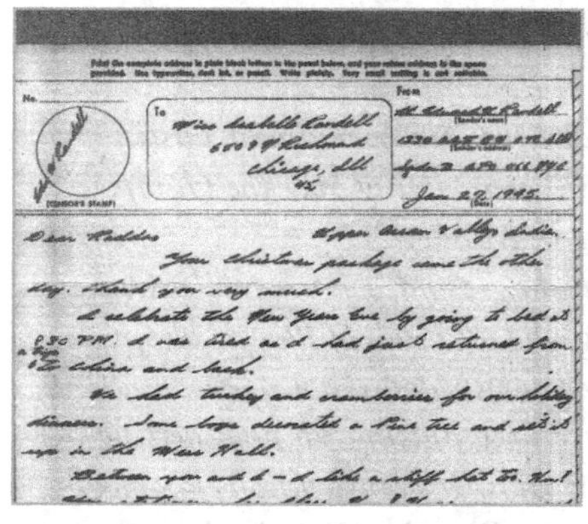

Edward wrote another of those tiny V-mails to Aunt Bunny (Radda.)

Copied below and on the following page…Translated might be a better word.

Jan. 27, 1945

Dear Radda,

Your Christmas package came the other day. Thank you very much.

I celebrated New Years Eve by going to bed at 8:30 P.M. I was tired as I had just returned from a trip to China and back.

We had turkey and cranberries for our holiday dinner. Some boys decorated a Pine tree and set it up in the Mess Hall.

Between you and I - I like the stiff hat, too. Hm!

Your stationery has class. Hm! Hope you can read this letter. We had a nice time during the holidays and are celebrating a second time now as our packages have finally reached us.

Am going on a rest leave this week and hope to go tiger hunting. Dad wants a tiger skin.

What would you like from India or China?

Love and a Happy New Year,
Ed.

April 22, 1945

Dear Folks,

I have not written of late because I thought maybe your address would be changed. So you now live on the river. How nice. Dotty wrote me about it.

Yes, I am now a Captain. I hope my next promotion is to a civilian.

Yes! I have been awarded the Air Medal and Distinguished Flying Cross for 300 hours flying over the Hump.

Are you building a place in Muskegon?

I have a head cold and am grounded for a while. Our spring is here, birds singing and all kinds of flowers blooming. We had a storm last week, which blew down a few buildings. The carpenters are here now putting up new netting and new roofs. The roofing is grass. The construction of homes in India is very simple. What is Grandma Pratt's address?

Love, Ed.

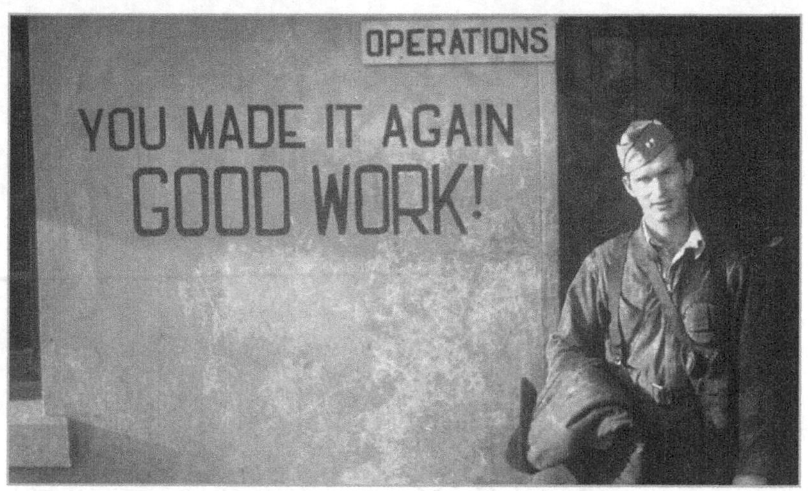

This picture shows a tired Edward returning from a trip to China. He has a pistol strapped across his body in case they were forced down.

Below is a picture of a B-24. The type of plane Edward flew.

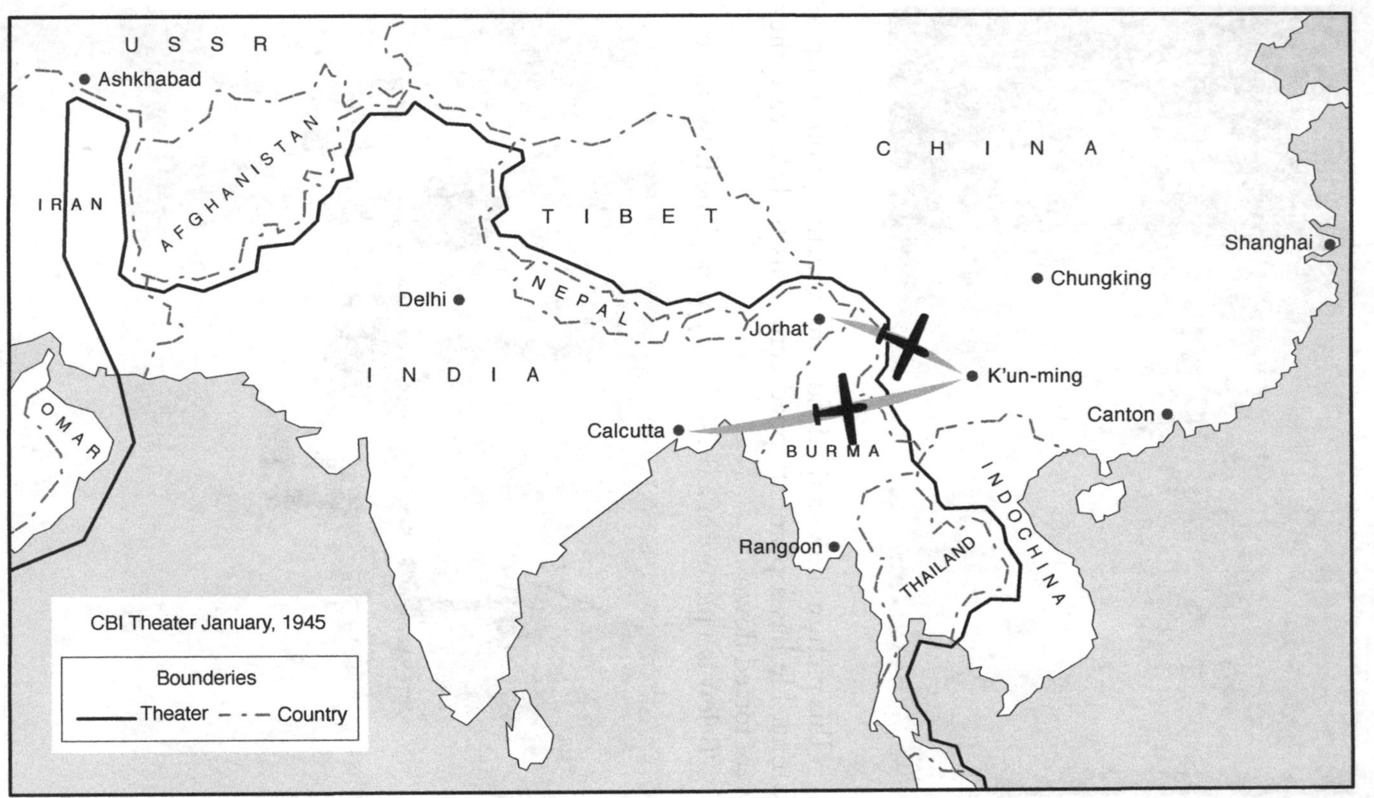

U S S R
Ashkhabad
IRAN
AFGHANISTAN
OMAR
TIBET
NEPAL
Delhi
INDIA
CHINA
Shanghai
Chungking
Jorhat
K'un-ming
Canton
Calcutta
BURMA
INDOCHINA
Rangoon
THAILAND
CBI Theater January, 1945
Bounderies
Theater
Country

The map on the previous page shows the route Edward flew...over the highest mountains in the world...the Himalayas...for a whole year, the cargo...large barrels of gasoline.

After the barrels were unloaded in China the gasoline was removed from the wings of the plane so that there was just enough for the crew to get back to their base in India. There was no reserve for any unplanned emergency detour or change of flight plan due to the weather!

After learning of all of this I marvel that Edward came home safe and sound. But he was a dedicated pilot, no taking of chances. It brought him home to his anxious family.

Thank you, thank you, dear Lord...thank you.

May 18,1945

Dear Folks,

Welcome from the Oriental land of China. We are staying here a few days while our ship is being repaired. Nothing serious, just a minor repair. I went to town to buy some gifts. The inflation is terrible.

I have bought you a small tapestry, Chinese machine made, which costs 3,000. Chinese dollars.

I hope you like it.

I can buy a 40-yard bolt of silk at $3.00 a yard. Is that high! Wow!!

Love and Happy Landings,
Ed.

Edward was sent to India to the Assam Valley and flew over the highest mountains in the world... the Himalayas... for a year. He flew from India to China carrying barrels and *huge tanks of gasoline!* I am thankful I didn't know what the cargo was. The route became known as the "Aluminum Trail" because of all the planes that went down during the years of flying over those high, high mountains. But Edward was a careful pilot who didn't try any tricks or shortcuts. He was a responsible person, which proved to be a lifesaver for him.

I have found no letter written when Edward learned of the birth of his son. However, I found something he *did* save. It was a very small envelope in which there is a note I had written to him while I was in the hospital after his first son was born. It's a cute note card with a drawing of a little bonneted baby on hands and knees touching noses with an equally small pink-eared white bunny.

Here he is, Darling! *May I present your son* ___
Edward William Randell, Jr.

Inside it reads:

Butterworth Hospital, Grand Rapids, Jan. 25, 1945

My Darling,

We have a son! He is really here and what a little pink bundle he is! I have only seen him twice, once yesterday at ten o 'clock and this morning at ten. I am to "have" him again tonight at six. I honestly don't know who he looks like. He makes the cutest faces and eats like a veteran. I'm not used to handling him & with my being flat on my back it's a bit awkward. "Daddy Randy," you should be here to help! (Don't think I wouldn't like to be!" I can hear you now. Hm!) I still can hardly believe he is actually <u>ours</u> and is actually <u>here</u>! Pinch me, will you? Oh! Oh! Time out... flowers are coming in! So beautiful! Three of them!

Later, Evening. A huge bouquet from "the gang" at Capital Lumber, another from Mom and Daddy, and a plant from Virginia & Freddy Pressman! Yesterday "Grandma & Grandpa Randell" brought a lovely geranium plant. The room is filled. My roommate is very nice & has a boy, too. She goes home Sunday. Mom and Daddy came up this afternoon. There is so much to write you about but it is dreadfully hard to write "flat" in bed. I can't even sit up to eat until the fifth day. They tell me just what I can do & when! Hm! Will you forgive me then for not writing more for now? Darling "Daddy Randy," I love you with all my heart and miss you so much.

Now I have a "miniature Randy" to fill my time but there still is an awful empty place for you to fill. I am still lonesome.

Goodnight, Sweetheart. I love you… love you… love you! I'm the proudest gal here! I'm the mother of your son!

All my love,
Muggins

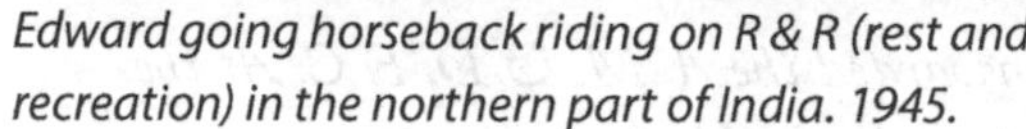

Edward going horseback riding on R & R (rest and recreation) in the northern part of India. 1945.

Back in Jorhat… scanning the horizon.

Edward didn't learn of his son's arrival until three weeks after the baby was born. He was happy and proud to have a son, a son to whom I gave the name of Edward, Jr. just as he asked me to do.

The next letter I've found that he wrote from India is a regular Air Mail letter from overseas written to his mother.

May 27, 1945

Dear Mom,

Enclosed is my tapestry to you. Hm! Do you like it? Do you think Mrs. Irish would like one?

I have been receiving your letters okay. I have four to answer right now.

The days are very hot and humid. A person sticks to everything and my envelopes are stuck together.

On our Rest Tour we visited the spot which has the

highest rain fall a year of all those which are measured. The nearest town to this spot is Cherripunji.

There is a Welch missionary in the town.

In the trees and bushes about we found some very beautiful, white with red streaks, orchids. Confusing sentence, isn't it? Hm!

You are right. Rabies are caused by a germ. The Doc says the monkeys and jackals here a bout could have and carry the germ. And when Ding (a puppy Edward "adopted" and named Ding How.) was small she played rather roughly with her neighbor's pet monkey and may have been bit by the monk.

Speaking of the Lord's coming what is to happen to all the people who are not Christians?

I have received Marjorie's birthday box but not yours yet.

Lt. Langhorst has loaned me his camera, the film size for it is 35 mm.

Yes, I have been awarded the A. M. & D. F. C. At the end of the year I get to go home. Hm!

We were not able to go to Calcutta because of a smallpox epidemic, also cholera.

I hope by this time your ankle is okay. My cold is gone and I am flying again.

I sometimes wonder how industry is going to absorb all the workers after the war. By taking advantage of the G. I. Bill of Rights I will be able to attend four years of College and Marjorie two years.

Under the point system I have 73. However, in order to be discharged, one has to be declared surplus and non-essential to the Army. We understand the Air Force will be the last to be let out of the Army, and the Air Transport Command will be the last to be let out of the Air Corps.

Thanks for all the news. I hope LaVerne is well again; I shall write Jack.

The last Observer I received was dated March 8th.

Our Bashas are built on the ground. The floors are con-*

crete. There are small ditches around each building to carry away the water.

* The Basha is the building in which they live when not flying.

Personally I don't think we need to fear Russia just yet, however, I don't like their Communistic ideas. And I don't believe in lend-lease after the War or building Europe over again. If they want to destroy their country let them work to build it up themselves.

I do hope Jack will show some improvement soon. It's been two years.

Love and Happy Landings
Son Ed

This is the last letter written by Edward from India that I can find.

I did find a list Edward compiled years later when he was planning to write his own story. It covers all of his time overseas in India, China, and the Philippines.

HPA Newsletter
Langhorst
Metzler
Capt. Christianson
Beckwith
Fenwick
Nagasaki Aug. 9, 1945
Hiroshima Aug. 11, 1945
Japan surrenders Aug. 15, 1945
Carrying money to China. Arbitration. Three-Way Trade with American (Dollars) Indian (Rupees) and Chinese (Yuan)
Were you the first pilot into Shanghai? (No, second day)

Flying American POW's to Manila, Philippines, Aug. 7-9, '45 - Lay Over - food for Officers - cost - Flight over Subic Bay and Cavite - Landing in Manila

Layover in Manila - Special Services boat - swim in the Bay - visit with cousin.

Capture on Corregidor. Major LaBrun, years later, tells about losing pens, rings & watches to the Japs, and money ankle deep in the tunnels on Corregidor.

End of the War

I believe he was thinking about the POW's from Manchuria here when he wrote notes of the "Surrender" on August 15, 1945.

Non-verbal mask suppressing an internal excitement- disappointed too many times - hidden hopes - no excitement or jubilation - emotions were held in check - gaunt.

Book- **"90 Days of Rice"** *by R. Jackson Scott*

Published by... California Traveler, Inc. Pioneer, Calif. 95666

Edward made a list of locations en route from the U.S. to India, in October 1944 - Mitchell Field, L. I., - Bangor, Maine - Gander, Newfoundland - Santa Maria, Azores - Marrakech, French Morocco - Tunis, French Tunisia - Cairo, Egypt - Abadan, Iran - ABA DHAB UARB, Emirates - Karachi, India.

Another penciled list of notations -

10 - 44 Kurmitola,

11 - 44 Jorhat,

7 - 45 Barrackpore.

August '45. (The war was over) Gave a C-87 Cargo Plane to the Raja of Bangalore with which to start an Airline.

Edward wrote about carrying newly printed boxes of Chinese money from India to China. The Philidelphia Bank Note Company printed it and one could make money by a three-way trade due to the arbitration between American Dollars, Indian Rupees and Chinese Yuans. For this reason the pilots were limited by the amount of money they were allowed to carry on the flights.

More of Edward's adventures…

> *On August 9, 1945 I was assigned to fly a C54 with a passenger load of American Prisoners of War from Kunming, China, to Manila, Philippines. I was told they had been flown in from a Japanese Base in Manchuria and were on their way home.*

Historical note insert here:

Manchuria is a mountainous region that forms the northeastern portion of China and comprises the provinces of Jilin, Liaoning, and Heilongjiang. In 1932, it was declared an independent state by Japan and renamed Manchukuo. It was restored to China in 1945. On with Edward's letter:

> *As they gathered near the aircraft I couldn't help but notice they were all quiet, no smiles, no signs of excitement or happiness. They were all wearing new uniforms with no indication of rank. However, they all seemed to know who were officers and who were enlisted as they gathered into two groups.*
>
> *Presently, an older gentleman from the smaller group walked up to me and introduced himself as Colonel Moore. His first question was, "Where did you get such a huge aircraft?" (The C-54)*
>
> *Because it was going to be a long flight the group were told to go to Operations and obtain a box lunch. The officers were told they had to pay a dollar for theirs. I couldn't believe what I heard. Now you tell me… where would you find a dollar after being a Prisoner of War for three years,*

and having all your possessions stolen from you? I took up a collection from my crew and we paid for their lunch.

We loaded up and took off, settling down for the flight to Manila. After flying for an hour or so the radio operator alerted me to tell me we were to land at the closest base as there was a typhoon over the China Sea heading for Manila. We landed at XXXXXXXX and were all assigned to a tent. That evening some Chinese bearers came into the tent and lit candles. You remember... the kind that pop and crackle as they burn.

Someone turned on a radio and we listened to Tokyo Rose playing all the new recordings from the USA. After a bit the Armed Forces Radio announcer broke into the program to tell us that the U.S. had dropped an atom bomb on Nagasaki and that it had reduced the entire city to rubble. In addition... no one dare walk near the city for 70 years, as the radiation would kill you. The tent was quiet for a few minutes and then everyone broke out laughing. What propaganda! We knew it was impossible; we had all seen the damage a 50- pound bomb caused, but destroying a whole city? What rubbish! What is an atom bomb anyway? No one ever heard of such a thing.

The next day we learned that the typhoon had dissipated and it was clear to fly to Manila. As we were approaching Manila Colonel Moore came into the cockpit and asked if I would fly over Subic Bay, as that was where he had been captured. He related that he would have been 65 in April 1942 and would have rotated back to the States for Retirement. He had missed it by two weeks.

As we circled Subic Bay and environs, Manila tower called us asking for our position. I told them we were just a few minutes to the north at 10,000 feet and asked for a straight in landing from the west. We were cleared to land and told to park at Base Operations.

The landing was uneventful and as we taxied toward Operations we saw a large crowd of people. When we de-

planed we learned they were doctors, nurses, press and onlookers. As we were checking the plane for a return flight, a cute nurse approached me and asked me if I was the pilot.

When I answered in the affirmative, she said, "You're a Hump Pilot, aren't you?"

To which I answered, "How did you know?"

She said "I watched you make your let down from 10,000 feet and I've heard about you guys making steep letdowns to land in mountain valleys."

I thought, 'Our fame goes before us.'

When I went to Operations to check on our return flight, I was told that all aircraft were grounded and that the typhoon was back. They would call me when it was clear. I was taken to a V O Q... Visiting Officer's Quarters... a tent on a wood platform, west of the famous Ball Field, on the south edge of Manila Bay. It was adjacent to an east west road that ran past General McArthur's Manila home with the centuries old Ming vases that the General was afraid the G. I. s would smash fighting the Japs.

With nothing to do I wandered down to the Bay, and found some guys that had a Special Services jeep boat that they were using for water skiing and fishing. Only they didn't have any skis, and were just towing guys by a rope. So I undressed down to my skivvies and took a turn. I tell you, it is a thrill to be towed behind a fast boat. What a wild ride! The first thing you do is lose your skivvies. By crossing your legs you can spin like a top, and by reversing your legs you spin in the opposite direction. Because it was salt water you float on the water not in the water.

On August 11, two days later, we learned that another atom bomb had been dropped on Hiroshima wiping out the entire city. There was now a lot of talk about Japan surrendering.

In retrospect… the two "typhoons" were actually the times the USA dropped two atomic bombs. They grounded all flights during that time as they didn't actually know how far the damage might go! They wanted no damage to our aircraft in the area. Now, back to the story.

Marjorie had written that her cousin was in Manila, waiting to be sent to Japan as part of the Invasion Force. I was able to hitch a ride and I did eventually find Earl. He looked very serious, but we had a good visit.

One of the nights in Manila I woke up to hear a girl screaming. Upon investigating I saw an enlisted man running down the road carrying a GI mattress and the girl running after him. Later I was told the military had given the mattresses to the natives, and the GI's had none. This GI was on a midnight requisition.

The days dragged along until the evening of August 15, 1945. I was sitting in my tent reading when I heard these god-awful explosions and machine gun fire. I ran down to the Bay and saw tracers streaking westward, red and green flares shooting upward, the big guns on the ships at anchor shooting, and small arms firing. I finally found a guy on the beach and asked if we were being invaded.

*He said, "**No! The war is over!**"*

I went back to my tent, sat on my cot and cried, thinking of all the friends I had lost in this war.

First, my brother-in-law, Howard H. Irish, Jr., Coast Artillery Officer stationed a few miles from where I sat, captured on Corregidor Island April 1942 and a Prisoner of War until he was killed by friendly fire September 7, 1944. Before I went to the Hump I knew he had been captured and I always wanted to bring him home.

There is an aside note here of Edward telling his future readers of my writing a book with my brother's story entitled, **"Searching For Friday's Child."**

My second friend lost was my bunkmate at Jorhat, Lt. Fred Langhorst. A week before Fred's last flight he confided in me that he was not going to make it.

I told him, "Of course you are."

I showed him all the stuff I carried for Good Luck charms… a New Testament with a steel cover in my left front shirt pocket, because I was told my heart was in the right place even though it was on the left side, a four-leaf clover and a 4" yarn doll, made and sent to me by Marjorie, which I always hung on the compass each flight.

An aside note here: Originally the little yarn doll was white and a pretty blue colored yarn, but the years have changed her to look as she does now.

He ended our conversation by saying, "No, I just feel I am not going to make it."

Days later, I was returning from a flight and found a stranger going thru Fred's belongings and asked him what he was doing, to which he answered, "Lt. Langhorst didn't make it."

Later I learned that my C-109 Crew Chief on the flight from the States to India, Sgt. Metzler, was on the same aircraft. I hate to think that it was the same Aircraft we flew from the States as more than once I smelled raw gasoline in the cockpit and I would shout to the co-pilot, "Shut off the gasoline heater!"

Special entry here from my computer:

U.S. Army Air Forces 1st Lt. Frederick W. Langhorst, killed during World War II, has now been accounted for.

On July 17, 1945, Langhorst was assigned to the 1330 Army Air Force Base Unit, Air Transport Command, as the co-pilot of a C-109 aircraft with three other crewmembers on a routine cargo transport mission from Jorhat, India, to Hsinching, China, when it crashed in a remote area.

An extensive search of the area failed to identify the crash site and the crew was declared deceased on July 18, 1946.

Between 2007 and 2009, aircraft wreckage was located and remains were found.

A lab analysis, in conjunction with the total of circumstantial evidence available, identified Langhorst's remains as included.

Interment services are pending.

Welcome home and rest in peace, 1st Lt. Langhorst.

When I saw the notice on the computer that Lt. Langhorst was found and his remains were being sent home I wrote Including Edward's letter where Lt. Langhorst told Edward he thought he wasn't going to make it. This is their reply:

Families and Supporters of America's Arunachal Missing in Action shared your post.

39 mins ·

Hello Marjorie, thank you for that new information about 1st Lt. Fred Langhorst and what he is reported to have said before he died. In the interest of historical accuracy, S/Sgt. Jacob Metzler, Jr. was not killed in the same crash that killed 1st Lt. Langhorst. As pointed out in Mrs. Chick Marss Quinn's book The Aluminum Trail, 1st Lt. Langhorst was lost on 17 July 1945, in the crash of C-109 44-49628. S/Sgt. Metzler is not listed as part of that crew. S/Sgt. Metzler is, however, listed in that book as a member of the crew of C-109 44-52000, which crashed on 27 February 1945. S/Sgt. Metzler and Pvt. Elmer F. Wang are still listed as missing in action from that February crash.

Edward's list continues:

> *Then, I lost a friend, Capt. Vern Christianson. The two of us, with our wives, had made many unauthorized 'escapes' from the Base in Memphis, Tennessee while waiting to be sent overseas.*
>
> *Fifth friend I lost was a student pilot on a C-109, Lt. Richard Beckwith.*

Sad, sad stories.

Little Known Facts of History: Fifteen Minutes of Fame. Edward writes:

> *When you read those great stories of fame and fortune, of those intrepid airmen who flew the airplanes across the Hump, and you come to the part where it says on the last day of the month in the summer of 1945 at Jorhat, India the record was broken for the largest number of tons of material ever to be hauled over the HUMP in one month - did you ever wonder who was in that crew? Or who was the first pilot of that crew?*
>
> *On the last day of June '45, in Operations at Jorhat, I was approached by a man who said he was a reporter and he wanted to interview me and have me tell him all about my crew because, when we take off we would break the record for hauling the most tonnage over the HUMP.*
>
> *After our conversation we took off and never heard another word about it until a month later when Mr. Reporter was back in Operations and said, "Oh, I'm sorry. I did not get in touch with you, but after you took off I decided to write up the next Crew, which set the* <u>*new*</u> *record for the most tonnage hauled over the HUMP in 24 hours.*

Shame on you, Mr. Reporter!!

Here is another of Edward's Hump Pilot stories:

I wondered if any of my fellow pilots flying over the Hump had ever seen a rainbow at night. For me, it was a moonlight night with a localized rain near the ground. I was heading west back to Jorhat when I looked out the left window and down below to the south I could see this rainbow. I have asked many Hump Pilots and none have seen a night rainbow. Many years later I received a National Geographic Magazine and... you guessed it!

There was a photo of a 'Rainbow in Moonlight.' And I had begun to think perhaps I imagined or hallucinated the rainbow I'd seen while flying back to Jorhat at night.

Edward made a carefully printed list of his medals:

Distinguished Flying Cross
Air Medal
Presidential Unit Citation
Asiatic - Pacific Campaign Medal
American Campaign Medal
WWII Victory Medal
Air Force Longevity Service Award Ribbon
National Defense Service Medal
Armed Forces Reserve Medal

There is also another list, this one hastily written, of things Edward wanted to put into his Autobiography when he wrote it up. He didn't ever do it... at least I have not found it among his papers.

After this is Edward's list of his occupations during WWII and the following years.

Student Pilot Class of 42-I

ATC Ferrying division (ATC is the Air Transport Command)

ATC Transport Division

Graduate Engineer, UCLA

Command and Staff School
Johnston Island
Chanute AFB
Jet pilot
Base Civil Engineer
R. I. F. (Reduction in Force)
Minute Man Missile
Project Engineer
Apollo
Manned Orbital Lab
Boy Scout Aviation
C. A. P. - Red Cross
Search & Rescue - 20 years

Edward, in the Ferrying Division, was ferrying new planes from factories to bases located hither and yon. In the Transport Division he was in India flying large tanks of gasoline over the highest mountains in the world, taking them to China for fueling the planes that were to bomb Tokyo.

After he returned from WWII and we moved from Michigan Edward attended college at U. C. L. A. in Westwood, California, graduating in June of 1951. He *did* eventually earn his promotion to full Colonel, even if it was many years later in the Civil Air Patrol.

When he was made Colonel at the award ceremony I had the honor of helping Col. Bidwell pin the new Bird Colonel insignia on his shoulders. See the photo on the following page.

Edward continued working with the Civil Air Patrol cadets until he retired. He was content. He had at last reached his goal.

Back up now to fill in the rest of Edward's story…

I have found some paragraphs Edward had written down, planning to include them in his autobiography. They are Interesting notes.

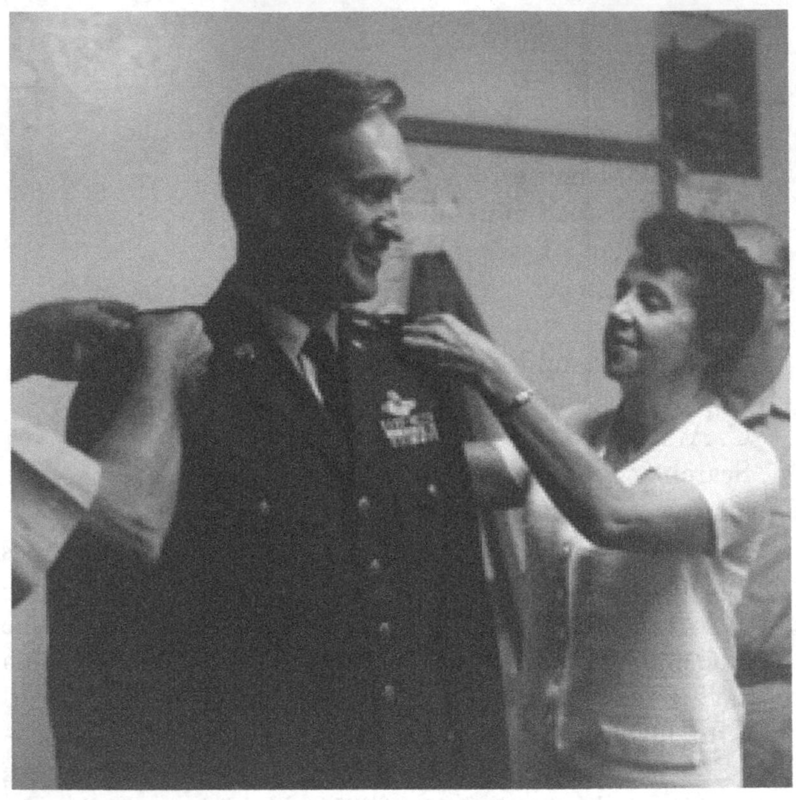

Bird Colonel at last!

I remember being on a flight as a Co-Pilot delivering a new B-25 to Italy. The aircraft had a 20MM cannon built into the area where the Co-Pilot sat. We flew it from the factory in the States southeast to Natal, Brazil, then east across the mid-Atlantic to Ascension Island, east to Monrovia, Liberia, north to Marrakech, Morocco, east to Tunis, Tunisia. When we arrived in Tunis I said to myself, "I know someone with that name, and I wonder where he is right now."

Edward was referring to his friend and neighbor from his days on the farm in Michigan… Tunis (Tony) Busman.

We never did fly the aircraft to Italy as a Bomber Crew

took command of the aircraft.

The Germans built the base at Tunis, Tunisia. The Quarters were excellent permanent concrete buildings. Either the Germans were out of explosives or they thought they were going to return, as they did not destroy the buildings. The Quarters were like apartments with a bedroom, sitting room, and a bathroom. However, before the Germans left for Italy they poured concrete into the toilets and sinks. Thus we had to use the old outhouses and water from the blister bags.

Another little story Edward made note of.

I have told several Hump Pilot friends when we flew across the mid-Atlantic that the Navigator carried two homing pigeons in a little cage, and they said, "I've never heard of such a thing. You're kidding."

The pigeons were equipped with tiny aluminum capsules attached to their legs. If we, GOD forbid, had to land in the ocean the Navigator was to write our longitude and latitude on a piece of paper, place it in the capsule and let the pigeon go. I asked him how the pigeon was going to survive if we dropped them during flight.

"Easy," he said, "I just place them in a paper bag, toss them out the bomb bay door, and after the bag and pigeon slow down, the pigeon backs out of the bag and flies home to his roost with all feathers intact."

The roosts he referred to were in Natal, Ascension Island and Monrovia, Africa.

took command of the aircraft.

The Germans had all [illegible] Town [illegible]. The [illegible] ers were excellent, permanent concrete buildings. [illegible] of the Germans [illegible] out of expensive or they thought they [illegible] going to return [illegible] the [illegible] the buildings. [illegible] [illegible] [illegible] living room and a bathroom. [illegible] [illegible] they [illegible] into the [illegible] tanks. [illegible] [illegible] we [illegible] the [illegible]

Another little story [illegible] made note of.

I have told [illegible] [illegible] we [illegible] [illegible] [illegible] [illegible] [illegible] never heard of such a [illegible] thing.

The pigeon [illegible] equipped [illegible] [illegible] attached [illegible] and [illegible] [illegible] longitude and latitude [illegible] [illegible] the [illegible] [illegible] [illegible] the pigeon [illegible] [illegible] dropped them [illegible] flight.

[illegible] [illegible] [illegible] [illegible] and after the [illegible] [illegible] [illegible] of [illegible] [illegible]

[illegible] and [illegible] [illegible]

Chapter Six

One year from the date he left to go to India Edward came home safely to his young son Edward, Jr. and me. The war was over! Edward wrote asking that I come to Chicago to meet him alone. He obviously wanted to take his homecoming in stages. I went to Chicago, leaving our young son with my parents. By this time "Randy" was a BIG boy at ten months old. When Edward and I came home by train from Chicago he could hardly believe this big, smiley baby was his son. Edward was home and we were all together at last! What happy days those were!

My parents, very thoughtfully, drove to California to spend the winter of 1945-46, leaving Edward, his new son and me to be together alone. We were supremely happy.

After my parents came back from California we stayed on at their home. Edward painted the big red barn for my dad. We visited his parents in Muskegon often.

One Sunday Edward took me up in one of those little yellow airplanes similar to the one in which he first learned to fly. He came home from a year of flying heavy bombers over the highest mountains in the world; I didn't have the heart to tell him I was scared to death in this little plane. I didn't dare grasp his arm to have the comfort of his safety, either. *He was the pilot!* I had flown with him during the war, when we were both in the service, in a big B-24, but this little toy airplane? Oh my! There *was* a difference! A big difference!

Edward had dreamed of going to M. I. T. after the war in order to get his engineering education. We drove with brother George and his wife Vi to Boston to check it out. Edward was very disappointed to learn that he would have to have a few more credits before they would admit him. We came home feeling more than a little deflated. Edward kept mulling things over as he worked now with his dad every day in Muskegon building houses. He came back to Coopersville every night. Bud (brother George) and Vi were in Muskegon and Bud worked along with Edward too, but he and Vi soon left to follow her mother and stepfather to California.

Life perked along from day to day until one morning when I was in the basement at my parent's home doing the family laundry. Machines were noisily churning when Edward came down to see me.

He cupped his hand over his mouth and spoke loud into my ear, "How would you like to live in California?"

I looked up at him and with barely a moment's hesitation said, "Okay."

The whole idea of moving west was put into motion. Edward flew out to meet Bud and look the situation over. Vi's parents were living in Westwood, just south of the University of California at Los Angeles... barely two miles. This was great news for Edward. He switched his ideas for an education from M. I. T. to U. C. L. A.

The two brothers needed to find a place to live. They found a brand new triplex in Westwood. It had two one-bedroom apartments and one two-bedroom apartment. It was perfect with a place for everyone. Bud and Vi could live in the front unit of 1945-7-9 Overland Ave., Edward, Randy and I could be in the rear two-bedroom apartment and Vi's parents in the middle. The fellows made an offer to buy the triplex, which was accepted! We were so excited when Edward flew back to

1945-7-9 Overland Avenue

help me pack up our things and get ready to leave for California. I tried to ignore the sadness in my parents as they watched us, tried not to feel bad about the tears in my mother's eyes, tears she willed not to spill, as we said our farewells. After all, we were all they had now that my brother had been declared dead*. There was a real reason for them to shed tears, to be sad.

** My brother, Howard Irish, Jr., had been a prisoner of war of the Japanese for two years when MacArthur was coming back to the Philippines as he had promised he would. The Japanese became alarmed and crammed prisoners into the holds of ships heading to Japan. My brother was in the hold of an unmarked freighter along with 750 fellow prisoners. They were steaming along in convoy with other Japanese ships when the U.S. Paddle,*

> *an American submarine, spotted them. The Paddle had no way of knowing that the unmarked freighter carried POW's... they torpedoed the Shinyu Maru in which my brother was held. Of the approximately 750 men only 93 of them survived the torpedoing. Three of those 93 survivors came to see my parents. Edward and I joined a group called "The Survivors of the Shinyo Maru." A few years later we met the man who was closest to my brother during the war. He had had a dreadful time returning to a normal life, and now, so many years later was extremely nervous while talking to us. It was several months after the survivors returned to the States that the other two men came to see my parents.*

My parents were grateful that Edward had survived and was home with his little family. It was very hard for them to bid us goodbye that morning we left for California.

Edward and I were grateful as well and we hated to leave them as we went forward on our way to a new life together.

Young, year-and-nine-months old Randy sat between us on a little wooden footstool in the front seat of the car. There were no seatbelts then, of course, but both Edward's and my arms went out automatically to hold him whenever we stopped suddenly.

The little guy was so thrilled with seeing so many American flags flying everywhere.

"Flag!" He would laugh as he pointed, "Flag!'

We used all of the money we had saved while Ed was overseas for our portion of the down payment on the new triplex. The monthly payments would be made by the two brothers... an amount no different than the rent we would pay somewhere else. That, combined with the rent paid by Vi's parents would be exactly the amount of the mortgage payments. Edward's G. I. Bill money for going to school each month would help toward our portion of the payments. However, he couldn't apply for the G. I. Bill until he earned the extra credits to enter UCLA the same as had been required at MIT. Edward found work as a meter reader for the Edison Electric Company in Santa Monica. He came home with stories of all the back fences he had hopped over; all the angry dogs he managed to escape... all kinds of wild stories. It was a far cry from flying the four-engine heavy bombers of WWII, but it was a job. Edward was the eternal optimist making the most of any situation, good or bad.

The new setup looked so perfect… *and it was…* for a while.

For living quarters we had the two-bedroom apartment of the triplex because we had Randy and a second baby on the way. As Edward was working we had enough money to buy a few pieces of furniture. We already had two bedroom outfits and a maple drop-leaf table and four chairs for meals, but lacked living room furniture. We went to Sears in Westwood Village and picked out a sofa and matching chair. Those pieces, along with the black Boston rocker from Grandma Bowser, my sewing machine table and a coffee table wedding gift made up our living room furniture! Edward made shelves to go on either side of the sofa out of six boards, each of which was about four feet long. He stained and varnished the boards, then put them together with beige-colored bricks. Two sets of bricks under one board, more bricks on top of the board, another board, more bricks with a final board to wind up on top. Bookshelves! Edward made two of the three board and brick sets, one for each side of the sofa. They looked wonderful to us as they were making an attractive and useful place to keep our books and magazines.

My grandmother Bowser (my mother's mother) came out to visit us and planned her trip to arrive in time for Randy's second birthday on January 23rd. While she was with us we went sight seeing a lot as southern California was new to all three of us. Grandma was interested in ceramics. We stopped at one of the many 'vacant' lots that displayed tiles, ceramics, vases and clay pots. We picked out two ceramic jars about twelve inches high. They were Grandma's gift to us! Edward partially filled the jars with pea gravel, bought parts at the hardware store, and we soon had two lamps, one for each side of the sofa on our new shelves. Edward was so good at making and building things. But there were no shades for the lamp bases he had prepared. It was Grandma Bowser to the rescue again. She somehow managed to find two shades at Sears to surprise us and make our lamps complete!

Grandma Bowser stayed with us until the very last few days of March when she had an opportunity to ride home with a family friend from Michigan, Miss Edith C. Gray. Grandma hated to leave us just a couple of weeks before the new baby was due, but it couldn't be helped. Edward's brother George's wife Vi, promised to look after two-year-old Randy while I was in the hospital, which she did. Edward at home alone, looked after his young namesake evenings and early mornings before going to work.

As we drove down Wilshire Blvd. toward the Good Samaritan Hospital at six o'clock in the morning on April 8th of 1947 Edward ran every red light! There was no traffic, at least very, very little and fortunately he was not stopped. You must remember, this was like a first baby for him as he hadn't been around to take me to the hospital when Randy was born. We arrived in plenty of time as Edward's second son arrived at 9:18 a.m., weighing in at 8 pounds 7 ounces. Another boy! We had planned on a girl, of course, and she was to have been named Claudia Jean. I had been reading a series of stories in the Good Housekeeping Magazine called the Claudia & David stories … hence my suggestion of calling our little girl Claudia. Edward had concurred.

We now pondered and pondered over a name for a little boy. At last I had a brilliant idea. When Edward came to the hospital to visit me one evening I told him of my idea.

"If we can't have Claudia we could have David."

Bingo! He liked the idea.

"How about a middle name?" he asked.

I hesitated.

"What would you think of Howard, after my brother? It would be David Howard Randell. That sounds about right, don't you think?"

"Sounds good to me. *David Howard* sounds *really* good." Edward grinned at me. "Two boys. How about that? Edward William, Jr. and David Howard."

We were happy with our little family.

It was after this when the peaceful coexistence of three divergent families living in the triplex on Overland Avenue began to crumble.

Chapter Seven

It was painful to live. It is painful to remember, even now so many years later. Parts are unbelievable, but I feel I must write about them, as it is a portion of Edward's life… and mine.

It all began when G. K. Holt's son came home from the Merchant Marines after the war. G. K. was Vi's stepfather who was living in the middle apartment in the triplex. We had a sample taste of what he was like when he started pounding on the wall between our apartments. The floors in the apartments were on a raised foundation and were made of hardwood. We had no money for rugs so whenever little Randy ran through our living room it sounded boom, boom in G. K.'s bedroom next door. Unfortunately, he worked nights and slept days. We tried to keep quiet, but it's hard to shush a two-year old. Besides, we felt it wasn't right to shush our little guy all the time.

How we reacted to all of this is hard to understand from a vantage point of a number of years later. Why should we shush our child? *We owned the building! We established the rules. If they didn't like it they could move!* We were young and inexperienced. We cringed at the thought of this man.

Back again to my story. G. K.'s son was named Dallas. There was no room for him in their apartment at night so he slept on a cot out in the Holt's single car garage space. George's car and ours shared the double-car garage space. All three garages were in one building. Gradually Dallas was becoming acquainted with Vi and her mother. More and more Dallas and Vi walked by our apartment together, laughing and obviously enjoying each other. George worked every day, of course, and was not aware of it. After while we wound up telling him. His reaction was to ask Vi to go back to Chicago with him. Of course, she said no. George evidently felt he had already lost her as he soon left to go back to Chicago alone.

After George left Dallas moved into Vi's apartment with her. At this point we were barely speaking to any of them. That and the wall pounding were too much for us to take. The Holts were a different kind of people altogether. To add to all of that… our building was on a narrow lot and our bedroom windows were exactly opposite the bedroom windows of the people next door. When we brought David home from the hospital he shared the second bedroom with Randy. He cried every now and then as babies do. Some nights I didn't get to him soon enough before the woman next door started swearing a blue streak… such words as I had never heard before. She slammed down her windows. I had always lived in the country with no close neighbors and noise to be concerned about.

Life at 1945 Overland Avenue was becoming almost more than we could stand. We learned years and years later that during that time Vi's mother Dolly was *molesting our young Edward, Jr.* Had we known it then I am afraid we would not have been responsible for what we might have done to that woman. Even today, as I type this story into the computer my heart pounds and I feel the same strong anger all over again.

She should be burning in hell!

There was a lawsuit when Vi tried to sell her quarter interest in the triplex. We were not familiar with the community property laws of California, but learned the hard way through a lawsuit.

When the verdict was handed down against us Edward took my hand and leaned to whisper in my ear... *"Don't you dare cry!"* I didn't cry, but it was hard not to.

After the lawsuit Vi sold her one-quarter interest in the triplex to her mother and stepfather. Vi, obviously pregnant by this time, moved away with Dallas. Dolly (Vi's mother) and G. K. moved up to the front apartment leaving the middle apartment empty. With no rent money from that apartment it was difficult for us, to say the least.

We had made friends with people named Nelson when Nelle Nelson was in the same hospital room with me at the time David was born. They had a little boy, too, naming him Timothy David. They were looking for larger space than the bachelor apartment they had in Hollywood so we suggested they move into our "vacancy." They did, but Nelle was so unhappy in California anyway and the situation with the Holts made it worse. She just wanted to go back to Nebraska where they had been born and raised, back where she felt at home. They were just with us a few weeks before they packed up and went back to Nebraska.

Somewhere in here… my memory is failing me a bit here… the Holts offered to sell us their one quarter interest in the triplex. Between George and Edward they came up with the money from somewhere. Thank heavens. *Those unthinkably cruel people were gone at last!*

My Uncle Ray's job was painting about then and he came to our rescue by painting both apartments, which looked great after that. Suddenly, I became an apartment manager! We even furnished the middle apartment and rented it that way. During the rest of the five years we lived there we had a number of different tenants. One family was the Glenn Browns, with whom we became good friends. They had a little boy just David's age and the two played well together. Glenn himself was a United States Marine and Kitty, his wife, had been an officer in the Marine Women's Reserve, all of which made points with me.

We lived at 1945 Overland Ave. for exactly five years. We sold the triplex and moved out on the very date we had arrived five years earlier, both of us older and definitely much wiser.

Note: Using Google Earth I checked on 1945 Overland Ave. the other day. Great surprise. Instead of the one-story triplex there is now a huge beautiful modern apartment building instead. A sign on the front of the building in huge numbers, reads… 1 9 4 5

ASSOCIATED STUDENTS
UNIVERSITY OF CALIFORNIA
AT LOS ANGELES

1950 MEMBERSHIP CARD 1951
PRICE $6.00 A SEMESTER

FROSH	SOPH	JUNIOR	SENIOR
1 2	1 2	1 2	1 2

SIGNATURE

GRADUATE MGR. ASUCLA

A B C D E F G

32 33 34 35 36 37 38
25 26 27 28 29 30 31
13 14 15 16 17 18 19 20 21 22 23 24
1 3 4 5 6 7 9 10 11 12

9107
NOT TRANSFERABLE
FORM 34

UCLA ASUCLA VOID MUTILATED

UCLA membership card with picture of EWR

While all of this activity was going on Edward was going to college at U. C. L. A. He worked as a gardener, a meter reader and anything else available while going to school. He graduated in June of 1951. At last he had realized his dream of an engineering degree. We were a happy little family as we watched Daddy walk across the stage at the Hollywood Bowl to receive his diploma. We took pictures right and left. This one, on the next page, was taken at home on the driveway of 1945-7-9 Overland Avenue.

Sweet Man Graduate!

Edward had walked across the stage of the Hollywood Bowl happy and relieved to have finally achieved his goal of an engineering degree. It wasn't until several weeks later… *he was notified he lacked a couple credits in order to graduate!*

The day after the graduation ceremony Edward was back in the Army Air Corps, unaware of any of this.

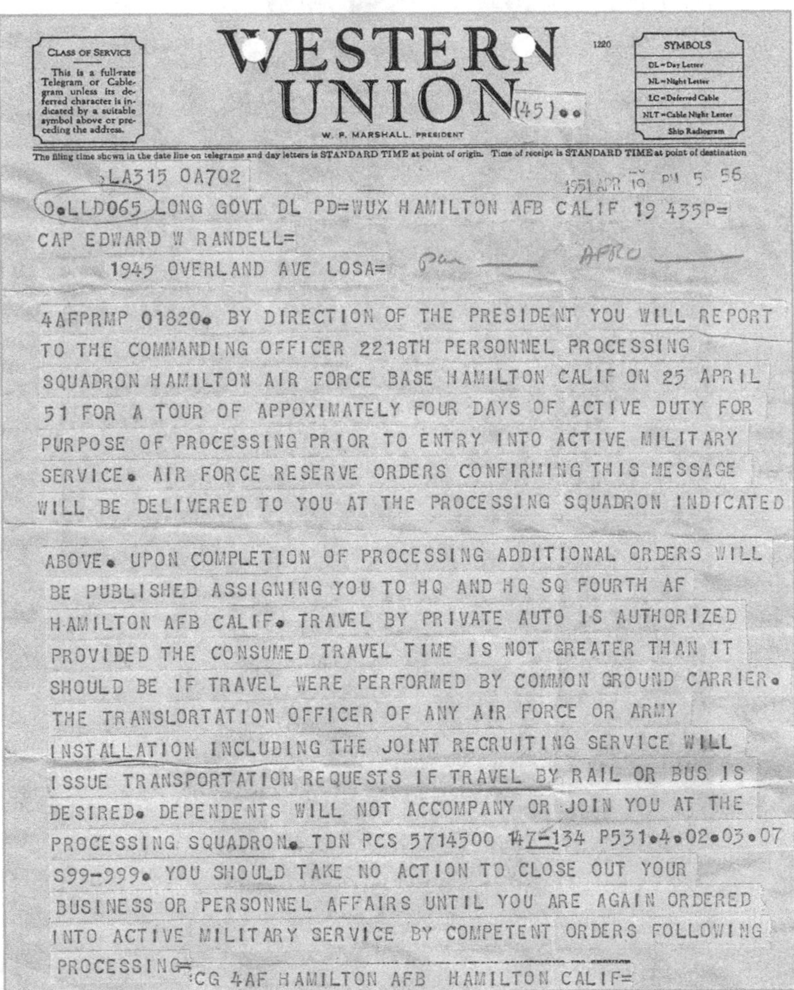

CLASS OF SERVICE
This is a full-rate Telegram or Cablegram unless its deferred character is indicated by a suitable symbol above or preceding the address.

WESTERN UNION (45)

W. P. MARSHALL, PRESIDENT

1220

SYMBOLS
DL=Day Letter
NL=Night Letter
LC=Deferred Cable
NLT=Cable Night Letter
Ship Radiogram

The filing time shown in the date line on telegrams and day letters is STANDARD TIME at point of origin. Time of receipt is STANDARD TIME at point of destination

LA315 OA702 1951 APR 19 PM 5 56

O.LLD065 LONG GOVT DL PD=WUX HAMILTON AFB CALIF 19 435P=

CAP EDWARD W RANDELL=

1945 OVERLAND AVE LOSA=

4AFPRMP 01820. BY DIRECTION OF THE PRESIDENT YOU WILL REPORT TO THE COMMANDING OFFICER 2218TH PERSONNEL PROCESSING SQUADRON HAMILTON AIR FORCE BASE HAMILTON CALIF ON 25 APRIL 51 FOR A TOUR OF APPOXIMATELY FOUR DAYS OF ACTIVE DUTY FOR PURPOSE OF PROCESSING PRIOR TO ENTRY INTO ACTIVE MILITARY SERVICE. AIR FORCE RESERVE ORDERS CONFIRMING THIS MESSAGE WILL BE DELIVERED TO YOU AT THE PROCESSING SQUADRON INDICATED ABOVE. UPON COMPLETION OF PROCESSING ADDITIONAL ORDERS WILL BE PUBLISHED ASSIGNING YOU TO HQ AND HQ SQ FOURTH AF HAMILTON AFB CALIF. TRAVEL BY PRIVATE AUTO IS AUTHORIZED PROVIDED THE CONSUMED TRAVEL TIME IS NOT GREATER THAN IT SHOULD BE IF TRAVEL WERE PERFORMED BY COMMON GROUND CARRIER. THE TRANSLORTATION OFFICER OF ANY AIR FORCE OR ARMY INSTALLATION INCLUDING THE JOINT RECRUITING SERVICE WILL ISSUE TRANSPORTATION REQUESTS IF TRAVEL BY RAIL OR BUS IS DESIRED. DEPENDENTS WILL NOT ACCOMPANY OR JOIN YOU AT THE PROCESSING SQUADRON. TDN PCS 5714500 147-134 P531.4.02.03.07 S99-999. YOU SHOULD TAKE NO ACTION TO CLOSE OUT YOUR BUSINESS OR PERSONNEL AFFAIRS UNTIL YOU ARE AGAIN ORDERED INTO ACTIVE MILITARY SERVICE BY COMPETENT ORDERS FOLLOWING PROCESSING=

CG 4AF HAMILTON AFB HAMILTON CALIF=

When Edward went to San Francisco he left me very pregnant with two little boys to look after. He kept assuring me he would be back to take me to the hospital. Needless to say, I was nervous. I did have a dear friend of my mother and grandma Bowser, a Mrs. Carson, coming to take care of the boys while I was in the hospital and to help me after I came home, but I had made no arrangements for getting to the Good Samaritan when baby signaled me it was time to go! We had no car as we had sold the brown Oldsmobile during the years Edward went to U. C. L. A. as we couldn't afford to use the car, or pay insurance for it.

Edward had gone to an Air Corps school in the East right after graduation. Classes were finished now right on schedule and he arrived back at 1945 Overland Ave. on August 11th driving a brand new Ford Victoria hardtop convertible! *Oh, my goodness, Edward!*

On the morning of August 13th I went into labor. Edward drove me to the hospital with me ringing his arm desperately each time I felt the strong contractions of labor. We had waited at home a little too long. While the Good Samaritan Hospital was undergoing remodeling and additions there was a small wooden bridge covering the debris left from some of the work. As we walked across the bridge I had to stop with a very strong contraction. I grasped the railing and looked at Edward, "Let's not do this again!"

Curtis Wiley Randell was born within forty-five minutes of our arrival at the Good Sam. *A nine-pound boy!* In spite of our having wanted a baby girl, it had been four years since David arrived and just having a baby was a big thrill for the whole family. I think, after we came home from the hospital, four-year-old David got down from the supper table at least three, maybe four times, to go check in the basket to make sure the baby was all right.

While I was in the Good Samaritan, Edward and our backyard neighbor, Mr. Case put up a cinderblock fence. The Cases felt they couldn't luck out twice with good neighbors after we sold the triplex and left the area, as we were planning to do. I almost forgot to tell you in here that Edward had also built a two-car garage for the Cases to match the style of their home some time before he was back in the Air Corps. The Cases were delighted with the garage and with us as neighbors. As we were with them!

Curtis was only three months old when we left Westwood and moved to Bellflower to be closer to Long Beach Airport where Edward was assigned duty. Edward had rented the house on his own. 6123 Oliva Ave. When we arrived on moving day I was devastated to find the house wide open, no screens on the windows, flies buzzing everywhere, and when I checked the other rooms the long hallway walls were covered almost black with dirty finger and hand prints! I was in tears. The renting agent came just then, bringing and installing brand new screens for all the windows. When I complained about the fingerprints he brought me a couple gallons of paint! Guess who put it on? Right. Edward. He painted all the walls of the long hallway. I was more than a little busy with a three-month old baby to look after and two young boys to get to school. David was only four so it was a day care center nearby for him and Randy was picked up by the school bus. Edward headed off early each morning for the Air Base at Long Beach.

My parents had not seen this new little guy Curtis Wiley, so they came out to California for the winter. Edward moved Curt's crib into our room and set up our spare double bed in Curt's room for the visiting grandparents. It was such a busy period in our lives in that location. We entertained my parents for the winter. My cousin LaVerne Irish on leave from the Navy joined us at Thanksgiving for a few days. I asked for more paint to paint the large shabby looking wooden shingles that covered the whole front of the house outside and my dad painted those for us while they were there. My parents had just left to go back to Michigan when Edward's brother George and his new bride Nancy and Edward's sister Dotty came for a visit.

We were in the house in Bellflower for those short, busy six months when Edward received orders for going to Wright/

Patterson Field in Dayton, Ohio. We packed up the things we felt we couldn't get along without, put the rest of our belongings in storage and headed east, pulling a fully loaded stake trailer behind us. The trailer was one that Edward's brother George had built and "stored" with us. It came in handy a number of times through the years.

Chapter Eight

We went to Michigan first and Edward left the boys and me there with my parents while he signed in at Wright Patterson Air Force Base at Dayton, Ohio. He was once again left on his own to find a place for his family to live. He thought he was doing the right thing to rent a place in the country, which proved to be a cottage on an "island" several miles from the Air Base. Weeds grew at least six feet tall along the country road into the island. No phone, no car after Edward left each morning, no neighbors and in a sort of makeshift cottage. Randy and David were in their element playing on the dam in the creek that went around the cottage. I was terrified. I did manage to keep track of the boys, but spent a lot of time in tears. I clung to Edward when he came home. Inevitably I broke under all of it. Edward had to take us back to Michigan. I look back on it now and realize I had had a nervous breakdown. My folks looked after us while Edward went back to Ohio to duty. This time he found a furnished apartment for us to live in directly within the town of Fairborn. It was the downstairs of a two-story house just outside the gate of Wright Patterson Field.

It was 24 "A" Miller Ave., Fairborn, Ohio.

All was well now for the moment. But, guess what? Another baby was on the way! In the midst of the sickish feeling of early pregnancy, while we were living in Fairborn young Curtis, just over a year old, came down with a bad case of vomiting and diarrhea. I managed to help him get over the vomiting but still the diarrhea persisted. Edward and I took him to sick call at the base. The doctor prescribed sulfa to which Curtis proved to be allergic and he began vomiting again.

Edward had gone to class one morning where he was studying to become an Installations Engineer and I was getting the boys off to school. I looked to see Curtis standing up in his crib, hanging onto the top bar of the side just weaving back and forth with the look of death itself on his face. Alarmed, I called Edward out of his class; he came home and we took Curtis to sick bay again. They told us, "Wait your turn."

While Edward held Curtis I went up to the window and asked if they would please come out and *just look* at him. As soon as they saw him they immediately said, "Bring him in!" They put him into a bed in the hospital, tied him down with soft cloth ties while they taped a tube running into his ankle with fluids and penicillin. They then proceeded to tell us they didn't know if they could save him!

When they were taking down his history and asked how old he was I broke down in tears as I told them, "Thirteen months." They sent us home, telling us there was no need for us to be there and that they would let us know if he responded to the treatment. Edward and I went home reluctantly. Within the hour the hospital called to tell us Curtis was responding to treatment and that we could visit the next day. *We were limp with relief!* Curtis recovered well and was soon home. For a number of years after that, however, he was alarmed and frightened by any man wearing a white jacket… doctors, barbers or waiters.

We stayed on at Wright Patterson until Edward finished the course qualifying him as an Installations Engineer, after which we headed back to California. Edward drove the Ford

Victoria, had Randy and David riding with him and he was pulling a loaded stake trailer. Edward's sister Dotty, Curtis and I followed behind him in a new dark green four-door Mercury. It was quite a trip, traveling in tandem, but we made it safely to Long Beach.

I should have mentioned earlier during the stint in Ohio at Wright Patterson we had been communicating with my Uncle Ray Irish in Hollywood, California. He wrote telling us about a brand new tract of homes being built fairly close to the Air Base in Long Beach. When we expressed interest he sent the sales brochure with floor plans and colored pictures showing everything to entice us. We succumbed and Edward sent him the down payment along with our choice of floor plan and exterior style. We were quite excited to finally arrive in California. Uncle Ray had come out to Lakewood, at that time a suburb north of Long Beach. He stayed with his son Louis and his wife UnaFaye around the time he felt we might be arriving.

Edward thought it best to cross the desert at night and then we just kept right on driving, which resulted in us arriving in Long Beach about four o'clock in the morning! Both Uncle Ray and UnaFaye, when we woke them up, were game to get up and lead us down to our new home, even at four in the morning. Bless their hearts. *We are forever grateful to them both.*

They had been working hard! Not only was a beautiful lawn all planted in the front yard of our brand new home, all of our furnishings had been brought from storage and were in place in the house! Oh my! Such excitement! Such delight! I think our delight was all the payment Uncle Ray and UnaFaye needed. We never did get to sleep that night. We were too excited to do that!

The only thing not done was the *big back yard!* Then we learned that no fences had been built and the huge yard was not *all* ours!

Edward had his work cut out for him, but he did it all. Very soon contractors were putting up a cinderblock wall across the back of our property. It was not long before we had neighbors on both sides. Together Edward and Bob Bowden on the west side had another matching cinderblock fence put in between their place and ours.

6608 Metz Sreet

Edward built a yard divider with a base of matching cinderblocks plus grape stake fencing fastened on top of them. This divider hid the clotheslines and later the playhouse Edward built for the boys. While all of this was happening construction was still going on in the new tract of homes, even right across the street from our house.

One day Edward commandeered a large truck to bring a huge wooden airplane engine box home from the Air Base. It had runners on the bottom for moving it easily when it held the engine. Now, however, it was empty and Edward went to work on it. He made a peaked roof for it, put windows and a Dutch door in three sides of it. He put on siding, shingled the roof and installed the windows and a half door. He stained the siding on the outside and painted the window frames white. Voila! The boys had a playhouse. What a beautiful little playhouse it was. It became not only a playhouse, it was a fort and any other thing those little guys could dream up to use it for. The boys were lucky having such a dad as Edward to build things for them.

Meanwhile, Dotty and I kept busy.

I knew I was pregnant again before we left Michigan but I never told my parents. When I confided in my mother before we had Curtis that we were planning on a third child she told me we shouldn't have any more children. We didn't know if Edward would come home safely from flying in the service. She kept going on and on about it. This time *I was not telling her!* We did, however, tell Dotty so she could change her mind about coming to California with us. She seemed to think it was all right to be having another baby. She was such a wonderful help while she lived with us. I don't know how we could have made it without her. She always liked to tell the story of the morning our fourth son was born.

Because Curtis was born so soon after we arrived at the hospital and now we lived further away, all the way down in Long Beach, Dr. McCausland, my obstetrician, advised us to start for the hospital as soon as the first labor pains began. They began at 2 a.m. the morning of May 26th, a week before the calculated arrival time. We woke Dotty to tell her we were leaving. She wished us well, and away we went. As soon as Edward and I arrived at the hospital and I was being "prepped" for the delivery everything stopped. No more contractions. However, doctors, nurses and student nurses were all stopping by to see me and listen to the fetal heartbeat. Why? *The heartbeat was far too rapid.* Dr. Mac thought the cord might be wrapped around the baby's neck so I was sent up for an x-ray. No. All was well. It was back to the labor room. Dr. decided we lived so far away and I was so close to the delivery date anyway it would be best to induce labor, so he had them give me castor oil, which only caused many trips to the bathroom. There were no more contractions. I learned later that Dr. Mac had obtained permission from Edward to do a Cesarean if it became necessary! At last, about 1 p.m. Dr. had me brought up to the labor room again and he broke the bag of waters. That did the trick.

Edward counted the time between contractions when the *real* labor pains began. Within the hour a healthy eight pound, eleven ounce baby was born.

"See… it's a dandy boy!"

I could hear Dr. Mac.

"You can't beat four of a kind."

I groaned. Another boy? Where were all those little girls we had dreamed about? Another boy? No. No. When they brought him in to me, though, *I changed my mind altogether.* Such a sweet little baby boy! How could I have wanted a girl? Footnote here: Some forty years later this fourth little boy gave us two lovely young grand*daughters!*

We couldn't seem to think of a name for a baby boy. After all, he was to have been Valerie Jean. We had dropped our ideas for Claudia by this time. Now, what in the world would we name this precious little boy? We hadn't found a name yet when it was time to leave the hospital and they weren't going to let us go until we named him, but they finally relented; our baby boy was put in the basket on the back seat of the car and Edward and I took our fourth son back to that lively place we knew as 6608 Metz St. in Long Beach.

It took us several days to finally come up with a name. We were both very fond of Hazen Pratt, our inadvertent wedding photographer. Finally I thought of Thomas.

"Thomas Hazen Randell. How does that sound?' I asked Edward.

"Hmmm… It goes together well. Let's call him Tom."

"Maybe Tommy while he's little."

"Done! Tommy it is. Fits this little fellow, doesn't it?"

I smiled at the love of my life, the father of our four sons. We were happy.

Chapter Nine

But all of that was not *Dotty's story!*

The morning of the 26th she got the two older boys off to the school bus on time and had closed & locked the front door, but young Curtis had just learned how to unlock and *open* that door. Which he did, and took off down the street toward the school bus where his big brothers had just gone. He usually followed them all over in the house and yard. He probably thought now, why not follow them to the school bus? Dotty ran out the front door chasing him and caught him before he reached the corner to cross the street. When they came back to the house, guess what? Dotty had inadvertently pushed the lock button on the front door as she went out. The front door was locked. The back door was locked. Keys were inside. There was no way to get back into the house! What she did with Curtis at this point is unclear, but she ended up getting a step-ladder from the garage and climbing in the *small* bathroom window that faced out on the driveway.

Dotty had made a cake and it was in the oven before Curtis took off so now the cake was a bit overdone. Throughout all of this she kept wondering, of course, why she hadn't heard from us in Los Angeles. Had the baby arrived? What was going on? She was greatly relieved when Edward called her after 2 P.M. to tell her she had another nephew.

She and Edward managed to hold everything together until I came back home after five days in the hospital.

Years later we looked back on our decision to name our new son. No one ever told us Thomas Hazen Pratt was the name of Mom Randell's younger brother. Edward didn't even know it. We learned many years later Thomas Hazen Pratt had been ostracized from his family for doing something or other of which they didn't approve. That was why we had never heard him spoken of. We still liked our choice though, and have been proud and very happy with *our* Thomas Hazen.

Life was a busy one, now more than ever, as Dotty was going to secretarial school, Edward was back at the base and I was caring for *four* young boys.

It was some time during these days that Edward obtained permission from the Air Corps to go back to UCLA to take the few courses he would need to have the degree. Life was so noisy, busy *and wild* around 6608 Metz St. Edward rented a one-room apartment in Westwood for the one semester so he could study in peace and quiet. He came home weekends to be with us. After the schooling Edward was back on active duty with the Air Corps based at the Long Beach Airport. It was wonderful to have him home again with his family full time.

Along about now… Father Randell kept bugging Dotty to come back home, telling her over and over, "You're needed at home. You should come home." He would go on and on. She had finished her secretarial course and with Edward living at home again, she finally gave in and flew back to Michigan.

Fortunately, it was late August when Dotty left and school started in September. Randy and David were soon enrolled and going every day, still catching a bus that took them to another school until Cubberly Elementary was built nearby. One afternoon when the school bus was bringing children home,

Randy got off the bus too soon and couldn't find our house! He kept walking and walking expecting to see home around every corner he turned. Edward went out in the car looking for him while I stayed at home in case he turned up there. Eventually we found him. He didn't seem to be as concerned about the whole thing as his parents were!

Edward encouraged me to attend activities at the Air Base and to join the Officer's Wives Club. Childcare was available at the Base. One day in the fall Edward greeted me as I came down the steps of the Officer's Club after having been at a Wives Club luncheon there. He showed me new orders he had just received. They were his first orders for duty as an *Installations Engineer!* The duty, however, was on the mile long atoll of Johnston Island eight hundred miles southwest of Hawaii on which there were no vacant accommodations for his family at the moment. The bad part of Edward's new assignment was the miles and miles of ocean between us.

Capt. Randell at his desk on Johnston Island.

Letters flew back and forth between us. Edward was as lonesome for me as I was for him. He had a two weeks leave due him soon and he suggested I find someone to take care of the boys, then fly out and meet him in Hawaii. I finally located a woman by trying out different sitters from ads I'd found. She was a large hefty lady I thought at first would work out. I tried her a few times when I went to group meetings for church or the Officer's Wives Club. She was so careless about cleaning things up after meals. She *did* look after the boys, however. I bought new luggage, then began feeling very unsure of myself. I was almost on the verge of another breakdown. I called Louis's wife, UnaFaye. When she came she talked with me, then she called Uncle Ray. He came out and he talked to me, then *he* called my mother in Michigan. He told her she should come to California. I remember hearing him tell her, "You will never be sorry that you came."

She came.

Uncle Ray stayed with me until Mom arrived. In the meantime I was seeing a psychiatrist recommended by our family doctor.

When my mother came I went to bed with a temperature of a hundred and two degrees. Here she was, a woman who had raised only two children, stuck with a sick daughter, four boys, an automatic washing machine which was like Greek to her, in a strange house, a strange neighborhood, a strange part of the country altogether! What did she do?

She coped. Amazingly, she did.

What about Edward during all of this? He was hundreds of miles away and not able to comfort me or help in any way, as he wanted to.

Earlier I had written to Edward's sister Dotty telling of Ed's early experiences on Johnston Island.

> *Ed says the island is larger and higher than he had imagined it to be. There are about 600 people on the island including the civilians that are working on the construction projects. They are now trying to replace the shack-like temporary buildings on the base with concrete permanent type buildings. This, of course, is Ed's work as the Installations Engineer on the island. Top man_not an assistant this time!*

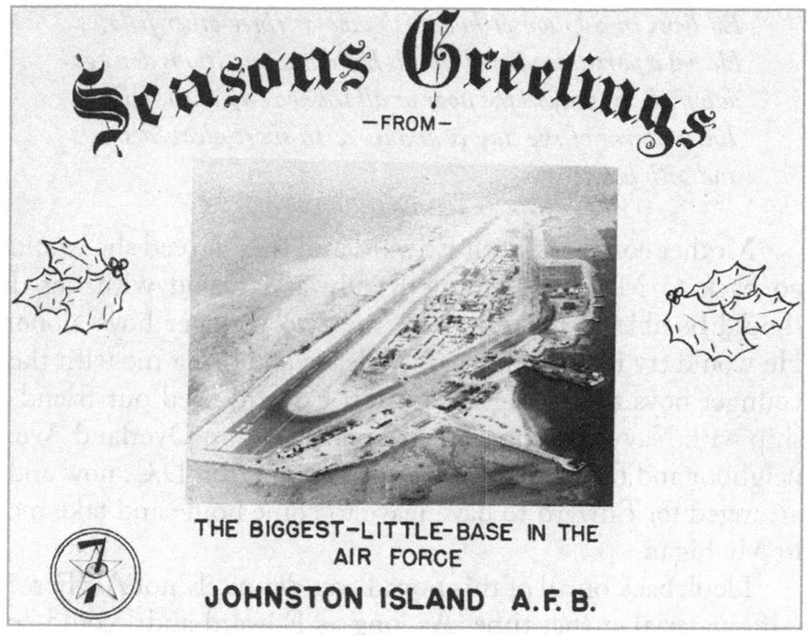

Johnston Island Christmas card.

The Installations Engineer had been gone from the island since last March so he was really welcomed. There are two "turnaround" flights a week from Hawaii that bring mail and passengers, two air sea rescue flights a week, otherwise other planes land only for emergency purposes. There is a large supply barge that comes in from Hawaii once a month and a small supply barge that comes once a week. He sends his khakis to Hawaii on the latter to be laundered, does his sox himself and does his underwear at a Laundromat machine in the Post Exchange. He mentioned in his last letter about the natives of the island being ants, cockroaches and termites!! Also there is a lot of rust and corrosion because of the salt air. They keep their clothes in a closet that is built about a foot off the floor and has an electric light bulb burning in it all the time to keep the clothes dry and keep mildew away. Sounds a good deal like India did when he was writing ten years ago from there.

> *Ed lives in a Quonset hut with two or three other fellows. He has a partitioned area that is his alone; partitions don't go down all the way to the floor or all the way up to the ceiling. The uniform of the day is khakis with short-sleeved shirts and pith helmets.*

Mother conferred with Edward and they agreed she would go back to Michigan taking Randy and David with her. I should be able to make it with the two younger boys alone. He would try for a compassionate leave and bring me with the younger boys to Michigan himself. Edward used our friendship with Navy Captain Farrell McFarland, an Overland Ave. neighbor and friend. Farrell was in Washington D.C. now and arranged for Edward to have leave to come home and take me to Michigan.

I look back on all of this now. I was definitely not Air Force wife material at that time. As long as Edward and I could be together I was fine, but without him *I was not*. Even now I feel so guilty for what seems like letting him down. He, however, was loyal to me always, doing his level best to make me happy. He did make me happy. Edward lives in my heart now, forever making me happy. How fortunate I am to have been married to him.

Back to our story...

Edward flew home, we packed up, stored our household things and headed for Michigan by car, in that Mercury Dotty and I had driven west. What happened to the Ford Victoria convertible Edward had brought home? We must have sold it as the only car we had now was the dark green Mercury. Edward cut a large board to fit exactly across the back seat of the car and touching the back of the front seats. He padded it, covered it with Naugahyde and put two legs on the side touching the front seats. It made a flat surface for the two little guys to lie down for naps plus letting them be up at a level to play where they could see outside as we drove on the long two thousand mile trip to Michigan.

Edward left us at my parent's home on the farm. The older boys, Curtis and I stayed with my parents while Tommy went to Muskegon to stay with Edward's mother and father. Edward flew back to Johnston Island to finish out his year there.

Chapter Ten

Edward's next duty assignment after Johnston Island was Chanute Field, at Rantoul, Illinois. When he went to Chanute he found the only available housing was a two-bedroom unit. As the older boys had already started school in Coopersville my parents suggested they stay on in Michigan with them and we take the two little guys down to Chanute until a three-bedroom unit became available, which is what we wound up doing. Randy and David stayed in Michigan on the farm until after Christmas when we finally had a three-bedroom unit.

Moving from one small cluster of apartments to another, going up and down stairs in both apartments was not exactly our idea of fun but if it meant we would finally all be together again as a family it was worth it.

Edward's job at Chanute Field was in the Installations section of the base. He worked under Major Jerman and met and worked with Lt. Charles Smith. We became well acquainted with all of the department people and their wives as Mrs. Jerman was an excellent hostess and she was forever having parties and get-togethers in the nicely furnished basement of their quarters. We also lived in Base Housing, which was a first for me. We were at Chanute for three years and really hated to leave.

In 1957 or 58, I'm not exactly sure of that date, the President put through an order for a "Reduction in Force." R. I. F. Because Edward was a Reserve Officer, not a regular career officer, he was put on the RIF list.

Suddenly we were out of the Air Force.

Out of the service and no job. We had rented our home in California to the McFarlands for three years. Yes, Farrell and Josephine, our Navy friends. Their lease wasn't up until September. This was January. What were we to do until September?

Edward's oldest brother Jim, who stood up with him as best man at our wedding, was going through a tough time as his wife had left him. He came home from work one day to an absolutely empty house. Mary Lee had left him with only what the law decreed… one bed, one table, one chair, one stove and one refrigerator. When we talked with him about our situation he suggested we come live with him, as his house was empty. He lived in Mt. Prospect, Illinois, on the north side of Chicago.

He saved our lives and we saved his.

While we lived with Jim Edward went to school taking some extra classes. Right now in 2016 I cannot recall the name of the college where he was going. That man was forever going to school. He loved to learn new things.

I spent a great deal of time getting to really know Edward's brother George's then new wife Nancy Wilbur Randell. They had a little boy who was born on New Year's Day 1954 and was close to the age of our Thomas Hazen. George and Nan's son was George, Jr. or Jordi, as the family called him. In 1955 they had a little girl they named Suzanne. I would take our two younger boys, while the older boys were in school, and go to Deerfield to spend the day with Nancy. Those months spent in Mt. Prospect were a wonderful time in our lives. Both Edward and I always looked back on them with pleasure and happy memories. Edward and George had opportunity to spend time together, sharing their great ideas and finally a few years later actually putting them into reality. Plus, Nancy and I became the best of friends.

Jim, in that interval, was beginning the courtship of a woman he had met at work, Stephanie Zyzak. She had several children but only one still living at home with her. When we left Mt. Prospect in late August or early September he and Stephanie were making plans to be married soon. We were leaving at exactly the right time. While we lived with Jim his oldest son, who had left with Jim's wife Mary Lee, came back to live with his dad. Jim and Herb shared one of the two bedrooms upstairs at Jim's house while we were there. Jim's other two children, Johnny and Melody, came to visit every Wednesday evening, staying for dinner with us. They also came every other weekend, which gave our boys and their cousins opportunity to become friends, which they are to this day.

When the time came to head for California once more, David and Curtis went to Michigan by train to spend the last few weeks with their Irish grandparents. By this time we had another new larger Mercury. Edward had negotiated on the price until it was down to what he thought was acceptable and he brought it out to Jim's. *It turned out to be pink and white...* a 1957 four-door Mercury. Maybe it was the pink and white color combination that made it easier to get the price down. I have a snapshot of Edward and me, with all four of our boys, ready to leave Michigan and standing beside the pink and white Mercury which had the forever-with-us stake trailer hooked up to the back of it. All of our pictures taken at that time show us looking so happy to be going back home to California and my parents looking not as happy but trying valiantly not to look sad. We Edward Randells were *almost singing out loud, "California, here we come ___ right back where we started from____."*

Edward had flown out to California to check our house when the McFalands moved out. He discovered much had to be done. He called Uncle Ray for help. Once again our great friend and helper Uncle Ray came down to our place on Metz St. and together with his son Louis, painted the entire interior of the house! Our furniture had arrived from Illinois and it, too, was in place! This time we had a key to the house so it wasn't necessary to wake anyone up when we arrived once more in the early, early hours of the day. It was August 12th, the day before Curt's birthday. He kept asking, "When is my birthday? Mom, *when is my birthday?*" I told him, as we drove along nearly home, that it would be tomorrow. When he woke up in the morning, having crawled into bed after we arrived, he thought it was his birthday! But it wasn't. It was to be "tomorrow" as I had said. He didn't realize that it was just earlier that very morning that I had told him, "tomorrow."

Sometimes being a kid is tough.

Tom had been only fourteen months old when we left Metz St. Now he was lost. I found him in tears. All of his brothers were running around excited to find their own beds in their own rooms. But Tom couldn't find his crib. *Where was it?* Everything looked so strange. I hugged him and talked to him trying to explain it to him. We made up a bed for him on the living room sofa and told him that tomorrow his very own *brand new* bed would be here and he could sleep in his own bed then. We didn't have the heart to tell him we had left his crib in Illinois… *poor little guy*. I stayed with him until he fell asleep at last.

This time when we returned to California the two older boys would have their own room, Curtis and Tom would have their own room,… *and… ah!* Edward and I would have our own room, too… *our own room in our own home.*

We were back home in California! How wonderful it was. Even Tom felt much better the next day.

We arrived in Long Beach with twenty dollars in Edward's pocket and no job! The first thing Edward did, of course, was look for work. Uncle Ray loaned us fifty dollars so we could eat.

When we left L. B. in 1955 the brand new Disneyland was about to open and we were going to miss it. Edward promised his boys at that time when we came back to California and he got a job, with his very first paycheck he would take the whole family to Disneyland. He found a job at North American Aviation in Downey. First payday came. *Edward kept his promise!*

It was October 1st and southern California was in the midst of an unprecedented dreadful heat wave with temperatures well over a hundred degrees. We went to Disneyland anyway and not one of us noticed the temperature! What a thrilling day it was, for *all* of us. 1958.

The next years of our lives flew by. Being the parents of four boys doesn't leave much time for anything beyond the raising of those boys. Life was great in many ways and traumatic in others. But, I wouldn't trade it for anything else in the world. Good times and bad times both to look back on and fondly remember.

Somewhere in here, Edward's brother George lost his job in Chicago. Nancy suggested he come to California to a dryer climate to look for work as she suffered from a lung problem and her Dr. prescribed a milder climate such as in California. George refused, so she and the children drove down to Mexico to spend time with her father and stepmother in Ajijic, Jalisco en route to California… without him. She asked him one more time to come to California. When he still refused, Nancy drove up to Long Beach from Mexico, filed for divorce and lived with us while she looked for work.

Nancy got a job north of where we lived and rode to and from work with Edward when he drove to North American in Downey each day.

This story becomes a bit confused in my mind now… fifty years later. One of the times Nancy came to Long Beach she had the children with her and one time she was alone. How she met my cousin Louis Irish eludes me but he became smitten with her, so that when she fell at work and was seriously ill afterward Louis helped care for the children. Louis was my Uncle Ray's only son. He cared for one of Nan and George's children and Edward and I the other and we switched periodically. Louis brought whichever one he was taking care of down to Cubberly School, near us, each school day. Nancy was in the hospital for six long months and Louis visited her there *every single day.*

Edward, in addition to working at North American had been going to Real Estate School in the evenings. When he obtained his license as a real estate broker and was going to quit at North American and start selling real estate he asked me if I would mind going back to work. He told me if I just made enough money to buy the groceries while he got started it would be all he asked. Thus, when Nancy was ill I was working at Allstate Insurance Company every day, which made it an extremely busy time in our lives.

During this trauma Edward and I talked about Louis falling in love with Nancy; we both felt it wouldn't work. Edward would just shake his head and shrug. Truthfully, there was nothing we could do. Eventually after her hospital stay and a month long recovery in Mexico with her parents, Nancy and the children moved to northern California leaving Louis behind, heartbroken.

The children had forged a relationship with us that resulted in their feeling toward us almost as child to parent. We have been particularly close with Suzanne who still lives in California.

Nancy became ill again when they lived in northern California. Jordi called me at work to see if I could come up as his mom was asking for me. I told him I must stay just one more day to close a real estate deal I was working on, but 'one more day' made it too late. Nancy died before we could get there. I was devastated. Bless her, she had hung in there until both children were graduated from High School and Jordi was working.

Nancy would be so proud of Suzanne, her husband and her family, and of Jordi, his wife and his family… if she were here today.

It was a sad, sad time for all of us. *We still miss her.*

Chapter Eleven

The story backs up a bit now, backs up to Edward asking me to go to work until he could establish himself in the business of selling real estate. I applied for work with Allstate Insurance who had an office in the local shopping center very close to our home. Luck was with me as the office manager was a former Marine. Because I filled out the 'jobs held' portion of the application with my time in the Marine Corps, he hired me. I had a job, plus I could *walk* to work every day!

Youngest son Tom was twelve years old by this time and I felt it would be all right for me to go to work. I would leave instructions for the boys each morning before I left. They were expected to have finished all of the things on the list before I came home. I told them it didn't matter when they did their chores, just so they were done by the time I got there. Later, they were able to have dinner started and took turns doing the cooking plus the clean up and dishes after dinner. As I look back, it was probably a good thing I went to work. The boys learned how to do a lot of things on their own which has stood them in good stead as husbands and fathers in later years. It's been nice for me too, hearing the words of appreciation from their wives.

One day while I worked in the Drive-In Claims portion of Allstate Insurance a man came in with a claim for a cigarette burn on the seat of his car. His job was selling houses and he loved telling me all about it, of how he was Salesman of the Month and had made $4,000. in just one month! In the nineteen-sixties $4,000 a month was definitely a suitable income. I was intrigued. Without telling Allstate I began going to real estate school in the evenings. After completing the course I gave two weeks notice and left Allstate. I spent the first week, before taking the big two-day exam with the Real Estate Department in downtown Los Angeles, attending the classes all over again, driving to a number of different locations to do so. The second week I crammed. I'm happy to say, I passed the two-day exam with flying colors. I had my license.

Edward was busy in the area of Downey, not selling so much as he was working in investments, real estate investments. He had met Rod Smith while he was working at North American. Rod and his wife Bernice owned a real estate company and Edward thought working for Rod and his wife would be the best place for me to start as a real estate agent. Their office was in Westminster, California and Rod was a good, patient boss. Getting a license to sell real estate doesn't teach you how to actually *sell*, but Rod taught me. He was still working at North American but he took time to teach me.

We go back now to Edward's list: Minute Man Missile - Project Engineer - Apollo - Manned Orbital Lab. He worked on all of these projects, about which I have no details or additional information. I am so sorry Edward himself didn't get to write all of this, with full details. It is unclear to me just when, but Edward also worked for MacDonald Douglas.

I learned about a packaging company through one of my cohorts in the real estate business. It was for sale with nothing down and payments to be made later. Edward investigated and found it to be **Consolidated Bubble Pac**, a company which made those little rigid plastic covers one finds on merchandise fastened to a card in stores everywhere. He was excited by the whole idea and bought the company, lock, stock and barrel… with nothing down. Only a signature and his monthly payments were required. Edward really, really liked the idea of owning his own business and being his own boss. The main thing wrong with such an idea is that as an owner one is tied to the business 24-7, with no vacations, no days off, on and on… .

But Edward's mind went on and on too, while doing all this mundane work, the work of pulling blisters off a wide strip of clear plastic which kept coming out of the mouths of those machines!

While stripping "bubbles" off the plastic Edward dreamed up the **Missions of California,** which entailed having Joseph Madas engrave dies to use in stamping out silver bars depicting the twenty-one Missions, plus one more depicting Father Junipero Serra, founder of the original California Missions. My cousin Louis Irish not only helped Edward at the Bubble Pac plant but he drew the original artwork used by Joseph Madas to engrave the dies. Someone else designed and made the small book-like containers for all twenty-two silver bars. Ads were placed in papers and magazines. Ebay today has ads for an occasional Missions silver bar.

Consolidated Bubble Pac even did some *sealing* of items on cards. One item Edward did was earrings. They were the gold starter earrings used right after ears are pierced. There were a dozen small squares of white foam mounted on a card with one pair of the gold earrings in each tiny square of foam. A dozen starter sets together on each card. He hired extra help for all of this, as the earrings had to be mounted in those squares of white foam before being sealed and sterilized. Busy boy that Edward!

He had a sign hanging in his office printed in large capital letters.

DO NOT
DILUTE YOUR ATTENTION

Edward's brother George came out to live with us somewhere in here, a number of years after Nancy passed away. He and Edward dreamed up the business of manufacturing and selling an invention of George's called a lawn edger. It was a round concave *sharp* blade about seven inches in diameter that was attached to a long handle, enabling the user to *easily* edge a lawn standing up, easily being the key word here. They decided to name it the Gay Blade. This was well before the term gay was used to identify a homosexual. At that time a "gay blade" was an up and coming young man-about-town. The fellows even ran an ad in House Beautiful magazine. All of these adventures into the manufacturing and selling business began well but didn't last, which, however, didn't stop Edward. He was always on to the next project. His mind was never still, even after the Missions of California there was a silver medallion of Halley's Comet issued. He made those at the time the Comet flew by the earth.

Then there was Skylark Adventures, Sierra Camps for Boys, on and on… the very last one was Pacific Sunways. There is a sad story with Pacific Sunways and why it never came to fruition. It was an airline that Edward and his friend Charles Wolverton, a friend from his North American days, were planning to start. The route was to be flying exclusively from Long Beach, California to Mexico. They made trips to Mexico, checking out planes and routes. Plans were progressing well until Charles flew to Idaho in his own plane taking some doctors on a special fishing jaunt to a five-mile long lake there. Today in 2016 I cannot remember the name of the lake and in checking maps there are two or three very large lakes in Idaho. The one where Charles had taken the doctors was large enough to have an island in the middle of it so it might have been the American Falls Reservoir. The group camped on the island and as a storm was approaching they decided it might be a good idea to leave the island. There was not room in the small boat they were using for all of them so Charles was bringing the second group from the island when the storm hit. The small boat went down, Charles with it.

It was *months* before the bodies were recovered.

Edward was devastated with the loss of his friend. He had no desire to continue with any plans for an airline.

Let's go back to Edward's story from 1980 or '81.

Edward had set the date of retiring and quitting the business… and quit it he did. He sold the Bubble Plant and was free of responsibilities there at last. *He was going to retire!*

We began making trips out and away from the Los Angeles basin each weekend looking at possible places for our retirement as I was retiring, too. One of our weekend forays out of the area was to Tehachapi, which was not far from Mojave.

Edward had learned of a special airplane called a Sky Commuter, which looked like a small car with tiny wings when on the ground. It was a plane that took off vertically. One could fly to an airstrip near work, land… then *drive* the rest of the way to work, all in this fabulous invention.

It was definitely a good-looking vehicle…

The Sky Commuter

Of course, Edward wanted to build one! He bought the plans, then he thought we should live near an airport and *Tehachapi had an airport!* We investigated and found the nearby area of Bear Valley Springs where we could live while Edward built one of these Sky Commuters.

Here is our hangar among all of the others.

Edward bought a new vacant hangar in Tehachapi where he could build the plane. He rented a brand new solar house in BVS in which we could live.

Bear Valley Springs was a lovely place. We bought a lot on top of a hill, or some would call it a rise, which ran down the middle of the valley. It was

a hill to me as we could look straight down from our lot and if you tried going down and then climbing back up… you would call it a hill.

All I was asking through all of this adventuring was to live in a place near a college or university where I could go to school and get a degree.

Edward set about immediately drawing house plans for building our retirement home in Bear Valley Springs. In the meantime, we lived in the small solar house in the Valley. I had checked mileage and found I would be able to drive down to Bakersfield to the Community College. I had a very enjoyable time going to school in Bakersfield while Edward worked designing our new home and investigating the possibility of also building a Sky Commuter. We loved the valley and looked forward to a permanent home there.

We were living in a gated community and felt secure in spite of being only 40 miles from a prison!

We lived in Bear Valley Springs for nearly two years, met interesting people, joined their Social Club and were looking forward to making it our permanent home. In fact, Edward had finished his drawings and was ready to take his blueprints *of our new home* for approval the very day our niece Suzanne came for a visit. He put it off for a bit while she was there.

One day during her visit Suzanne said, "Oh, Uncle Ed, you should see this place up near Sacramento! You can live right beside the Air Strip. Bob's brother lives near the airport and showed it to us this weekend."

This conversation was on Thursday.

On Saturday we were in northern California… in Cameron Park.

It is truly amazing how fast plans can change. Very shortly after the visit in Cameron Park we *moved* north, renting another nearly new house in the town. Again, I would be able to go to college here. The University of California at Sacramento this time, plus Edward was happy to be living in a town with an airstrip adjacent to it.

One day there was a paper flyer dropped on our doorstep. I showed it to Edward. It advertised a four-bedroom, family room home in the Cameron Air Park. We realtors called it a FSBO (fizzbo) or “For Sale by Owner.” We drove by. The streets in the Air Park were eight lanes wide and served as taxiways for the planes as well as for automobiles. There was indeed a homemade ‘For Sale’ sign out front. The house looked small, with no landscaping but lots of green grass. There was a weed-filled ditch running alongside it. We asked to see the interior. Mrs. Emerson had four little children, plus she was caring for a small baby. She was embarrassed for us to see her house so cluttered, but we weren’t looking at any of that. The house was larger inside than it looked from the front. It had a total of twenty-two hundred square feet. We went home, mulling the idea of purchase over and over and finally asking if we could look at the house once more. This time we had an appointment. The house was picked up and everything looked very nice indeed inside, plus, and a big plus here, there was a huge back yard *right beside the airstrip*. We could watch the planes landing and taking off as we ate our breakfast. We met Tony Emerson himself this time and he and Edward talked a mile a minute.

2953 Boeing Road

The ending of this little part of Edward’s story was not a great surprise to me. The airplane in Emerson’s hangar stayed there when we bought the place. Now Edward had his own airplane, a four-passenger Cessna 210 and I could easily drive down the hill to Sacramento State for classes.

We were a happy pair.

Our Cessna 210 # N3922Y

In 1986 Edward invited the entire Randell family to a "Randell Reunion" in sunny California. We had fun researching areas and finally decided on having the reunion in Arnold, California, which was a hundred and seventy-five miles south and east of Cameron Park. Edward paid for the rent of three completely furnished homes in Arnold, homes that were kept strictly as rentals for summer visitors. Ahead of time Edward and I assigned certain families to be together and we gave them directions for getting to the house to which they were assigned. We tied big yellow bows on trees along the routes to each home. We arranged and left bags of basic groceries in each house with notes telling the families they were to make out their own menus and buy any additional food they would need for the week they were there. We had a central meeting place where we all met to get acquainted. There was a huge green grass-covered area in Arnold where we could all meet for games and fun. We provided lists of all the various activities available, times, directions for getting there, etc. It was great to see the families together having fun.

The first night Edward and I had dinner catered as a buffet in a large hall in the same park as the green grass area. The rest of the time each family was responsible for their own meals, snacks and food. The Reunion lasted a week, with rafting trips down the rapids of a fast moving river, gold panning, canoeing, hiking in the mountains, on and on. The very last night we had another dinner, potluck this time, with all of us together. Unbeknown to us the families took up a collection and gave us the gift of a rafting trip down that same fast moving river later at our convenience! *What a pleasant surprise!* Several weeks later Carl and Lucy Stoner (David's wife Jamie's parents) joined us for a fun day of rafting down the river.

Up until the reunion we had been renting a house in Cameron Park. Escrow on 2953 Boeing Rd. in the Air Park closed just before the reunion, thus, we had not moved yet. After the reunion we had such *letdown* feeling to have everyone gone! There was no rest, however, as we immediately gathered ourselves together and started work on our "new" home.

Every wall in our new home on Boeing Rd. was covered with wallpaper! We armed ourselves with a big sprayer for water, scrapers and lots of elbow grease! Edward found a young fellow to help us and we all went to work. On the walls that had cloth like paper on them it came off easily in great swathes; for the rest… it was spray and scrape, scrape, *scrape*. Then it was wash, dry and paint the same walls. I think Edward hired someone to do the painting, bless his heart. I think he felt enough was enough after we had done all the wall scraping and scrubbing we had!

It wasn't very much later that I discovered a thickened place on my upper chest. I assumed it was just a newly developed muscle from all the work we had been doing. However, the Dr.

at Mather Air Force Base felt they should biopsy the thickened place. I was still very foggy from the anesthetic when the Dr. came into my room at the hospital saying, "I'm afraid it isn't good news, Mrs. Randell. The tissue was malignant."

Of course, I was in tears at home telling Edward. He said, "You're going to make it. Don't let this get you down. You're going to make it." He held me in his arms and kept telling me that I was going to be fine. Major surgery three weeks later removed the whole breast and a great deal of tissue from under my arm and across my chest. I woke up with my arm strapped to a board. Learning to write and do everything temporarily with my left hand and arm was a challenge, but Edward kept encouraging me… always telling me, "You're going to make it."

With Edward's help I *did* make it. He was so good to me. He helped with everything. Three weeks later there was radiation. He drove me to each session in downtown Sacramento and insisted, the day after the last radiation treatment, that I attend a special dinner with him given by the Investment Club he belonged to. I dressed up for the first time in weeks and wore a loose, velvet vest-type jacket, which covered the fact that I was flat on one side. He was so right. I believe going with him that night was the turning point in my complete recovery. What a wonderful husband, helpmate, lover and advisor he was for me… *he was everything.*

I make it sound as if Edward and I never disagreed, never quarreled, never were on the outs with each other, which is far from the truth. We had our times for all of those things, but basically we were on the same page. He cared for me always, just as I cared for him. We made a good team with many *fond memories.*

Again, back to Edward's story.

Even with his own plane, the Cessna, Edward still wanted to build a Sky Commuter with its vertical takeoff. He spent more than a little time and money building it as far as he did. There were trips to Seattle, finding space to store it as a work in progress in our hangar in Cameron Park, on and on. There is a big "however" here. The designers of the Sky Commuter were never able to find a way to get it off the ground. *No power to lift it up to the sky.* Edward's ten thousand dollar investment in the company was gone. A few years later the company, Flight Innovations, Inc., offered to buy his partially finished Sky Commuter, which was stored in our hangar in Cameron Park. Edward hauled it north to Seattle and left it with them. They bought it… oh yes, they bought it. They paid for it with $5,000 in stock certificates in their company. The company did not last long. It folded and the stock was worthless. I think Edward kept those certificates in a notebook just to remind himself to never get carried away like that again.

We flew in the Cessna on a few trips. One flight was down to Mojave to see the famous plane, the Voyager, the plane that flew all the way around the world without ever landing. It was on display in Mojave, wingtips frayed just as we had heard they were. Because the plane had been so loaded with gasoline when they took off the wingtips scraped the runway. It wasn't enough to cause the trip to be postponed. It had been an amazing flight by Dick Rutan and Jeana Yeager.

While in Cameron Park Edward joined an Investment Club, as I mentioned before, driving down to Sacramento every week to attend meetings and learn more about investing, about the stock market, etc. It occupied a great deal of his time. He did, however, build an office in the hangar that was attached to our house. He insulated it, built it strong enough to be able to store things above and on it. He set up his clocks on the wall, computers, a worktable and chairs. He even put in surround sound. Later yet, Edward put insulation into the walls of the hangar itself. Grandson Jonathan came out from Oakland to help on that project. Edward built a new deck across the entire back of our home, put on new siding where it was needed, plus he put new shingles over the entire house and hangar. When he was up so high on that hangar roof I insisted he wear a safety belt attaching him by a line to the peak of the roof. I was happy *he did do it.* Last of all we hired the entire house and hangar painted. It looked wonderful with all the things Edward had done and then to have it painted was like putting frosting on a cake. There was a saying in the real estate business at the time which is this… if you want a house to sell you paint it yellow. Our house was yellow with white trim. Even those huge hangar doors were painted yellow to blend in with the house, but we didn't intend to sell it!

Somewhere in here, while we lived near Sacramento, Edward was impressed with my cataract removal surgery and decided he wanted to have the same thing done. His first operation was a great success. He then *insisted*, against the Dr.'s advice, on having the second surgery *right away,* which was reluctantly done a week later. In the process the Dr. accidentally nipped a nerve that caused Edward to have a permanently dilated eye. This, of course, made him squint and scowl whenever he was in the sun or a bright light. Any pictures taken after that nerve snipping show him frowning and squinting. Either that, or he would be wearing dark glasses. It was a real shame, because Edward had such a beautiful smile, as you have seen from earlier photos of him.

On one of our many trips together we were in New Mexico visiting Curtis and Patti, parents of grandson Jesse Brian. Jesse was graduating from High School. Curt's daughter Althea was visiting there too, of course. Conversations were flying.

Althea told us about trying to get her college education. It was hard to work and study, plus attend classes.

Some time during the visit her grandfather Edward said to Althea, quite casually, half in jest, "You should come to live with us. You wouldn't have to pay rent and you could go to college."

It was shortly after that when Althea phoned to say she had decided to take her grandpa up on his offer to come live with us! I was overwhelmed! After nearly a lifetime of raising four boys we finally had our own place, no responsibilities and the freedom to enjoy each other for a change. It was indeed a very sour grandmother who reluctantly prepared the guest room of our home to be a live-in student's room.

Althea was a sensitive girl. She could feel my resentment

and she was not the kind to suffer in silence as I was. She confronted me one day. We talked. I must admit, it did clear the air. I learned a great deal from that young woman. She has told us over and over since living with us for three years just how grateful she was and still is, for both of us being a wonderful influence in her life. We love her dearly. She had a very special place in her grandfather's heart. She was the daughter he never had… a very special granddaughter. By her living with us for those years she has become a very special granddaughter to me, too. She has now, by the year 2016, provided us with grandson-in-law Chad. The two of them, in turn, have given us two great grandsons, Simon Edward DeBeer and Crosby Randell DeBeer. Edward met Simon but Crosby was born just four years ago.

We were both grateful to Althea for coming to live with us, showing us the way to *really* be grandparents!

Edward and I had the great good fortune of having *two more granddaughters* born some twenty years later. Thomas Hazen and Lorianne Scott had two lovely daughters born to them, six years apart. Heather and Brooke Randell. Both girls, now at twenty-two and sixteen, are Scottish Highland dancers! We have had the joy of watching them in competitions, and seeing them win! We have felt most fortunate. *Three granddaughters!* All three of them are as wonderful as anyone could ever hope for.

How lucky could Edward and I be?

We lived on Boeing Road in Cameron Park for twenty-two years. Twenty-two years for Edward to associate with other pilots, watch the planes taking off and landing practically in his back yard, and part of that time to be flying his own plane. Three of our four sons lived in southern California and kept begging us to move south so they didn't have to travel four-hundred miles to come see us.

In 2008 Edward had a stroke, which did not affect his looks or his ability to walk and get around as he always had. But the stroke took away his memory! I must admit we had some fun times after that with me telling him about a lot of the things he didn't remember.

As I told him stories, he would say, "Oh, that does sound so familiar!" and we would dissolve in laughter.

Our southern California sons won the contest with us as we finally gave in and in 2009 we sold our home… *our yellow house…* on Boeing Road and moved south to live in a retirement community called Leisure World in Seal Beach, only two miles from the ocean. Edward had a great time sitting out in front of our pretty corner unit apartment and inviting his neighbors to join him. He loved to talk to people, tell all his stories and listen to theirs.

13380 Danbury Lane, 130G, Seal Beach, California

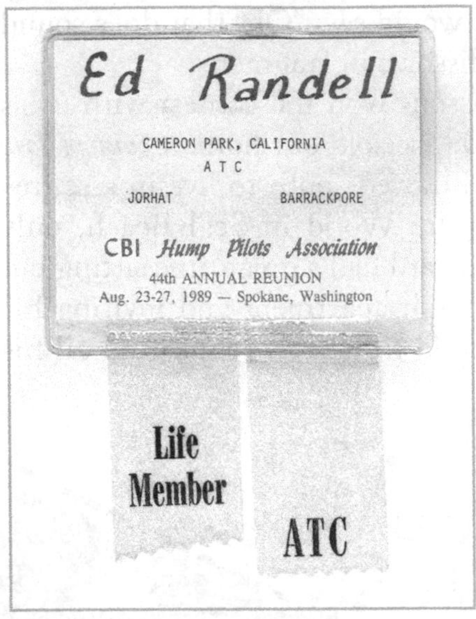

Hump Pilots badge

Prior to this in his retirement years Edward was invited to join the newly formed Hump Pilots Association. The group held annual gatherings in various cities across the United States. Edward and I attended many, if not all, of them. At the very beginning of these meetings we didn't know anyone, but gradually some of Edward's wartime buddies turned up, plus we made new

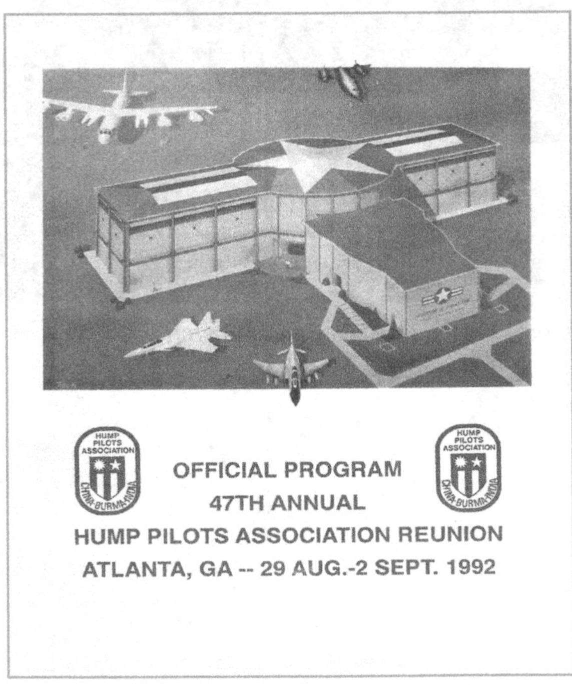

HPA Atlanta meeting program

friends of the other pilots and their wives who attended. It became our annual vacation. The gatherings were usually about five days long with meetings, tours of the surrounding country and on the final night there was always a banquet with everyone dressed to the nines. Dancing would follow the banquet and the brief program. Those WWII Air Corps men and their wives could still 'cut a rug' in great style.

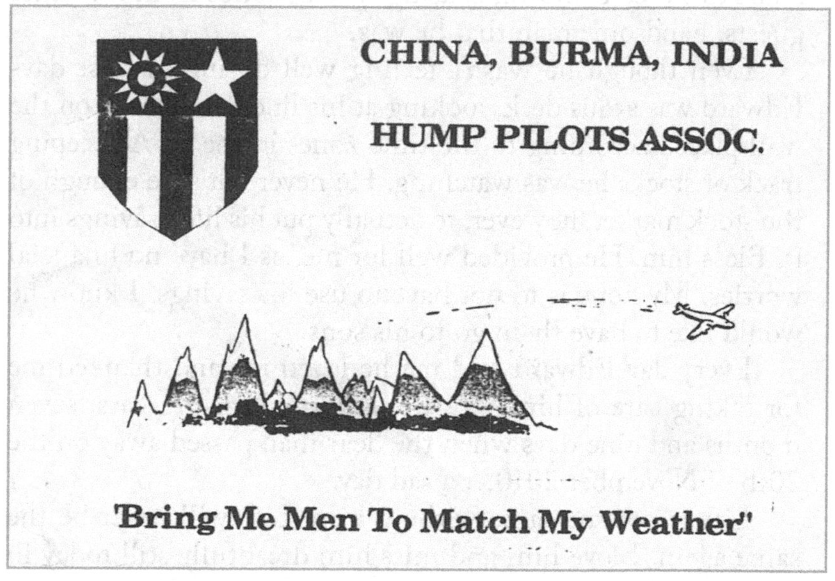

CHINA, BURMA, INDIA
HUMP PILOTS ASSOC.
'Bring Me Men To Match My Weather"

The motto for those intrepid Hump Pilots was
"PILOTS WHO ARE ELITE IN THAT THEIR FLYING WAS UNIQUE"

Edward loved these gatherings. One year he and others from the Sacramento, California area were the hosts of the annual meeting. So much work and thought and planning went into those gatherings. We hadn't realized just how much until we helped put on one of the affairs. Edward received many compliments from the attendees after all of his hard work when they came to Sacramento.

At this Sacramento meeting he put on his Army Air Corps

Uniform of olive drab blouse with "pink" pants. Most of the comments then from the rest of the fellows were that *they* weren't able to get into their uniforms any more! Edward was always slender and trim with never an extra pound. He could very comfortably fit into that Army Air Corps Uniform from WWII.

The very last meeting he was able to attend he wore his blue Air Force Uniform, causing special notice from the other guests, handsome man that he was.

Even though he wasn't feeling well during his last days Edward was at his desk, looking at his lineup of clocks on the wall placed according to the time zones in the USA, keeping track of stocks he was watching. He never felt sure enough of the stock market, however, to actually put his life's savings into it. Bless him. He provided well for me, as I have no financial worries. My hope is to not have to use his savings. I know he would like to have them go to his sons.

Every day Edward told me he loved me and thanked me for taking care of him. We were married for 67 years, seven months and nine days when the dear man passed away on the 20th of November 2010… a sad day.

Life is not the same without him. Life will never be the same again. I love him and miss him dreadfully still today in the year 2016.

How fortunate I am to have been married to him!

Edward William Randell, Sr. was an exceptional man. I feel privileged to have been part of his life.

Co-pilot on the flight.

2010

Edward's 90th birthday celebration

Edward flying as a Civil Air Patrol Pilot

Major Edward W. Randell

CERTIFICATE OF SERVICE
ARMED FORCES OF THE UNITED STATES

THIS IS TO CERTIFY THAT
EDWARD WILLIAM RANDELL AO 665 862
Major
HONORABLY SERVED ON ACTIVE DUTY IN THE
Air Force of the United States

DD FORM 217AF-1 JAN 50

Edward's Certificate of Service

Here is Civilian Edward Randell. This was taken when he and I were both working for California Western Financial Investments - 1979-80

Edward and I with CWFI - late 1970's &; early 80's
"Tuck in your collar, Ed!" **Too late! Picture is taken.**

Colonel Edward W. Randell, USAF Retired
Handsome man.

Colonel Edward W. Randell, USAF Retired
"Scrambled Eggs" on the brim of his hat at last!
The star on his wings identifies him as a Sr. Pilot.

"Where is your famous smile, Edward?"
"Taking this picture is serious business, Marjorie!"
Love that man!!!!

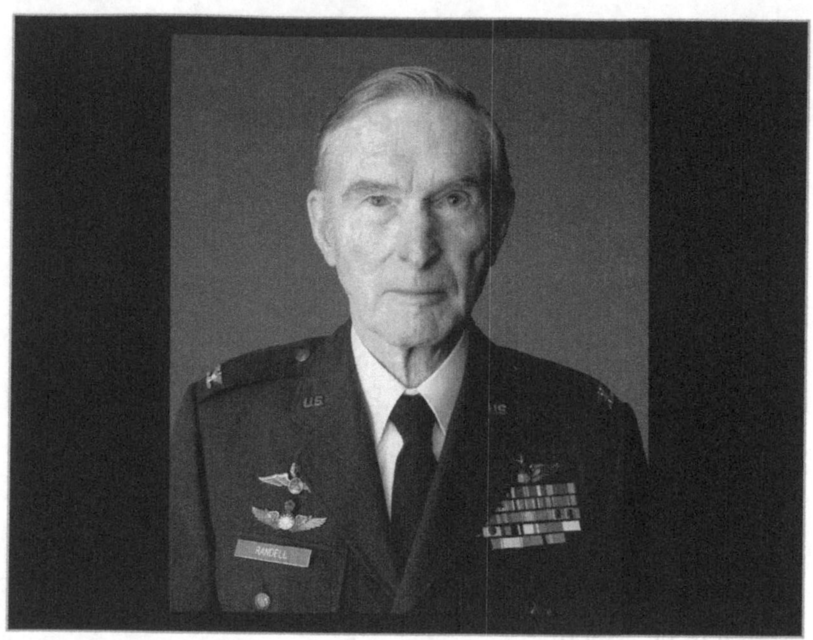

Civil Air Patrol Colonel
U.S. Air Force Reserve Officer

Here he is again!
This is the one with the smile… the fellow on the left.
I really, really do love that man!
Always have. Always will.
Either smiling or serious. Edward.

Places Edward and I have lived together:

1943 - 1944	Various places, with both of us in the service.
1944 -	Cambria Court, Romulus, Wayne Co., Michigan
1944 - 1946	Irish Farm, Coopersville, Michigan
1946 - 1951	1945 Overland Ave., Los Angeles, California
1951 - 1952	6123 Oliva Ave., Bellflower, California
1952 -	Xenia, Ohio 'Island' in the country, then
1952 -	24-"A" Miller Ave., Fairborn, Ohio
1952 - 1955	6608 Metz St., Long Beach, California
1955 - 1958	Chanute Field, Illinois
1958 - 1958	Pine Ave., Mt. Prospect, Illinois

1958 - 1983	6608 Metz St., Long Beach, California - 25 years
1983 - 1985	Bear Valley Springs, California (Tehachapi)
1985 - 1986	3785 Milbrae, Cameron Park, California
1986 - 2009	2953 Boeing Rd., Cameron Park, California
2009 - ?	13380 Danbury Lane, Unit 130G, Seal Beach, CA
2010	Edward back to Coopersville, Michigan alone.

Edward was taken back to Coopersville, Michigan… his last flight… in early December 2010. I shall join him there one of these days.

2016

Appendix

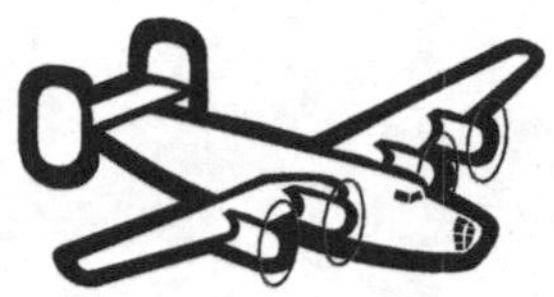

Graphic designer Edward W. Randell, Jr. did the scanning of all of the pictures used in this book, as well as designing the interior and the cover, plus making the small drawing of the B-24.

Genealogy Notes

Joseph Henry Pratt and Anne Hazen Pratt

John Francis Pratt
William Henry Pratt
Eugene Arthur Pratt
George Hazen Pratt *
Elizabeth Roxanne Pratt

*George Hazen Pratt and Emma E. Clarke,

Dorothy Pratt Randell *
Thomas Hazen Pratt had two daughters

*Dorothy Pratt and James Paul Randell

James Pratt Randell
George Milton Randell
Edward William Randell *
John Rogers Randell
Dorothy Isabelle Randell Thomas

*Edward William Randell and Marjorie Jean Irish

Edward W. Randell, Jr*.
David Howard Randell*
Curtis Wiley Randell*
Thomas Hazen Randell*

*Edward W. Randell, Jr. and Patricia Cady

Jonathan Wilson Randell

*David Howard Randell and Jamie Stoner Randell

Nathan John Randell
James Adam Randell
Edward David Randell (Ted).

*Curtis Wiley Randell and Dana Ledesm

Althea Libra Randell DeBeer.

*Curtis Randell and Patti Littlefield Randell

Jesse Brian Randell.

*Thomas Hazen Randell and Lorianne Scott

Heather Randell
Brooke Randell.

Great Grandchildren

Nathan John Randell and Sabrina Patrick Randell are the parents of:
Katelyn Patrick Randell
Quinn Riley Randell
Violet Lorelei Randell.

Althea Randell DeBeer and Chad DeBeer are the parents of:

Simon Edward DeBeer
Crosby Randell DeBeer

Above information regarding great grandchildren is current as of this date:
26 July 2016.

Genealogy Notes for Randell

Milton Paul Randell was the thirteenth child born to his father and the father's second wife. He was born in Cincinnati, Ohio. Gracie Rogers is the daughter of Dr. Charles Harvey James, dentist, also from Cincinnati.

Milton Paul Randell and Gracie Rogers

James Paul Randell*
Isabelle Randell

*James Paul Randell and Dorothy Pratt

James Pratt Randell
George Milton Randell
Edward William Randell*
John Rogers Randell
Dorothy Isabelle Randell

*Edward William Randell and Marjorie Jean Irish

Edward William Randell, Jr.
David Howard Randell
Curtis Wiley Randell
Thomas Hazen Randell

Edward W. Randell, Jr. and Patricia Cady Spangler

Jonathan Wilson Randell

David Howard Randell and Jamie Lou Stoner

Nathan John Randell *
James Adam Randell
Edward David Randell (Ted)

Curtis Wiley Randell and Dana Ledesma

Althea Libra Randell DeBeer *

Curtis Wiley Randell and Patti Littlefield

Jesse Brian Randell *

Curtis & son Jesse are the only descendants of Edward interested in airplanes and flying.

Thomas Hazen Randell and Lorianne Scott
Heather Randell
Brooke Randell

Great Grandchildren of Edward and Marjorie Randell are:

* Nathan John Randell and Sabrina Patrick Randell are the parents of
Katelyn Patrick Randell
Quinn Riley Randell
Violet Lordlei Randell

* Althea Randell DeBeer and Chad DeBeer are the parents of
Simon Edward DeBeer
Crosby Randell DeBeer

This information is believed to be accurate – October 2016.

I have copied a tiny folded note I found among Dorothy Pratt Randell's letters, which she had saved. It tells yet another story of her relationship with her Grandfather Clarke, a part not covered in "Emma Clarke Pratt-One Life," or in this book.

32-W-27th Street
New York, N.Y.
June 2nd. 1901

My dear granddaughter Dorothy:

I thank you very much for your nice letter, and I am glad to learn of you having been given a red wagon and that you and Thomas have such happy times. Do not let Thomas fall in the creek, or is it a river you call it? I have forgotten. I may not be able to visit you this year, but Aunt Myra will and she will make it very pleasant for you all. Sometime you may come on a visit to me. Would not that be nice? Well, I will see when Myra comes to me, for we certainly will talk about it.

When I go down town I will get Thomas another toy – one of the sort you can wind up and make go yourselves – and hope it will please him. Let me know what he thinks of it when you write again.

How are all your friends? I forget their names but you know who I mean. Mable was one you thought most of. The children had two days of holiday last year because of Decoration Day. That is the holiday when we remember the soldiers who died in the war of the rebellion, and whom it should be the delight of everyone now and hereafter to honor by strewing their graves once a year with those sweet flowers. My brother Henry was killed in that war in what was called the second battle of Bull Run, and is buried at Arlington Heights in what was called a grave for the "Unknown" for they were buried so quickly that the graves were not marked, as was the case for thousands of others. But they are all there and equally honored. It is a day to forget as well as remember. You will not forget this story, will you? Ask your Mama to tell you and Thomas about that war.

> *I hope you will have plenty of flowers in your yard. The tiny things look so nice when well fed and watered – seeming to thank you for your kind attention by giving you fragrance and a pretty look. Do you think they ever know? Please give Thomas a kiss for me. My love to you both, and Mamma.*
>
> *Your Grandpa – T. D. Clarke*

Thomas Dowling Clarke typed this letter on somewhat sheer paper, which has creases and tears in it now. The typing is in a greenish blue color.

He wrote "Your Grandpa" and signed the letter in longhand with black ink.

Remember, this was written in 1901, more than a hundred years from when I am writing this. How wonderful to have this bit of history with which to connect to your ancestor family! Many thanks go to the one saving this note. No doubt it was Dorothy Pratt Randell, as she must have treasured it. Dorothy Pratt Randell, Edward's mother.

Historical Note defining "The Hump."

The operation began in April 1942, after the Japanese blocked the Burma Road, and continued daily to August 1945, when the effort began to scale down.

The India-China airlift delivered approximately 650,000 tons of materiel to China at great cost in men and aircraft during its 42-month history. For its efforts and sacrifices, the India-China Wing of the Air Transport Command (ATC) was awarded the Presidential Unit Citation on 29 January 1944 at the personal direction of President Franklin D. Roosevelt, the first such award made to a non-combat organization.

Printed in the United States
By Bookmasters

Printed in the United States
By Bookmasters